HELL & EARTH

Ophelia Wolf

ISBN 979-8-9878368-5-9

Cover art by Meredith Alden Lewis
Author photograph by Tatiana Daubek
Book design by Jesse Pinho and Meredith Alden Lewis

To this world's Jeremy and Azrael, for teaching me more about being human than pets should have any right to know.

ACKNOWLEDGMENTS

First of all, I would like to thank you, Dear Reader, for going on this adventure with me. If you're reading this, you've probably read *Gods & Angels* and come back for more. For that, you have my deepest gratitude. As I've said before, publishing a book is a little bit like asking people to hang out with your imaginary friends. It's a vulnerable, joyful, loving, and all-around weird act. Your support means the world to me.

Next, I owe a deep debt of gratitude to the two people who took pains to edit various drafts of this book. I couldn't have done it without the two of them. Brace Negron, thank you for listening to a very rough first version of this story, thank you for kindly pointing out all the places that were lacking, and thank you for your continued enthusiasm for Lyla's world. A big thank you also to Brian Oliver, for your detailed feedback on the middle draft and for having the very rare skill of giving notes not on the story you want to read, but on the story you know I am writing. You truly helped me elevate the final draft to a whole new level.

My gratitude goes out to Madelyn Bayles, for swooping in at

the last minute and saving the day, painstakingly proof-reading the final draft for missing Oxford commas and much more after having already given story notes and feedback.

Moreover, I'd like to thank Meredith Alden Lewis for her gorgeous cover art, for all her help and patience in formatting and designing the physical and electronic versions of this book, and for holding my hand through what I consider to be the most harrowing part of this process.

Sandi Johnson, and Sandon Berg, I owe you for reading early versions of this story, giving feedback, and cheering me on in this process.

And last but certainly not least, I would like to thank the Merry Band of Misfits without whom I would not be alive to publish this book today. You know who you are. I owe you my life and, for that, I will forever be grateful.

For a Spotify playlist, courtesy of Brace Negron, inspired
by Gods & Angels, follow:

playlist.godsandangels.com

HELL & EARTH

PROLOGUE

Azrael

They'd been scouring the face of the earth for weeks now. When Lyla had kicked them out, Jeremy and Azrael had lost their purpose. In their respective ways, they'd both been soldiers for Hermes in this war for the soul of humanity. Azrael and the other angels of Hermes' line fought on the ground. Jeremy and his fellow acolytes of Aphrodite's healed them at home. But being exiled by Lyla meant that they couldn't get near the God either. He'd be watching her like a hawk now that he'd found his long-lost daughter. For all his sharp, nigh-immortal edges, at his core, Hermes was just a concerned, somewhat overbearing father. Lyla didn't know the latter part yet. After all, she'd barely had a chance to get to know him. Azrael, on the other hand, had been made to give Hermes daily reports on his daughter every single day during the fall. That overprotectiveness would only be further cemented now that father and daughter were finally reunited. There'd be no circumventing Lyla to continue working for Hermes.

Knowing Lyla, Azrael had expected an explosive reaction the day she'd found out Max had betrayed her. The human had after all been a lifelong companion to her and she'd probably never trusted anyone as much as she'd trusted him. That thought made him physically ill. He knew what Max had done. He'd heard it from the boy's own lips. He'd ruined Lyla's life in the most consistent of ways. And yet, she'd loved and grieved him as if he'd been a saint, as the human expression went. Azrael's reaction once he'd realized Max's betrayal – to beat up the boy and get him to confess – wasn't something he was proud of. Priests of Hermes' were supposed to act from a place of empathy and compassion, not rage. His violence hadn't been rooted in kindness. It had come from that angry little part of him that would never forget what it felt like to be small, vulnerable, and at the mercy of those around you. He hadn't known Lyla at the time, thank the Gods. If he'd been in Max's presence after meeting her, who knew what he would have been capable of.

That jealousy, those primitive instincts that had kicked up again when she'd been endangered in Hell, those weren't feelings he cared to dwell on or explore. Besides, he was in no position to feel morally superior. After all, wasn't he the one who'd physically assaulted and almost dragged her back to their enemies just a few weeks ago? He remembered the proximity of their bodies, as he'd smashed her against the wall. The heat and fear radiating from her, as he'd stepped between her legs and immobilized her, pinning her in place, robbing her of any chance to defend herself. His hands wrapped all the way around her skinny arms... he'd have broken them if only he'd squeezed a little bit more. And all along in his head, the voice telling him to incapacitate her and deliver her to the Fallen...

Azrael's hands started shaking at the recollection of how fragile her bones had felt in that moment, at how she'd looked up at him, scared and yet resigned. He was no better than Max. And he really needed to find some purpose beyond sitting in the freezing cold, looking for an angel who may very well have killed herself. Something to make him feel a little bit less like a monster.

Besides, he couldn't afford the distractions that were guilt, shame, jealousy, or that sharp spike of desire he'd felt in those last few days with Lyla. Much like they could not afford this petty feud. While he'd expected her to have a strong reaction and to deny the truth, he hadn't expected her to take it out on him and to indefinitely kick him out of her life. He should have known better. When he'd first met her, he'd tried to keep her at arm's length for weeks. He should have listened to that instinct. Instead, he'd slowly let her get close, until he'd thought they were friends. When, in reality, said friendship couldn't even survive a single argument. Though he hadn't forgiven himself for what he'd done, she had seemed to still want and crave his company even after that... incident. He'd truly believed they were close enough to work through such a thing as Max's betrayal. How wrong he'd been. And how much he wished he could go back and keep things professional between them, teach her, but not get to know her beyond the training ring. Sleeping in her bed that one night sure had been a colossal mistake. And yet, he hadn't been able to say no. She'd looked so small and scared that night. And her hand had been so tiny in his. He'd thought of her as this innocent fledgling in need of protection. But there was nothing innocent about the way she'd flared her wings at him before kicking him out, threatening to blast him with her powerful magic.

His thoughts were blissfully interrupted by Jeremy running into the shelter they'd built to survive the cold, and yelling, "I found her! I found her! There's a town east of here with a pub. She was drinking herself into a stupor."

In lieu of a mission, he and Jeremy had set out to find Zadkiel. The latter had given four of her fellow priests a mercy killing. All five had been captured and injected with a serum that made them kill all villagers and temple dwellers on Hermes' island. The five priests had even slaughtered the children. They hadn't been able to live with themselves, so she'd killed her four companions by cutting off their wings. But no one had been able to do the same for her.

If she hadn't already taken her own life, Azrael and Jeremy knew that she would go to the most punishing place she could possibly find. Hoping against hope, they'd searched for her in the harshest climates they knew she'd been deployed to on past missions. Azrael would name a place, and Jeremy would open a portal straight to it. Finally, they'd made it to a far corner of Canada, deep in the Northern woods between Seattle and Alaska, where they knew she'd once been sent to by Hermes.

"Did you talk to her?" Azrael asked.

"No. I stayed away. She didn't seem in any state to have a conversation. Besides, I think you should be the one to approach her."

Azrael knew what Jeremy meant but didn't say. That he too had been infected with the serum. That only sheer luck had made him let go of Lyla and come back to his senses. That Jeremy knew that the things he could have done, the things he'd almost done, still kept him up at night. That he, unlike his friend, understood what it meant to have blood on his hands. He hated that Jeremy was right.

The next morning, they made their way into the nearby village. Coming to this place had been a complete shot in the dark, but Azrael had remembered that Zadkiel had vehemently hated her mission in this part of the world. Hermes had sent her out west a few years ago to take down an encampment of demons that had been placed near Mount Fairweather by the

Fallen. The cold hadn't bothered her, seeing as Hermes' island was located off the shore of Greenland and covered in snow for most of the year. What had driven her to near insanity was that she'd been working for weeks on an attack plan with priests of Ares'. "Droppings for brains," as she had called them. Zadkiel couldn't stand their punch-first-ask-questions-later attitude. As a priestess of Hermes, much of her power centered around empathy, whereas Ares' acolytes used brute force... just for the fun of it. She'd hated being stuck with an entire group of the more primitive angels for weeks on end.

Azrael had had a hunch she'd punish herself by going to a place she had particularly loathsome memories of. What he hadn't expected was to find an entire fishing village in a place that had been deserted not ten years ago. Well, "village" might have been an exaggeration. It was a hamlet, made up of one long street and a dozen cabins, including the one that housed the tavern Jeremy had mentioned.

They'd hoped to find Zadkiel in the establishment, and, as if on cue, she stepped out, leaving the pub and staggering down the street, as they rounded the corner. Not wanting to attract any human attention, Azrael and Jeremy followed at a distance, as she walked down the narrow street, past the last few houses and toward a wooded area. Azrael lost sight of her for a moment as they followed her into the darker coverage of the trees. Afraid she might have heard the crunching of their footsteps in the snow and tried to lose them, he quietly unfurled his grey wings, signaling Jeremy to do the same, and flew down the path. Around a sharp corner, he found her, sitting in a clearing.

Nothing could have prepared him for the sight.

Zadkiel was sitting in a frozen pool of pink blood, sunken into the snow and ice around her. At first, Azrael wondered if she'd been attacked, but as he got closer, he realized that it was so much worse.

Crouching in the snow, Zadkiel was ripping out her own feathers. Their wings were sacred; there was nothing more painful than losing feathers. It was a pain that pierced their very souls. Zadkiel was self-mutilating. She was adding fresh bright red drops of blood to the older shade of pink that must have accumulated over time. This was a daily ritual, he realized. After drinking herself into a stupor, she'd come to this clearing to self-harm.

Approaching her, Azrael saw the pained look on the angel's face. She wasn't crying, but with every feather she ripped out, her body twitched and she suppressed a pained moan. Her wings were a mess of frozen blood on membrane, feathers, old and fresh, littering the ground in front of her.

Azrael cautiously knelt in front of her and put his hand on hers, where she was ready to tear out another feather. She was freezing and shaking but still tried to pluck it, until he grabbed her and forced her to stop.

"Zadkiel," he said in as soft a voice as he was able to, vaguely aware that Jeremy had stopped at the edge of the clearing, giving him space to reach out to her. "Zadkiel, look at me."

Slowly she lifted her head, and what he saw in her eyes shook him to his core. It wasn't grief, or even self-loathing. Her eyes were empty, devoid of any life, as if her very soul had left her body.

He grabbed both of her frozen hands in his own and slowly touched his forehead to hers.

"Zadkiel, you are not alone anymore," he said. "I'm here, I'm with you."

She neither moved nor replied. Pulling back and looking into her eyes, he realized that she didn't even see him. "It's me. Azrael," he tried to remind her, but there was no recognition in her eyes. The angel who had followed him on missions for over two decades, who'd fought alongside him, laughed and grieved with him, looked through and past him, a vacant, weary look in her gaze.

"Stand up," Azrael encouraged her. But she wouldn't move. When she remained sitting on the frozen ground, no apparent motivation to go anywhere, he turned to Jeremy for help—

Only to find a much larger male holding his friend still, one hand covering his mouth, the other holding a knife up to his throat. In the split second it took Azrael to realize someone had gotten the jump on them, several threatening shapes walked into the clearing through the dark trees, all sporting large, pitch black wings.

Only one kind of creature moved with that stealth: they'd been fooled by the simple look of the fishing village, and they'd stepped right into the territory of a tribe of lost children.

"You even think about using those wings, and I'm slitting his throat," threatened the scrawny lost holding Jeremy, who looked alarmed, if not flat-out scared.

Azrael slowly put his hands in the air, making a show of his benign intentions. He was too far away to charge the male and they were surrounded. As he looked around though, something caught his eye. Their attackers all looked... jumpy, erratic. He knew the look in their eyes. He'd seen it too many times on creatures he'd had to execute; souls who'd lost their way, and no longer knew how to redeem themselves. Yes, that was desperation in their eyes. What had happened to this tribe?

"What are you?" the leader, he assumed, asked.

"I'm an angel. Like you," Azrael replied, holding his hands up, his wings drooping limply to the ground.

"You're nothing like me. And I'm not an angel," was the reply.

No, technically they weren't. They were the so-called "lost children," Lucifer's first generation of offspring. But genetically speaking, they were the same. Just born on different sides of the war. Their wings may have been black, but that made them no less cousins.

"What kind of angel are you?"

"Ah," Azrael replied. "I'm a priest of Hermes'. And my brother here, is of Aphrodite's line," he added, nodding toward Jeremy.

Something flickered in the lost's eyes.

"Perfect. You're coming with us."

In a motion swifter than Azrael would have expected from such a clearly burned-out lost child, he moved the knife to Jeremy's back, keeping a hold on his left arm, and started guiding him back toward the village. At the same time, the other dozen or so lost circled around Azrael, making it very clear he had better follow. All of them kept their ink-black wings on display, threatening to blast him with magic if he stepped out of line. As for Zadkiel, she stood up, that same vacant look still in her eyes, and simply followed, no threat or force needed to make her comply.

It wasn't long before they arrived in the hamlet. The road that had been deserted just half an hour earlier was now full of anxious looking lost of all ages, standing outside the doors to their homes. What had happened here? This village had not existed a mere ten years earlier. This tribe had clearly built it and made it their home. But why were they all so anxious? They didn't look hungry or abused. They looked sickly and scared.

Finally, their captors stopped in front of a house that looked just as modest as the others, and knocked. The reply came soon enough: a young female cracked the door open and, upon seeing the scrawny lost and Jeremy, opened it wide to let them enter.

The inside was just as humble as the outside. An area rug, simple furniture, low candle lighting. Jeremy, Zadkiel, and Azrael found themselves in front of a middle-aged lost, sitting in an armchair, his jet-black wings proudly displayed over the back of the chair, as their captors fanned out, creating a circle around the room.

"What's this, Stevie?" asked their leader.

"I brought a solution. He's an angel of Aphrodite's line. A healer."

"What–" Azrael began, but Jeremy interrupted him with a calm hand on his shoulder.

"What do you need a healer for?" the angel said in his kindest voice.

"For what this one has been trying to do, but wasn't able to," the male said, with a nod of his head toward Zadkiel.

"What is happening to your tribe?" Jeremy continued. "Tell us. I will do whatever I can to help."

Azrael threw Jeremy a dark look the latter actively ignored. But he understood what his brother in arms wasn't saying. This was who Jeremy was. Even threatened, he couldn't help wanting to heal, wanting to help others be better. Priests of Aphrodite's weren't martyrs, but they approached everything and everyone, even their sworn enemies, with nothing but love in their hearts. It was who they were, from the depths of their being all the way to the surface. Theirs was the most potent magic Azrael had ever experienced.

Indeed, just like that, the conflict was resolved and the leader folded his wings away. Bowing his head, he replied, "Our people are dying. An ailment is plaguing us. It came from humans. We got word that it has been slowly spreading among them, killing some, and leaving most sick for weeks. But it seems deadly to our kind."

LYLA

It had been weeks since she'd seen him, weeks since she'd kicked him out of her house. And yet, Lyla still dreamed of Azrael every single night. Sometimes she relived their fight, sometimes it was their heated kiss she re-experienced, sometimes she dreamt that he was asleep next to her. But every morning, she woke up to cold, empty sheets on the pull-out couch she'd taken over as her own. That, and a large serving of regret. She'd once heard from one of her New York acquaintances that addicts needed to pay attention to feelings of hunger, anger, loneliness, and tiredness – all of which spelled out the acronym "HALT." When they'd returned from Hell and Azrael had told her of Max's betrayal, she'd felt all of those sensations, and she really wished she had taken a moment to halt and eat something before figuratively sending her two strongest allies right back to Hell. Their lie of omission had conflated in her mind with Max's insurmountable betrayal, and before she'd known what she was doing, she had threatened to throw the same kind of magic at them that had just paused Lucifer himself in his tracks. No wonder they hadn't come back.

Azrael had criticized her impulsivity over and over again during her training and their subsequent mission to rescue her father from the clutches of Hell. She'd always given him a petulant comeback. But he was right. She was a twenty-five-year-old angel and it was probably time her brain learned to outpace her mouth.

As for Max, she wished she could drag him back from whatever ghastly place his soul currently occupied and kick his ass. And yet, she still missed him. Even though she now knew he'd been the one funneling information to the Fallen and helping them torture her and try to emotionally break her, he still populated all the best memories of her life. She couldn't quite match this new information to the Max she'd grown up with. Her friend didn't fit in with the creatures she'd seen in Hell, the almost mechanical demons, the sheer madness in every fiber of Lucifer's being...

She'd expected to have nightmares about it when they'd escaped that place. And yet facing the devil himself, seeing the torture he'd subjected her father to, hearing his psychotic propositions, being so outnumbered that it was a miracle they'd all made it out alive... Those things hadn't authored new nightmares, they'd put an end to her existing ones.

Boredom however, was threatening to become her newest ordeal, as she waited for her father to heal from the torment he'd been through. Hermes currently occupied the cabin's bedroom. It was the only place he could spread his wings and allow them to heal. He'd spent most days lying face down, waiting for his feathers to regrow and his spiritual body to heal, leaving Lyla to twiddle her thumbs for long periods of time. Thankfully, for the last week, he'd started getting out of bed and taking walks with her. He could go for hours not speaking, something that would make any shorter lived person feel incredibly awkward and uncomfortable, but that seemed normal for an almost immortal God like him. But then he'd ask exactly the question she needed to answer, making her talk about her feelings about Hell and helping her process things she didn't even know she needed to process. And he could also listen. Truly listen, without pity, without advice, and without judgment.

Sometimes, she was still overcome by a sense of alienation toward the seven-foot-tall, frightening creature she called "father," but they'd bonded since the day Azrael, Jeremy, and she had pulled him out of Hell with the help of a dozen other angels. After her impulsive fight with the two males who'd taught her everything she knew about being an angel, she'd proceeded to enter her father's room with a bucket and a clean towel. At the first contact of the cloth with his bloody wings, he'd snapped awake and she'd found herself in his grasp, his sharp canines at her throat, before she could blink.

"I'm sorry," he'd said, while lying back down, "I'm not used to feeling this vulnerable."

"I just wanted to clean the blood off of you. Is that all right?" she'd responded.

He'd looked at her for a long moment before nodding. She'd waited to see the powerful muscles on his shoulders and upper back relax into the mattress before she'd tried to touch him again. It wasn't her impotence that had frozen her as much as that she'd been on guard because she knew that he wouldn't quite be able to help his predatory nature. When he'd closed his eyes, showing his trust like a blinking tiger, she'd touched the cloth to the edge of his wing, distracting him all the while.

"How can we fly with feathers on membrane? I thought bats and birds have one or the other, but not both..."

He'd opened one eye and given her a strange look before responding in the gentlest tone she'd heard from him so far. "Actually, there's a Chinese dinosaur fossil which they believe had membrane and feathers. Whether it actually flew is a different story. We have both because we're overbuilt."

"What does that mean?" she inquired as she used the towel to soak his white feathers in enough water to not rip them out.

"Where we came from..." he slowly replied in his supernaturally echoey voice. "We almost went extinct. We survived by evolving powerful traits. Some of them became obsolete, some of them were never useful in the first place."

"Like vestigial structures?"

"Something like that. My raptor sight and hearing are useful. My teeth, on the other hand," he added, gesturing to the elongated saber-toothed tiger canines that had grown past his lower lip and down his chin, "they're really just in the way. I tried to pull them out when I was young. They just grew back. As for flight, it's the magic that propels us, not the wings themselves."

They'd had their first true conversation then, while she'd carefully softened weeks of crusted blood from the naked mess that had been his wings. He'd treated her like his own flesh and blood for the first time. More than that, he'd treated her with such love and care as she had never known. He'd apologized for some of his past behavior and had told her of the agony he'd undergone while searching for her for two and a half decades. He'd known that she'd been in the clutches of the Fallen, in one way or another, and he'd been in constant pain over the fact that he couldn't protect her from them.

In the meantime, his white feathers had mostly grown back, and with them, his powerful presence had returned.

Half an hour into one of their walks through the desert, he broke the silence. "You're agitated today, Lailah," he remarked, using the name she'd only heard from him and Lucifer.

"Are you reading my mind?" she responded.

"No. I can't read minds," he told her in an unusually heavy tone. "That was Aphrodite's power. It is Jeremy's now. But, like all Gods and Fallen, I am still connected to the hive in a way. Or at least to my own blood in my descendants' veins. I can't read your mind, but I can read your heart. And it is more distraught than usual today."

"I'm feeling... I'm not sure, actually. I guess I'm emotionally confused," she confessed.

There it was again. That mixture of love and deep resentment. Max had betrayed her. Her first friend, her first love, her first protector, the boy who'd always been there, the man who'd kept alive her faith in humanity. He may have played a large part in her suffering, yet she also owed him.

"Two decades of my life were based on lies," she explained. "I'm angry and disappointed. But, at the same time, I finally know. And, in spite of what he did, I miss him."

"Which one?" he asked.

He hadn't mentioned her argument with Azrael and Jeremy, but he must have heard every word of it. She thought about it for a moment before answering, "All three of them."

They continued walking in silence. When they finished their loop and found themselves back outside the cabin, he announced, "Tomorrow, we'll continue your training. I am almost back to full strength, and it's time for you to return to practicing and studying your magic."

Something twisted in her heart. Azrael had been her trainer for months. He'd been her teacher, he'd become her friend, and by the end she'd developed quite the crush on him. Training with someone else felt like admitting that that chapter might be over.

Hermes must have sensed her thoughts, because he added, "There are things you need to learn that Azrael can't teach you.

I was always going to take over your training sooner or later."

"I know. I read your journal. I just miss our old routine, back when the island was still... well, you know..."

When it was still full of life and joy, before everyone was killed.

"I miss it too. It's all right to love him, you know?" he answered cryptically.

"Which one?" she repeated his previous question.

"All three of them."

HERMES

Training Lailah was more frustrating than he could ever have imagined. No wonder Azrael had hated the job. She was stubborn, unpredictable, and erratic. She was good enough at the things the angel had taught her, but utterly hopeless in learning new techniques. For days now, he had had her sit cross legged in the desert sand, trying to get her to channel her magic through the ground and into the nearest tree to make it flower.

He'd trained thousands upon thousands of angels over the centuries and he couldn't remember any of them being this headstrong or aggravating. But they hadn't been Lailah. Some of them had been his direct children, but none of them had been *her* daughter. None of them had had that kind of unknown power coursing through their veins. And none of them remind-ed him of the female he'd loved for what felt like an eternity, the one whose absence was still a constant shard of ice pushing through his brain.

Lailah might have been testing his patience, but he needed to keep his temper in check. He knew all too well what could happen if he didn't. He was still ashamed that he had attacked her weeks ago, when she had tried to clean his wings. It had been his first interaction with his daughter outside of a public space, and he had nearly killed her before realizing what he was doing. And yet, she'd just calmly looked at him, knowing to stand her ground and not run from a potentially aggressive bear. Not only that, but she had been brave enough to stay, to tend to him, and to talk to him.

Right now though, he wanted to pick her off the ground and throw her into the tree her magic wasn't reaching. Funny, he might have had all the time in the world and yet, since his love's death, he'd become increasingly impatient. He could sense Lailah's frustration during training. Her sorrow. And her deep anger. It was the latter that concerned him the most. He'd made it a daily habit to make her talk through her feelings in the hope she'd learn to recognize, befriend, and manage them, but she had yet to realize that something inside her was constantly raging at the world. She still hadn't told him of her childhood, of the horrible experiences she had undergone, being thrown from one abusive home to the next. He was secretly grateful that she hadn't. He wasn't sure he could bear to hear it. He didn't really want to know the details of all the things he hadn't protected her from.

"I don't understand how I'm supposed to do this without my wings or my voice," she complained.

"I'm just asking you to try," he sighed.

"But Azrael said–"

"That angels need their wings to use magic," he interrupted. "We've been over this. Your sonic attacks are proof that your magic isn't dependent on your wings."

"Fine."

She closed her eyes again and made another vain attempt. He was glad she'd grown comfortable enough to give him push-back, but he'd been hoping for the same kind of blind obedience from her that he was accustomed to from most of his priests. It made his work so much easier to not have to explain the things he knew she had every right to ask about.

Three weeks passed like that. The cabin she and her dead human friend had set up as a getaway years ago was a perfect hideout from the world. It was secluded, miles away from the nearest town, at the bottom of a canyon. A tiny stream ran through the valley, providing it with water, and food. No one would ever find them here... and the isolation was driving him utterly insane.

As the weeks passed, he sensed her slowly give up. Her motivation disappeared and was replaced by more and more of that fury inside of her. If only she channeled said fury into this exercise the way she did into her sonic attacks, they would have been done weeks ago. But she was too scared to do so. The few times she had used her powers to their full extent, she had destroyed everything around her. Azrael had reported those incidents to him, and he hadn't been surprised to hear it. Her lack of control whenever she felt threatened made this training that much more urgent. Yet, he knew he was at fault. She was working with partial information, and it had been several thousand years since he'd trained anyone in this particular fashion.

"I'm trying. I really am, but there is nothing going through my hands," she interrupted another one of their sessions.

With a sigh, Hermes stood and headed toward a hill on the horizon. "Walk with me," he told her, silently making for a boulder she enjoyed watching the sunset on.

How could he expect her to access her power, if she didn't know what that power was? He'd been trying to instill a daily emotional honesty in her that he himself hadn't been practicing in weeks. He hadn't been honest with himself about the turmoil in his heart. The grief he was afraid telling her the truth would cause him. The grief it would cause him to watch her grapple with the reality of what she was. He was afraid of the heartbreak she'd endure as the truth sank in over months and years. And most of all, he was afraid of thinking of her mother. The mother who would have been so much better equipped to handle everything Lailah needed. He never spoke of her, because he knew he'd mourn her until the end of time, and because he was afraid that the mere mention of her could trigger... it.

Yet, she needed to know. And she needed to know now. Sitting down on the edge of the rock, the precipice in front of them an invitation to take off into the skies, Hermes folded his hands in his lap and finally told his daughter the truth.

"I'm sorry for giving you instructions without explanations," he started, staring into the disk rapidly sinking toward the horizon. "I've been afraid of telling you the full truth about your lineage. The reason your magic doesn't operate the way Azrael's does, is that you aren't an angel like him."

"I thought you were my father..." she responded, with an edge of dread in her voice as to what he might say next.

"I am," he replied soothingly. "But your mother was not an angel. And that's why you have powers far beyond the angels of my bloodline."

"I don't understand," she replied. "My mother was human?"

"Your mother was a Goddess. Your mother was..."

He couldn't quite bring himself to say her name.

"I thought Gods couldn't procreate with one another," she interrupted.

"They can't," he told her. "They shouldn't be able to. But twenty-six years ago, Apollo had a vision. He saw that there would be a new God, born of... the two of us. Your mother and I..."

He couldn't bear the vivid memories that sprung up as he spoke of her out loud as a lover for the first time in over two decades. How well he remembered every single freckle on her face, every curve, groove, and indentation on the body he'd worshipped his entire existence.

"We had loved each other for millennia, but we would finally be able to have a fledgling of our own," he continued around the knot tightening in his throat. "Lailah, I know that most of how our species procreates is dispassionate and cold. It's necessary, but it lacks in depth and aftercare. But I want you to know that you were so wanted and loved long before you were even born."

Lailah turned around and looked at him with such deep emotion in those eyes she'd inherited from her mother. Her breathing had picked up somewhere along the way and he knew that, hard as it may be for him, he was giving her the answer to a long-lost dream, reigniting a candle of hope she'd smothered many years ago.

"I know you grew up not belonging anywhere," he continued. "But your home was always waiting for you. I just wish it was all of it, not only my half. We dreamed up a whole life together. We wanted to give you... everything. But most of all a family... a safe space to grow up and come into your own. The very thing you haven't had, and will never have now that things are as they are. I'm so sorry, Lailah."

Somewhere along the way, the sun had set, she'd leaned into him, and he'd wrapped his wing around her shoulders. Wrapping his other wing around her, he leaned his cheek on top of her head, cocooning her into all the safety he wished she hadn't been robbed of and started sobbing alongside her.

"I'm so sorry you had to grow up so fast and all alone. I'm so sorry, Lailah," he wept into her curls. "And I'm sorry I've been giving you half truths ever since you arrived on the island.

I thought I was protecting you by keeping you at arms length when really you needed me to just be your father. And I thought I was protecting you again these last few weeks by letting you believe you were a common angel... I've been doing this all wrong..."

"Why didn't you just tell me?" she asked, pulling away to look at him.

"I didn't want to burden you even more," he replied, wiping his face on the collar of his shirt. "Apollo's prophecy predicted that the child would have all the powers of the hive combined. The powers of every single God. She would be what we used to be before we fell to Earth and our magic was splintered."

He didn't want to continue, but she deserved the full story.

"We conceived you in secret, all the while making plans for how best to raise our prophesied offspring. But someone caught wind of Apollo's prophecy. I still don't know who or how. Exactly nine months later, they came for her island... While her priests were distracted by the attack, the Fallen snuck past her defenses and stole you from her... She'd never needed protection, but she went into labor and... I wasn't there to save her. Or you."

He took a deep breath, ready to say her name, that echo whispered from the future.

"Aphrodite?" Lailah asked when he paused.

"Yes," he confirmed with a nod. "She was... well, she was the best of us. And the love of my timeless existence." Sighing, he continued, "As for you, you're not an angel. You are a hatchling God. A miracle."

"I don't look like one," she questioned.

"Which makes you that much more powerful," he explained. "I'm forever doomed to be the stuff of nightmares to the species I swore to protect. But you look exactly like your charges. You look human."

"But why?" she asked.

"I'm not sure," he replied. "I wasn't expecting you to look like this either."

"So that's why I can access my power without the use of my wings?"

"And why you were able to hold Lucifer himself at bay for a minute."

He sensed the turmoil in her. Fear, hope, love, confusion, all intermixed as she pulled up her knees and wrapped her arms around them.

"That's why the Fallen want me. That's why I need to be able to fight them..."

He felt the panic course through her body as he heard her heartbeat speed up. She was beginning to understand. What was expected of her. What the Fallen would turn her into. That she truly could not turn away from this life, because she was the problem and the solution all in one.

"Lean into me," he whispered, wrapping his wings around her again. "I know it's hard. For a God, you are still but a hatchling. But you'll learn. And I'm not going anywhere."

He wanted that to be the truth. He hoped with all his might that it was. That he wouldn't end up letting her down. Pulling her toward him so she could lay her head against his arm, he found himself stroking hers with his feathers, holding her and soothing her the way he'd imagined he would twenty-six years ago.

"I know it's overwhelming," he murmured. "And I know that you've been feeling your power wanting to burst through the seams. I know you've been scared of letting it out. But I promise you that I will teach you everything I know about mastering it. You're not alone anymore, Lailah."

He and his nine "siblings," as they called each other for familiarity's sake, had broken off from the hive, and each had ended up with a tenth of their original power, which made them specialists at certain types of magic. But Lailah was whole. Some day she'd be as powerful as they'd once been. As powerful as their adversaries, the Fallen, had once been.

Some day, she'd be the most powerful creature to walk the Earth.

"I'm scared, Dad," she admitted. "I'm really scared."

"I know, sweet hatchling, I know. I'm right here. I'm right here. Breathe. Breathe," he repeated over and over again, rocking her like the hatchling she still was to him and realizing that his confession had finally locked a long-lost piece of him back into his heart.

Long after the moon had risen and the stars had come out to play, she pulled her head out of his feathered cocoon and sluggishly asked, "Does that mean Jeremy is my brother?"

"He doesn't know it, but yes, he is."

HERMES

He kept ruminating while scouring the hills for animals to hunt. They were remote enough from human settlements that the chances of being seen by a human were slim to none, at night in particular. He still remembered the last time he had encountered one. For a thousand years the Gods had been revered and worshipped by humanity. But when he was sighted a mere three hundred years ago, the human had fled and threatened to return with a mob. His large, white wings, his claws and fangs, the ear holes in his temples, and the down on his head had forever cursed him to scare the very people he had sworn to protect. A punishment fit for his crime of challenging the Fallen.

It was a lonely existence, not being able to return to the hive he so desperately missed, and only interacting with his descendants, his soldiers. That was why he had cherished the stolen moments with Aphrodite. Only she had truly known him. He called her "sister" in the tradition of the hive in which everyone, though not related, referred to each other as brothers and sisters, an acknowledgment of how few of their species remained here. But she'd been so much more to him than his other eight "siblings." She'd been his guidepost, the light illuminating his path, the safeguard on his otherwise decaying sanity.

He'd been afraid of facing the grief, yet sharing his story with Lailah had returned a sliver of that love to him, a semblance of the family he'd once prepared for. He hadn't realized until their heart-to-heart just how much she still needed a father. That need just might keep him on the right side of madness for a little while longer.

Instead of Aphrodite's magic, he'd decided to start Lailah's training with Artemis' power, which was that of an enhancer of magic. The latter would stand back on the battlefield, and channel her power into the soldiers, never getting into the fight herself. Ares and Artemis had had that symbiotic relationship; him on the battlefield, and her boosting his forces from afar. It took an inordinate amount of energy to send her magic out so far away into specific objects and angels. Maybe he was wrong in starting Lailah's training with such a complicated skill. Maybe he needed to rethink things. She had learned how to fight fairly well, both with and without magic. Why not start her off on Ares' simple battle skills instead?

Just as he made that decision, he spotted an oblivious coyote roaming in the distance. In a flash he was on top of the animal, his fangs sunk deep into its neck. The animal never knew what struck it, but Hermes felt peace overcome it, gratitude for being taken off this dangerous planet of predators.

Their training sessions improved over the next few days. He was no longer trying to teach her complicated skills. Instead, she was learning to channel her power into purely physical blows as Ares' priests did. They would spar or go at each other with weapons, and her job was only to amplify her skills with magic. The very nature of the task made it easier than anything she'd learned before. The first few times she'd channeled her magic, Azrael had reported to him that she'd used the infinite pit of resentment inside of her to get her power out into the world. Her body going through the motions of a physical conflict helped her unearth and direct her limitless rage.

By now she was beginning to excel at it. Each punch, each kick came at him surrounded by the shimmering halo of a magic she was slowly befriending. But he told her that they wouldn't stop until she'd bested him at least once. She'd asked him how she was supposed to best a God.

"Because you are one too," he'd simply responded.

He wanted her to try to outsmart him, as they floated ten feet off the ground, their wings flapping a few times a minute to keep them at eye level with one another, going at each other with staves he'd made out of wood on one of his hunting expeditions. He was working out excess energy on those hunting trips. Being cooped up in a small cabin was driving him quite steadily insane, and he didn't know how much longer he'd be able to bear it.

Every time their staves knocked into one another, or one of them hit the other, sparks of power showered down to the ground. At one point he'd even had to put out a fire when she'd accidentally set a bush ablaze. He'd now hit her in the same shoulder half a dozen times, and, though he was holding back, he could see it bruise. But that was just the thing about being a hatchling God: small injuries were beginning to heal as fast as she was acquiring them. At the same time as he saw the bruise grow, he watched her shoulder stitch itself back together.

She'd only gotten him once. Barely. She'd hit his fingers on the staff and he'd berated her for the fact that it was an accidental and sloppy hit.

She needed to find a way to outsmart him... She had to think outside the box... He wished he could will her to do so.

As she stared at his pristine white wings, he noticed the moment she had the idea. She was about to play dirty.

She kept going through the motions of mostly fighting him off of her, but began to hum, low enough to think she would not to be heard over the sound of staves knocking into one another. When he saw it appear in the cabin's doorway, he realized she'd been focusing on a coil of rope she and her human friend must have left in a corner of the house. She let out an ever so slight wisp of power and guided the rope to uncoil itself and slowly snake through the sand to a spot right under him. *Yes*, he thought. *Keep going.*

The last step would be the hardest. She lifted the rope into the air, until it was in her line of sight and let it hover just under his wings. He hit her in the gut and she almost dropped to the ground, but she kept the rope in place. Good on her. Flying back up to her father's level, she took a little more space from him, and let her hum turn into a clear, loud note, as she quickly twisted the rope around the base of his wings, effectively binding him.

Hermes fell to the ground and she came down after him, pushing her staff right to his throat.

"Well done!" he laughed. "I was waiting for you to combine your powers. That was the whole point of this exercise. You have more than one power, you need to start using them in unison."

Shocked at the fact she was holding a weapon to a God's throat, she stumbled back, unsure.

He sat up, and she asked, "You let me win, didn't you?"

"Of course, I did," he laughed, righting himself.

But he was so very proud of her.

LYLA

"Have you ever had any visions?" her father asked her after what felt like the longest training session. Gods, did he not sleep? She was comfortably wrapped in a light blanket on the couch, holding a steaming cup of tea, her freshly showered hair dripping into the mug.

He'd told her that he wanted to work through every God's fundamental skill with her. That she could dive into them in more depth later. He was satisfied for now with her use of his power and Ares'. And apparently she'd used her mother's to take away his pain when she'd held him in Hell. Her mother. He hadn't told her much about Aphrodite other than that he'd loved her and she'd been impatient to meet Lyla. She wanted to ask, she wanted to hear everything. Every story. Every description. Every memory. But the heaviness in him was palpable and told her to wait.

She'd once wondered what it would feel like to be loved by the Goddess of love herself. Never in a million years could she have imagined that that love was what had brought her into the world. That she'd been worthy of pure, unconditional love before ever even existing. That these two giants had wanted her. Not wanted her to be this or that, to do x, y, or z. Just wanted her. As she was. No matter what. That thought filled her with so much peace, she could almost forget about that little detail of being an immortal, all-powerful God-being. She couldn't get near the time component. Couldn't wrap her head around the fact she'd outlive–

"Lailah, stay on task. Please," her father's deep voice snapped her attention back to the present moment.

When Azrael had trained her, he'd often pushed her to her limits. But her limits had changed since she'd last seen him. Still, she felt completely beat up. Apollo's gift of foresight might be a respite from all the fighting they'd done, channeling Ares' powers.

"Visions? No."

"Any premonitions? Feelings about what was about to happen?"

"Come to think about it, I did. Once. I don't know if it was a premonition, but I knew Azrael and I shouldn't have gone into that house in Denning," she remembered.

"Set down the mug please."

She obeyed without questioning him and sat the mug onto a small side table to the couch she currently used as a bed.

"Close your eyes and focus on Azrael."

She really didn't want to. All that guilt and regret, intermixed with worry and lust, wasn't something she wanted to revisit, but she knew better than to argue with Hermes. She closed her eyes and thought of grey feathers.

"Now, find him."

She spent days focusing on nothing other than Azrael, outside of showering, sleeping, and eating. Hermes told her that it would be simplest to focus on a well-known entity, that a vision of Azrael might be the easiest thing she could possibly conjure. Everything after that would be significantly harder, but for now it would suffice. He mostly left her to meditate on the big guy.

She remembered her training sessions with him, how tightly he'd held her when she'd almost killed them both with her magic, how relaxed he would get when they had lunch at the tavern. She remembered how he'd fought and humiliated Michael for insulting her. She remembered the boot knife he'd shown her that so few knew about, the snowman he'd built with pure magic up on the Sacred Mountain. And she remembered how he'd held her hand and helped her drift to sleep when her nightmares had kept her awake.

Azrael himself had taught her how to meditate. He'd taught her how to let her mind go blank and how to let fleeting thoughts pass her by. Her mind had always gone black. She didn't picture the world around her when she closed her eyes to meditate. She simply saw a pitch-black darkness. Within that darkness, her white wings wrapped around her body, she tried to picture the beefy angel. It was all too easy. She pictured his height, his bulk, the large shoulders and pecs that chronically threatened to rip his uniform. She pictured his green-golden eyes and dark hair, his golden brown skin, and the way he always chewed on his lower lip when he was uncomfortable. And most of all, she pictured his beautiful grey wings. White-winged angels judged him for having the blood of the black-winged lost in him. But she'd always thought his wings were more beautiful than any white ones she'd seen. They were larger than most, as was his power, and the grey in them was so pure it would shine almost blue in the sunlight.

She pictured those wings, spread to their full extent, slowly flapping toward her, sending their magic in her direction. As she did, the darkness started disappearing and was replaced by a picture. There were woods, and a snowed-over field, and then appeared the ruins of a castle behind him. No, that wasn't a castle – that was Hermes' temple. She recognized the towers, even though they were partially destroyed. In fact, that was a massive stone replica of her father's head lying in the snow. Lastly, the body of a dead angel materialized at Azrael's feet. He picked it up as if it were a precious child, turned around, and started carrying it away, down the dark tunnel of her mind.

When she came to, Lyla was on the floor, breathing heavily. She had no idea how she'd gotten there, or what had happened, but she knew one thing.

"The island. They're on the island."

"Good," her father replied, helping her sit up and wrapping the blanket around her shoulders. "We need to go there anyhow."

PART ONE

I

She'd been apprehensive of seeing Jeremy and Azrael again, but she hadn't expected to find them rifling through Hermes' office right as she and her father stepped through the portal and onto the island.

She had no idea how the portal worked. All she knew was that it was created by Hermes' magic and it could take the user to any destination they desired, as long as they were very intent on where they were going. She had only ever seen another portal like it – made by Jeremy, the sole angel carrier of Aphrodite's full power. This portal always stood in the back of Hermes' office, on the top floor of the temple, the castle-like structure her father's priests worked and lived in.

Apparently, Azrael and Jeremy had not only made it back to the island before them, but they were also sorting through the paperwork and information Hermes had left behind when the island had been attacked. Seeing them, she froze and stared at the floor, avoiding their gazes. She needed to apologize somehow for overreacting the way she had the last time they'd been in a room together, but she wasn't prepared to see them this soon. Perhaps luckily, Azrael tensed up as well, and Jeremy looked away. Was that shame in his eyes? Or were they righteously irritated by her?

Thankfully, Hermes, either oblivious or not caring for their petty disagreement, cut right to the chase.

"Where have you been staying, and are there any more?"

Probably happy to have something to do, Azrael looked at him and answered, "In the infirmary. Zadkiel is also on the island. Her mind is not in good shape."

"I've been healing her to the best of my ability," Jeremy clarified. "But her mind is shattered and the pieces don't fit."

"I will speak with her tomorrow. We should all stay at the infirmary," Hermes answered. "I have to clean up this mess," he continued, gesturing around the office. "The Fallen managed to break through my wards during the attack. Who knows what they stole? Meanwhile, the four of you would do best to work on rebuilding this place. Clean it up and make it inhabitable for refugee angels."

That task felt like karmic punishment. Having to spend her days with Jeremy and Azrael, when she so very much wanted to run away from the conversations they needed to have, was just like bumping into an ex everywhere you go right after they've broken your heart.

Turning toward her, Hermes added, "And you'll resume your training with Azrael at six tomorrow morning."

Well, shit.

Ignoring his daughter's pleading look, Hermes walked out of the room and down the dark stairs and corridors toward the infirmary, the three of them in tow. Apparently none of them felt like talking.

When they arrived, Hermes strode right through the ward, toward the large window, where he stood for minutes without speaking. He was overseeing the damage to the island he had built thousands of years ago and which had been destroyed in a matter of hours.

When she'd first arrived here, months ago, she'd become fond of the view through the bay window. It looked down upon fields of green grass, entirely untouched by man. This island had belonged to Hermes' people for millennia, and remained magically protected from human or Fallen interference. It had become a haven to Lyla, with its fields of green, its rocky cliffs and beaches, and the beautiful village full of angels who knew nothing but peace and freedom.

Now, it stood in ruins. The snow-covered fields outside the infirmary were littered with chunks of grey rock that seemed to have been pulled straight out of the temple walls. But what was worse was the mess of pink blood and feathers that had been snowed and iced over before anyone could clean it up. There weren't any bodies in sight. Jeremy, Azrael, and Zadkiel must have given them funerals. But the remnants of the carnage were unmistakable.

Lyla didn't want to take a closer look at what it was her father was examining. Instead, she waited in the doorway, trying to figure out which beds were Azarel's and Jeremy's.

"We're all staying right here by the door," Azrael whispered behind her. "If you take the far-right corner, you and I won't have to look at each other."

She briefly turned toward him. The disdain in his eyes told her everything she needed to know about how he'd processed their argument. She didn't just need to apologize to him. She needed to make amends.

2

The next morning, she stood in the fighting ring at six a.m., just like she had countless times before. But this March morning felt nothing like the fall. For one, the fighting ring, though cleared of the bodies they'd had to leave behind when they'd escaped in late November, was surrounded by pieces of fallen rock that had been torn off the temple in the horrific battle she'd had no choice but to watch from the top of the Sacred Mountain. The fighting dummies were shredded to pieces, stuffing poking out of them and trailing onto the ground, and she couldn't unsee the dozens of broken and dead angel bodies they'd walked past the last time she'd been here. This inner courtyard of the temple had become a refuge to her in the past, a place where she could exert physical energy and feel free of her thoughts and emotions for a moment. Now it was just another depressing quadrant to mourn in.

But what was worse, was the icy look in Azrael's eyes, as she handed him a cup of steaming coffee and he simply put it on the ground and jumped into the ring without a "thank you," proceeding to go through their usual sparring motions as if they'd never left the island. She'd known a cup of coffee wouldn't cut it, but it had gotten her truly nowhere at all, which felt unfair. Her resentment toward him sparked again as he so casually dismissed her attempt to fix things between them. And yet, feeling his body heat so close to hers just made her forget everything and want him all over again.

Both of those emotions made it impossible to focus. She was usually very good at hand-to-hand combat, having had to learn out of necessity in a world that presented potential danger at every corner. But this morning, Azrael kept getting past her defense. He dropped her and pinned her to the ground time and time again. Until he silently turned away, walked out of the ring, and took a seat on a giant fallen chunk of the inside wall of the temple.

They never took breaks that early into a training session, but Lyla stepped through the ropes and followed him, wondering why he'd stopped.

"What are we doing?" she asked, crossing her arms.

"We're going to talk."

"Great. Look, I shouldn't have kicked you out the way I did. I know that," she started explaining, hoping they could clear things up once and for all. "I regretted it about five minutes after you were gone. But you have to understand—"

"That's not the conversation we need to have. I don't care about that. You acted like a fledgling. What a surprise. What we need to talk about is that I could have beat you in fifty different ways in the last five minutes alone," he grunted. "You're so angry at me, it's making you sloppy."

"You could kill me in fifty different ways every day of the week. That's been firmly established," she answered, unable to stop the simmering rage in her chest or the cruel part of her that wanted to remind him of how close he'd gotten to harming her in the fall.

"That's a low blow, Lyla," he replied, not taking the bait. "I taught you better than to let your emotions overpower you like this. You're so angry at me, you're letting your training go out the window."

"I'm not angry anymore," she snapped back. "I just need to explain that I trusted you. And the way you threw the truth in my face... It felt like you couldn't have cared less. I spent months mourning Max's death, feeling guilty over it, missing him. And you allowed it, knowing full well that he'd never been worth my tears. You let me drown in my loss, only to end up throwing what a fool I'd been in my face. Cut me a break already!"

"Are you done?" he asked, raising an eyebrow as if he couldn't care less about her explanations.

"I don't know, do you have anything to say about any of what I just said?" she asked, her voice raising with her mounting frustration.

"Like I said before, I have nothing to say about what happened three months ago. We're at war. We can't afford to be wasting time with emotional crap."

"I came here wanting to apologize!" she yelled.

"Apology accepted. Now get your shit together."

"It clearly isn't!" she argued.

"I said," he growled. "I'm not having this conversation. You acted like a fledgling in January and that's your problem to deal with. It wasn't my job to tell you the truth. And I don't regret snapping you out of your denial. I didn't betray you. Max did. Max was the shithead who ruined your life and if you can't accept that you trusted the wrong person, loved and fucked the wrong person, that's your problem. You don't get to put that weight on my shoulders."

There it was. She'd been sleeping with Max and that irked

him. She wanted to take that word, "fucked," and shove it straight back down his throat.

"I never asked you to apologize," she calmly pointed out. "But it's good to know what's really bugging you. Friend." She let that last word drip with sarcasm. Maybe she shouldn't make her grief his problem, but his jealousy sure wasn't hers either.

"We're not friends, you and I," he coldly replied. "My job is just to train you."

"So, we're back to that?" she asked, incredulous, remembering those first few weeks of her training, in which he'd treated her as if he'd rather be around just about anyone else.

"It's never been anything else. Your father tasked me with your education and your safety. That's why I'm here. So next time you let your mood affect your sparring skills, I won't be so gentle about it. Maybe once you get hurt, it'll get through to you."

His words hit her like a slap in the face. She knew he'd only taken over her training begrudgingly. She knew he'd never wanted to be her mentor. But they'd warmed up to each other. They'd shared secrets, they'd laughed together, and they'd kissed. And he was willing to throw it all away over one mistake of hers, one outburst too many.

Even in her anger, she hadn't forgotten how she'd felt about him toward the turn of the year. She'd dreamt about it. Daydreamed about it. Every day of the last three months. How much she'd wanted him. How she'd felt a pain to the very core of her own soul when Lucifer had hurt him. And mostly, she'd gone to sleep every night fantasizing about what he'd feel like on top of her. Every night, her anger had dissipated when she'd imagined that first moment he'd penetrate her.

Time to put those fantasies to rest.

"Good to know," she told him, turned on her heel, and

climbed back into the ring.

3

By the end of their session, Lyla was so furious that she stomped upstairs with the intention of skipping lunch and taking a protest nap. It was one thing to point out to her how childish she'd been during their falling out. But to refuse to talk it out, to put his jealousy on the table and to then ice her out like a teenage boy might have... She wasn't the only one who needed to grow up.

The wind was taken right out of her sails when she walked into the infirmary and found her father standing at the window again, his inhumanely large shoulders slouched in what she could only read as impossible grief. He was overlooking the devastated island, his home, the home of generation after generation of his descendants.

He had a direct connection to every single one of them, Azrael had told her. He could feel their presence, their emotions. He couldn't see where they were or why they felt the way they did. But he could sense their joys and their sorrows, their love and their anger. When he'd been a part of the hive, they'd all shared a mind. And, though he was now a separate individual, he was still attached to his blood in his descendants' veins.

When the island had been attacked, he must have felt the agony of hundreds upon hundreds of his children, she realized. He must have felt their deaths. She'd learned over the last few months that his feelings went deeper than those of humans. They were after all the feelings of an immortal. Humans had good reason to move on from their pain and grief: their lives were fleeting, over at any time. For him, not so much. There was no fear of death driving him onward and onward. And so, he carried with him millennia of raw, badly over-scarred pain. She couldn't even imagine how that would feel. How he could make it out of bed every morning and continue fighting for what he believed was right. The attack on the island must have driven him mad. No wonder he had demanded that at least she fly to safety.

And now, he contemplated the results of the carnage. The safe haven he'd built for his children lay destroyed. There were only forty-two angels of his line left alive. Lyla quietly stepped up to his side, looking at the fields ahead – fresh, clean snow betraying the gallons of blood frozen into the ground.

"I want you to work with Azrael, Jeremy, and Zadkiel on rebuilding the island," he began, without taking his eyes off the landscape. When she inhaled to respond, he quietly added, "Don't. I am asking you to do so, not because it needs rebuilding, but because you need to get over your resentments. All three of you do. But you in particular cannot afford to hang on to such things. Your magic is too important to allow you to indulge in petty passions. Besides, someday you'll be their superior. You need to learn to work with them, regardless of your own mood."

She nodded, but remained silent. He was right and arguing would get her nowhere.

Looking back at the large window, he asked, "I can sense that three angels are in a separate location from the other thirty-six. Do you know where they are?"

"They are with a tribe of the lost in Upstate New York. Two fledglings and a hatchling. Orphans. We left them in their care before making our way to California," she replied, remembering the echoes of how tight her bond with Azrael had been in those traumatic, blurry days.

"Good thinking," her father mused. "They were safer there. However, I want everyone back under my protection as soon as possible. Next week, Azrael will bring back the thirty-six who've been hiding out in France. And Jeremy will accompany you to pick up the little ones. They'll only return them to a familiar face."

"I could go on my own..." Lyla suggested timidly.

At that, he turned around and sighed. "You could. But Jerahmeel will portal you there. And the two of you are long overdue for a sincere conversation anyways."

"That's what I'm afraid of," she admitted.

"He's got a good track record at— well, at being less of a hothead than Azrael. I'm sure it'll be fine. Meanwhile, how many more mixed angels live with Julien?"

"Four," she replied, remembering the grey-winged warriors who cohabitated with Jeremy's husband in Paris.

Grey wings were the sign of angels who were born from a white-winged descendant of the Ten Gods and from a lost child, a black-winged descendant of the Fallen. While the lost didn't follow the Fallen and just kept to themselves, angels snubbed their noses at them, and mixed offspring tended to not be welcome on either side. Some, like Azrael, chose a side anyway, only to live half-ostracized from their fellows. Others, like Jeremy's husband Julien and his friends, chose to permanently fold away their wings and blend in with humans.

Julien and his four friends had helped them invade Hell to rescue her father months ago. They'd followed him and Jeremy without question, and had subsequently indefinitely hosted the thirty-six refugees from Hermes' island in the abandoned warehouse they inhabited, making space and sharing their resources without ever questioning what their own fate would have been, had the tables been turned.

"Good. Azrael will convince them to join us."

"I know we need numbers," she replied. "But how will he convince them to join a cause they've avoided their entire lives?"

"The same way they were convinced to join your Hell mission."

They'd followed Julien... who had joined out of loyalty for Jeremy...

"You're going to have Azrael offer Julien to come live here and hope they follow him. That's quite manipulative," she mused.

"Maybe so. But in the end, a whole lot of people who love each other will end up under the same roof. That seems like a fair trade to me."

He sounded weary in that way only he could, that way that reminded her that he had been around this planet since the dawn of humanity. Which made her "petty passions", as he'd called them, pretty insignificant indeed.

4

Her work on the island was efficient. She would set the funeral pyres ablaze with the hottest of fires, then they'd stand back in order to not inhale the smoke, while Azrael spoke the funeral rites that were still foreign to her. She'd done this once before, just before the grey-winged angel and she had left for California. Back then, it had been pure instinct. The island had lain devastated and they'd had to do something about the mutilated corpses of Zadkiel's fellow soldiers so they wouldn't rot in the sparring ring. Singing had been how she'd channeled her magic then and it was how she channeled it now. They lifted up and set the corpses onto funeral pyres, mostly by physical exertion because it felt lazy to use magic for such a mournful and sacred task. And Lyla would use her sonic magic to set fire to them. She'd close her eyes, picture the flames, and send her magic through her voice, like a ripple in the air going straight toward the pile of dead bodies. Azrael would then speak words in an ancient language she didn't know a word of and they would move on to the next bodies, while the flames continued to burn brightly, melting the snow and leaving nothing but ash and bone fragments behind.

It was beautiful and gave her closure of sorts. But it was also extremely unpleasant. She was polite with Zadkiel, but the latter didn't answer any of her pleasantries. It was like talking to an ostrich – empty eyes and no acknowledgment of anyone's existence. And Lyla hadn't spoken a single word with Azrael or Jeremy.

The former would give the occasional grunting order, determining where to set up the next funeral pyre, while Jeremy kept his head down and quietly helped carry limbs and bodies from all over the village, and Zadkiel added tinder and wood for her to set ablaze. They didn't eat lunch. They silently agreed that none of them felt hungry. Not with the work they were doing. Not with the suffering that had happened on these streets. At least they could agree on that.

Meanwhile, Lyla couldn't shake the realization of how much she'd changed. In the fall, these deaths had ripped her in half, torn out her heart and stuck it in a blender. And now she looked at them with detachment. It wasn't her mantra – to keep going at all costs – keeping her from breaking down. It was everything Hermes had told her about the endless war with the Fallen. It was the fact she had been to Hell and fought Lucifer himself, looked into his terrifying goat eyes and his black wings, the void of pure nothingness. It was the fact that, as much as she hated to admit it, Azrael's rejection had hurt her worse than any of the horrors she'd witnessed in the last few months.

Other than Max, she'd always avoided romantic entanglements like the plague. She'd left every man or woman before they could say, "I love you." Max had been the only person she'd ever allowed near her heart. And Max had been easy to let in: she'd never had to fight for his love. Or so she'd thought. Who knew what Max had really thought all those years he was selling her out to the Fallen? But it had always felt like he would love her no matter what, like she didn't need to earn his love or worry about losing it.

And then she'd opened up to Azrael. In her grief, she'd allowed herself to feel something, to want something. To want someone. And she'd so desperately wanted him to want her back. She'd stupidly allowed herself to imagine that he might feel the same way. That he'd act on it. Those little emotional paper cuts tore at her heart. And yet, she felt... hardened. As if she too was beginning to look at the larger picture, as if these deaths were becoming statistics. Or maybe she just needed to stay cold and calculating or she would truly fall apart and never recover from the horrors she'd witnessed since the infamous day she'd left her life in New York. Either way, she had changed and she wasn't sure that it was for the better.

By sunset they'd made their way through most of the village and had arrived at the orphanage. Lyla dreaded the next step. The orphanage had been a happy place once upon a time, a place of child-like wonder and imagination. But when she'd seen it after the attack, it had been strewn with bodies of fledgling angels and their caretakers. Very little blood had flown here, because they'd died from magical, not physical, attacks. Magic had been swung at them through the air and had snuffed the life out of them, broken them internally, or smashed them into walls and trees at speeds they couldn't survive. The same bodies now lay across the courtyard and hung from the trees, frozen, covered in a layer of ice.

Lyla walked up the stairs into the courtyard first. Without saying anything, she flew up to a tree, and gently lifted a small body up and off the branch it had been impaled on. She could have levitated it, but these fledglings each deserved to be carried to their rest. She flew down and laid the tiny body carefully down at the top of the stairs, folding their wings around their body. Zadkiel followed suit. Meanwhile, Jeremy and Azrael sprang into action. They entered the building and carried out fledglings and their caretakers, one by one, adding them to the growing pile.

She could barely look at them – their young, scared faces, their small white wings... They weighed next to nothing in her arms, so full of promise. And killed, for what? Because two powers were at odds? She knew this war was righteous, but in this moment, she hated it. She hated all of them. The Fallen. The Gods. The warriors. They were the reason these young angels' lives had been snuffed out before they'd had a chance to even start.

It was long after dark by the time they'd collected every corpse or piece thereof, and laid it onto the substantial pile. She wished they could give each of them their own farewell, but she knew time would never allow it. So, Lyla set the communal pyre ablaze, melting all the snow and ice in the courtyard, while they watched from the bottom of the steps. Azrael spoke their funeral words in the old language of the hive, and Jeremy and Zadkiel silently listened. Lyla wasn't talking to them, but she knew, in this very moment, that they all felt the same way. The same rage, the same sadness, the same grief.

As they were about to turn around and leave, Zadkiel gasped, fighting for air, and fell to her knees. Before Lyla knew what she was doing, she jumped to the female's side and wrapped her wings around her, holding her tightly in a cocoon of white feathers.

"What the– Lyla!" Jeremy exclaimed. But she barely heard him through the darkness that began to envelop her and Zadkiel. And then she was in. How she knew, she had no idea. But she could see into Zadkiel's heart. Jeremy had wanted to give her purpose by asking her to help with the cleanup. But instead, this was all too much for her frail mind. Within the dark void Azrael had taught her to channel during meditation, Lyla pictured the other angel's mind. What she saw was a brain, cut up into pieces and glued poorly back together, cracking at the seams, slowly breaking apart. It looked like a jigsaw puzzle that hadn't been put together right, one Lyla desperately wanted to solve beyond anything she had ever wanted.

And then, the unimaginable happened. She saw the broken pieces of the warrior's mind break apart, as if floating in the void Lyla had conjured, and coming back together in the right order, stitching themselves back together seamlessly. She saw that brain begin to shine with a beautiful light that seemed to come from its very core. One by one, the pieces sprung back into place, as Lyla realized that she was the one who had willed them to do so.

As she pulled away, after what felt like an eternity, Lyla stumbled back and opened her eyes, only to see the life return to Zadkiel's, a slow smile spreading on the latter's lips. She let her go and turned toward an incredulous Jeremy frowning at them. Lyla opened her mouth to explain what had just happened, but before she could speak a single word, her wings snapped back into her body and she fell to her side. As she drifted into unconsciousness, she heard the female warrior's voice for the first time. "Gentle males, I'll carry her up to the temple. Clearly, she doesn't want anything to do with either of you."

With that, Lyla disappeared into oblivion.

5

She'd been in this soft, warm cloud of sheets before. She remembered waking up, weary like today, in one of these cozy hospital beds like it was yesterday. Last time, she'd had a broken heart and a splitting headache. This time, her heart was hurting in a different way, but her forehead was warm. No, that was a warm hand on her forehead. She knew that hand. Its touch was the most comforting gesture in the world. It made every ache fall away, until all that was left was her and that hand that told her everything would be okay.

She so very much wanted to stay in that delusion that everything was just fine. If she focused enough, she could almost imagine the sounds of healers bustling around this place, their feathers scraping on beds as they went from one sick angel to another, whispering words of comfort and injecting them with their healing touch. That's how it had been the first time she'd awoken in one of these beds. Aphrodite's healers had been working their magic around the clock, making this the most restful place she'd ever set foot in. But they were all gone now, save for Jeremy. Not a single one had survived. Now the place was quiet, every motion echoing in its solitude.

With a sigh, she opened her eyes and looked into Jeremy's face, who immediately removed his hand from her forehead, and put it in his lap instead, casually leaning back as if to cover up the misstep. For a moment she just looked at him. She'd almost forgotten what he looked like. It was his touch and his voice she'd always recognized and trusted. But looking into his face had always felt bizarre. Like he was a stranger somehow.

He smiled at her, and she noticed the peaceful, happy lines that smile drew on his cheeks. How had she forgotten about that?

"You're not playing fair," she told him, as she sat up. "You know I can't stay mad at you, when you give me your magic."

"I'm the only one here who could heal you," he answered sheepishly. "And you'd worn yourself out. Again."

"I just needed to sleep it off. I've been practicing ten times as hard in the last few months. I would have been fine and you know it. You just wanted to use the opportunity to get back into my good graces."

"Did it work?"

He wasn't the one needing to make amends...

"I don't know if I was ever really mad at you," she replied, looking out the window. "I was just angry about finding out about Max after months and months of lying."

"You'd rather not have known?" he sincerely asked her.

"Yes. No. I honestly don't know. I'm not sure what I'm supposed to do with the information now."

"If I may make a suggestion," he replied." I think you may need to grieve."

Lyla scoffed. She couldn't imagine needing to grieve the bastard after all the tears she'd already shed thinking he'd been the best thing that had ever happened to her.

"I mean it," Jeremy intoned, unmoved by her sarcasm. "I know you mourned Max. But I don't think you've grieved the loss of your old life, the loss of everything you knew, and of who you used to be. It's just a thought."

He stood up to leave and she called after him, "By the way, It's completely inappropriate of you to bypass my boundaries by using your magic on me to gauge where I'm at."

He ground his teeth and said, "You're right, I'm sorry. And while we're on healing magic, how is it that you could heal Zadkiel, and heal her better in the span of a minute than I did in weeks?"

He left without waiting for an answer. Had he guessed? And was she ready to share that information with him?

She'd always thought of Jeremy as a friend, a confidant, a big brother. But, having just felt his magic seep through his hands and into her mind, she realized that, if it weren't for his touch, she might never have opened up to him. Come to think about it, she didn't know the first thing about him, other than the fact that he was married to a doctor and had once dated Azrael. Though maybe love didn't mean knowing everything about another person. Not caring had been the goal for most of her life, as she'd protected herself against any and all bonds outside of Max that could have made her vulnerable to pain, betrayal, or grief. Somehow, that didn't seem like such a sage goal anymore. Maybe extending love to people without assurances wasn't so bad.

On the other hand, if he found out who she was, he might very well hate her. After all, she was the reason his mother was dead. She was the reason his people were gone. If it hadn't been for her, Aphrodite's island would never have been attacked. Maybe she'd better keep her healing powers to herself for the time being.

6

A week later, they'd given everyone on the island decent funerals and Lyla's lessons with Azrael had become unbear-
ably frigid. Where there had used to be jokes and banter, there
was nothing but coldness and gravity left. Thankfully her father
decided it was time for Jeremy and her to return to Phoenicia
and regain custody of the orphaned fledglings. Her feelings for
Jeremy were complicated too, what with the secret she was hiding from him, but at least his attempts to kill her with kindness
were more bearable than Azrael's open spite.

Carrying a small backpack with everything she'd have
packed for a long hike – water, food, and a small armory's worth
of sharp weapons – Lyla waited in Hermes' empty office for Jeremy to join her on their mission to pick up the children from
their temporary home with the lost in Upstate New York. Hermes, who was currently out assessing structural damage to the
village, was certain that they would willingly return the three
children Lyla and Azrael had rescued from the attack on his
island, but she wasn't so sure. The three siblings, Cassiel, Raziel
and Sarathiel, had witnessed the Fallen's attack and been trau-

matized by it. It had taken everything they had to extend their trust to Azrael and her. But instead of keeping them safe themselves, they'd had to drop them off with a strange tribe of the lost with only Azrael's assurance that they'd be safe there. Now, they were about to uproot them again, months later. Lyla knew all too well how constant lack of stability could retraumatize a child until their body and mind knew only danger and could no longer recognize safety when they saw it.

Jeremy finally arrived, a smile on his face. He was so good at extending kindness and good humor in the face of her detachment. And it worked. Instead of trying to get her to open up to him again, he just showered her with love. He hadn't crossed any physical boundaries with her since that morning in the infirmary, nor did he invade her mind to influence it. He was simply kind at all times. Maybe he couldn't help it. Maybe that was what it meant to be a priest of Aphrodite's. But if it did – why couldn't she do the same? Why couldn't she extend unconditional love to those who'd hurt her? She knew she was capable of it; she'd done it with Max. And yet, she couldn't help that gnawing feeling in her stomach every time she thought of her love for Max. Had it truly been unconditional? Or had it been entirely circumstantial? Had she simply bonded with the only seemingly safe person around because she'd needed a lifeboat? Didn't unconditional mean that she should continue to love him in spite of his betrayal?

She was still deep in thought when she and Jeremy stepped from the portal into a brisk New York afternoon. This time, surprisingly, they were not greeted by a group of stealthy warriors. The lost weren't known for letting angels wander into their territory, she thought, as they silently stepped into the woods. In fact, there was a reason they had grown so secretive and well-prepared as a species: they were hiding in plain sight in the human world. This specific tribe lived just a short hike from Phoenicia, a touristy New York town full of locals and through-hikers, and they'd remained hidden through constant vigilance as well as by using magic to create frequent bear sightings in and around town, deterring people from hiking too far into certain parts of the woods.

Finally, twenty minutes into their walk, Lyla felt a pair of eyes on her. She could just sense it — they were being stalked. Jeremy stopped short, as soon as he too realized what was happening. "We come in peace," he said loudly. "Please save us the trouble, and show yourself so we may speak to your Eldest."

Last time she'd been here, Lyla had learned that a request to speak with their leader could not be refused. By asking for an audience with their Eldest, Jeremy had effectively stopped the lost from attacking.

It was a testimony to his stealth that Lyla saw the male stepping out of the bushes before hearing him. Unfortunately, she recognized him the second he looked at her. And from the way he looked at her, he did too. It was Marcus, the douchebag who'd spat in Azrael's face the last time they'd been here. But he looked different. His wings were folded away and he wasn't as well fed. Not as well groomed. He looked tired. And even angrier than last time.

"It's not a good time," he answered Jeremy's request, not taking his venomous eyes off Lyla. "What do you want?"

"I can't tell you that, I'm afraid," Jeremy carefully replied. "We need to speak with him directly."

"He's indisposed."

"We'll wait," Jeremy dug in his heels.

"Be my guest," Marcus spat out, angrily turning around to leave them in the middle of the woods. But there was something else on his face. Just as he took his eyes off her and looked into the distance for a moment, she saw it. There was a deep weariness in his features. And fear. Yes, that was unmistakably fear. Lyla closed her eyes and, just like that, she knew. She couldn't explain the flashing vision of the Eldest in bed, coughing his lungs out. But she knew, in the depths of her being, that it was the truth.

"He's sick, isn't he?" she called after Marcus.

The lost stopped in his tracks, but didn't turn around.

"You're afraid he's dying," she continued.

Jeremy turned around, wide eyed, but she ignored him. "We can help. My friend here is a healer. Let us repay you for taking in the fledglings."

Marcus stayed frozen, but she saw his shoulders sag just a little. Finally, he turned around. The look in his eyes broke her heart. She'd hated him when he'd called Azrael a "dog," but in this moment, all she saw was a male in pain, afraid to lose his leader, afraid for his fragile community. Marcus swallowed and nodded.

Without invitation, Lyla took a careful step toward him, and another, until Jeremy followed. They walked through the woods for over an hour, never looking at each other, keeping up the respectful silence of a funeral procession, before she saw them. A collection of abandoned trailers and cars, so old all color had peeled off of them until all that was left was rust. But there was a certain beauty to them, their oxidized color matching the dead leaves on the ground, almost like camouflage. The trailers seemed to be inhabited, while the cars had all sorts of other purposes: some had drying plants in them, others were full of cans of food and jugs of water. She knew this was where the tribe lived, cleverly disguised as a group of travelers, should anyone come upon their community. But there wasn't a soul around. The lost were fundamentally angels, descended from the Fallen as opposed to the Gods, but genetically the same. And if there was one thing she'd learned from her time on Hermes' island, it was that angels had a sense of community that had long since been lost in humans. They lived and breathed fellowship, and never shut themselves off from others. So, why were these lost all locked inside in the middle of the afternoon?

Marcus led them to a trailer that was indistinguishable from the others. He gestured for them to wait, ascended the steps, and quietly knocked on the door.

"It's Marcus. I brought someone who might be able to help."

Lyla didn't hear a reply, but Marcus slowly opened the door and all three entered the humble trailer. The outside hadn't betrayed any of its beauty. It was a true home, with tapestries on the walls, decorative weapons, and a sense of deep, deep love. At the end of the trailer, in a bed covered in pillows and cozy blankets, lay the bald man she had met all these months ago. But he looked so much frailer today than he had even then.

"Marcus," he inquired in a raspy voice he clearly hadn't used in days. "Marcus, you shouldn't bring people, I might infect them."

With the end of his sentence, he went into a coughing fit, the likes of which Lyla had only seen in the movies when you know a character is bound to die. Marcus stepped toward the old male, but stopped himself. She saw the pain etched into his face. Every fiber of his being wanted to help the Eldest, but he was scared of the disease, scared of spreading it to the rest of the community. Jeremy, on the other hand, wasn't so scared. He stepped right up to the bed, and sat down at the old male's side, ignoring the latter's weak motions to stay away.

"I've seen this before. A tribe Azrael and I visited last month in Western Canada was plagued by the same disease. I can help. How many more sick do you have?"

"A dozen," Marcus replied, bowing his head. "Nothing seems to help. It's spreading."

"Any dead?"

"Five. But half the sick could be dead by the end of the week."

Jeremy turned to Lyla and sprang into action. "Marcus, is it? I need you to take Lyla into town. Go to a drugstore and get all the surgical masks you can get. Stock up on multivitamins as well, cold medicine, disinfectant..."

Lyla turned toward the door, when he added, "And, Lyla– be safe."

She nodded and left, closely followed by Marcus.

7

It took them two hours to arrive in town. Two hours without a word said. Two hours with nothing but a cloud of gloom above them. Jeremy had said that he'd seen this in another tribe of the lost. A virus, then. But he'd said Western Canada. How the hell did a virus infect two tribes on opposite sides of the continent? Tribes that lived completely isolated lifestyles and never travelled? Unless it had been carried by humans. She couldn't quite remember her biology lessons, but she did remember that the bubonic plague had been erroneously blamed on rats, when it was actually fleas that had spread it. And if she remembered correctly, the fleas would get more aggressive and have trouble feeding when infected with the plague, so they'd eventually die of starvation, but they weren't actually dying of the plague. What if humans were the fleas in this case? With modern travel, they could easily be carriers of a plague that only affected angels.

When they finally arrived in town at four in the afternoon, she realized she was dead wrong. She'd been here mere months ago, and she remembered it for the touristy place it was. A very small community, it tended to have visitors and hikers alike populating its few streets. But today, it was deserted. Every storefront, the very stores that made their living from said hikers, had a "Closed" sign on it. Some were even boarded up. The campgrounds, usually crawling with hikers, were shut down, their cute bear signs turned morose rather than sweet. Marcus quietly walked her to the only open store: the pharmacy. They entered, and the pharmacist immediately started gesturing in a panic.

"Wear a mask or get out of my store!"

Lyla didn't understand the words at first. The pharmacist seemed threatened. She herself was wearing one of the light blue surgical masks Jeremy had mentioned. Above her, a television blurted the news. Horrific images of hospitals across the world... entire cities on lockdown... more sick than there were sickbeds...

And finally, it dawned on Lyla. This wasn't an angel problem. This was a global problem. A pandemic like they'd been warned about by disaster movies. Somehow, it had spread in the time in which she'd been isolated in the middle of nowhere with her father. And now people, humans and angels alike, were getting infected by the tens of thousands.

"I'm sorry," she said, pulling her sweater up to cover her mouth and nose, "I don't have a mask."

The pharmacist carefully handed them two masks, stretching her arm as far over the counter as it would go, the kinds of masks Lyla had never seen on anyone other than doctors, and the occasional tourist on the New York City subway.

"What do you need? I want you out of here as fast as possible," she told them, grabbing a spray bottle and disinfecting the counter in front of her.

Three hours later, Marcus and Lyla were back inside the Eldest's trailer with two backpacks full of supplies, though everything had been scarce at the pharmacy which must have been raided by the locals.

"We'll have to make do with this," Jeremy said, as he left a bottle of cold medicine and one of multivitamins on the Eldest's bedside table. "He is sleeping for now. Let me visit your other sick and I will come back to him in a few hours."

They spent the entire night going from one trailer to the next. Lyla would distribute supplies and leave, waiting around the dark woods for Jeremy. Finally, they visited a trailer covered in children's drawings. The moment they walked through the door, a familiar scent hit Lyla and she panicked. Turning toward the bed, she saw a small form she recognized. It was Cassiel, the brave pre-teen fledgling she had met all these months ago. Cassiel had been ready to sacrifice herself to save her younger siblings. She'd shown so much courage. But also, resignation. She'd reminded Lyla of Max when he'd been a child, so willing to throw himself into the fire to save those he cared about.

And now... Cassiel smelled of death. She was glistening with sweat, thrashing around in her bed, clearly hallucinating, and her breathing could only be described as a rattle.

Raziel and Sarathiel, her siblings, were nowhere to be seen. She must have been quarantined from them. But near her head hung a picture, drawn by a small untalented child, of three angels. The tallest one, a girl, stood with her wings wrapped around her little brother while she held the bundle that was her hatchling sister in her arms. At that sight, Lyla broke away from Jeremy and Marcus and ran toward the little form in the bed. She'd be goddamned if those fledglings lost their sister after everything they'd lost already.

"Lyla..." Jeremy cautioned.

He didn't want her to be discovered for how powerful she

was. She understood that. She knew her father would be furious. But no one here knew that she was of Hermes' lineage. They'd simply think her a young priestess of Aphrodite's. Besides, she didn't care. A fledgling's life was on the line. Protecting her anonymity was meaningless in comparison to that.

Before Jeremy could stop her, her hands were on Cassiel's head and she was lost inside the little one's soul and body.

She could see it. The virus. The enemy. She was in a dark space, a void, and Cassiel lay on the ground fighting, while the red and pink virus wrapped itself tighter and tighter around her, its numerous tentacles reaching into her mouth, eyes, ears, wrapping themselves around her to consume her whole.

She had no idea how regular descendants of Aphrodite's were trained to heal. She didn't know where Jeremy would have started. All she knew was what instinct told her to do, which was to untangle the enemy from the fledgling, and murder it.

So she did. Lyla pulled out her pristine white wings and screamed at the virus. Screamed uncontrollably in its direction. As she did, it turned its head toward her, its head which was just a red blob with pockmark-looking scars of deeper burgundy and sunken red eyes. And then it turned back toward its prey and grabbed the fledgling tighter than it had before, its tentacles slithering into her face, wrapping themselves around her throat to suffocate her.

Without hesitation, Lyla grabbed the arm creeping around the child's throat. It was slimy like a worm, but she held on to it. She instinctively reached into her boot and found the blade Azrael had given her all those months ago. Without ceremony, Lyla cut the tentacle and threw it to the side.

The monster hissed. But it was a virus and could only do the one thing: attach itself to another cell and infect it. So Lyla went about her business. One at a time, she ripped the tentacles off

Cassiel, and cut them away until there was only one left – going down the fledgling's throat. She grabbed it and pulled it out of the child's body, fighting against its resistance, this virus with only one mind: to survive, no matter what. And then, she looked it dead in its beady red eyes, bit through the tentacle, and spat it out into the corner of the void.

The thing detached itself from Cassiel, then shrieked and shriveled away as if it had never existed.

Lyla opened her eyes to find herself back in the trailer with a strange aftertaste in her mouth.

And then, everything went dark. Just like it had after she'd healed Zadkiel.

8

Lyla opened her eyes to Jeremy's smiling eyes. She was in Cassiel's bed, in the back of the fledglings' trailer, surrounded with their toys and stuffed animals. She must have passed out from healing the young female. The little ones were nowhere to be seen, probably reunited in another trailer.

"Good morning, little sister," Jeremy greeted her, a mischievous smile breaking through the concerned creases on his face.

Her brain went into overdrive. He knew. Why was he sitting there, grinning? They'd barely spoken in months and he'd just found out that she was the cause of his sorrow. Did he not hate her?

"You know? How long have you known?" she asked apprehensively.

"You healed a dying fledgling in minutes from a virus it would take me many sittings to heal in healthier subjects. I wondered after Zadkiel, suspected after Cassiel, and you just confirmed it yourself. Besides, now I get why Hermes keeps talking about how special you are, calling you a 'miracle' and whatnot. I don't understand how it's possible, but if you are who I think you are, you are quite the marvel indeed."

Gods, the love in his eyes... It was overpowering. No wonder Azrael had found it unbearable to be loved so deeply by another angel.

"I am..." she replied, tentatively.

"So, you have both Hermes' and Aphrodite's powers?" he inquired.

"Actually, more like all of the Ten's..."

Lyla sat up, uncomfortably twisting her hands in her lap.

"That's how you knew that the Eldest was sick. You have Apollo's foresight..." her brother replied, awed.

"I can barely wield any of my powers though. I just occasionally get lucky. I guess I'm pretty young for what I am..."

"What you are..." he repeated. "You're a Godling... You're one of the Ten..."

He paused, shaking his head and probably wrapping his brain around this new reality. Finally, he cracked a smile. "I'll call you 'Eleven'..."

"I'm not shaving my head," she laughed, then added, more seriously, "You don't hate me?"

"Why on Earth would I hate you?" he replied, frowning.

"Because I'm the reason they're all dead. I'm the reason she's dead," Lyla told him, looking out the small window.

"Being the cause of something doesn't make it your fault," he told her, seriously. "I thought I'd lost everything that day. My people. My mother. My life in Paris. And my unborn little sister. I just got one of those things back. That is nothing short of a miracle as far as I'm concerned."

He kept grinning at her, and the knot in Lyla's stomach slowly untied itself. She'd projected her own resentments onto him. Hating the cause instead of the person responsible... That was something she did. But not Jeremy.

Shame began to replace her fear.

"Now I understand why you always felt so familiar to me," he continued. "You're one of mine."

"I'm sorry, Jeremy. I'm sorry for kicking you out. For holding on to my grudge. For distancing myself these last couple of weeks. It wasn't fair to you. I know you never meant to hurt me. But I've just been so angry and confused and..." The words poured out of her.

"I know," he replied simply, as if it was all far in the past and irrelevant now. "I'm sorry too. I didn't tell you about Max because you needed something to hold on to. And it wasn't going to be Hermes' island. And it wasn't going to be me. I didn't want you to fully lose your sense of identity. But I know it hurt you to find out that I'd kept the truth from you. I know I broke some of your trust. And for that I'm sorry."

He cocked his head to the side and gave her that look, so typical of him, that told her he was seeing right through to her soul.

"It's ok that you grieved him, you know?"

"Is it?"

"Everybody deserves to be loved and to be remembered. Even those who betray us. People are complicated and nuanced. We all do good things and bad things and things we can't even really explain. Life and people aren't black and white. They're full of strange and contradictory colors. His betrayal was only one aspect of your story."

She wasn't sure she agreed. More so, she knew she couldn't. Her world had always been black and white. Good or bad. Mostly bad... She needed to focus on Max's betrayal, to let him become his betrayal in her mind. She didn't have room for nuance. Anger was easier than grief and she'd had too much of the latter already. She didn't think she could survive any more.

"There's something else for which I've been meaning to apologize, Lyla," Jeremy added, speaking slowly, as if the words cost him.

"What do you have to be sorry for?" she asked, perplexed.

"For healing you."

"What do you mean? You think you shouldn't have healed me? Jeremy, I'd have died from grief if it weren't for you," she exclaimed, before he could explain himself. He'd spent months healing her emotional pain, helping her back onto her feet after she'd wanted nothing more than to die alongside Max. If it hadn't been for him, she'd have given up on life, given up on herself. But with his help, she'd started to heal and grow and move on. She'd even started to fall in love again. Not that she wanted to think of Azrael right now.

"I know. And that's why I did it. I couldn't help myself. When I met you... You were like this little baby bird with broken wings, and I had to mend them for you. But I healed you too fast, Lyla. I robbed you of the opportunity to heal yourself. I believe that's why you're so angry. If you'd moved on at your own pace, you'd eventually have gotten to a place of acceptance. You would have been able to let things go better. But I skipped the steps that would have allowed you to get there. And for that, I am so sorry."

He looked out the window as he spoke. It had always struck her how his "I'm sorry" truly sounded like he felt sorrow over his own actions.

"Maybe..." she replied, grabbing his hand and catching his attention. "But I can fly again. I'm fairly certain I'd be dead if it weren't for you... big brother."

That felt very unnatural to say, but she was glad their family ties might bring them closer together after all. He smiled a deep grin full of love, ran a hand over his face, and sighed.

"I'm very glad you aren't. Now. Let's go heal some lost. Your father is going to worry if it takes us too long to get back. And you really should just help me heal the patients. They already think of you as a healer, so you might as well do what you clearly are better at than me."

9

It took them another two days to heal all the sick and recover from the exhaustion the work put on them. Two days before they sat with the Eldest and Jeremy gave last words of advice.

"Don't go into town unless strictly necessary," he explained. "If you have to, send as few people as possible, make sure they wear face coverings, and quarantine them upon their return. Wash what they bring back. Wash your hands at all times. Wear masks when interacting with others. The virus could still be dormant inside some of your tribe..."

"Thank you," the old lost replied, his cataract-heavy eyes suddenly looking as sharp as they must have in his youth. "And in return, your secret is safe with us."

"Excuse me?" Lyla replied.

"I know who you are, Lailah of Hermes' line," he explained.

That wasn't good. Not only did he know the name only her father and Lucifer used for her, but he also knew that she was a healer and simultaneously from Hermes' blood line.

"Not to worry. I already knew last time I met you," he continued, pointing at his own milky white eyes and adding, "These aren't from old age. I've always had them. And I've always seen and known things. But you are starting to discover your own sight, aren't you, young one?"

Lyla swallowed. This would be very dangerous information in the wrong hands. But what truly disturbed her was that the Eldest had known what she was before she had. Why was he telling them now? Why was he threatening her with the information he knew right after she'd saved his tribe? Holding it over her head like some future leverage? Frankly, that just pissed her off.

"That's all well and good," she replied, covering up the anxiety in the pit of her stomach with nonchalance. "But that's not what we came for. And, no offense, but keeping my anonymity isn't worth the same as your life and the survival of your entire tribe."

"Fine, I'll bite," the old male replied. "What did you come for?"

"The fledglings—"

"No," he interrupted her with finality before she could finish her sentence. "They're staying here. You aren't uprooting them again."

"I'm not uprooting them. I'm bringing them back home!" Lyla exclaimed.

"This is their home! You brought them here, because you couldn't take care of them! Why should I trust that you can now?" the Eldest thundered in a voice louder than his frail body should have been capable of.

"They belong with their God!" Lyla retorted.

"Don't make me laugh," he scoffed in response. "As if he was going to raise them. As if he ever raised anyone."

"Don't you dare, old man. That's my father you're talking about..." she threatened.

"Oh, I know. Remember, I know more about you than you do yourself..."

"Enough with the threats. The Fallen know who I am. Who else are you going to tell?" she called his bluff.

"There are plenty of people in this world who'd pay good money for that kind of information."

"And that's how you'd repay me for saving your people? No wonder Azrael left you!"

Azrael had briefly lived among this specific tribe many, many years ago, but he'd left after an ugly fight with the Eldest. Probably just as ugly as this one was turning.

"And no wonder he and you get along so well," the old male replied sweetly and quietly. "Do you really think fledglings should be around either of your tempers?"

He'd baited her to make a point. And perhaps he even had a point. But she couldn't let that stand. She didn't know the fledglings. She'd met them for all of an hour. And yet, she felt responsible. When they'd left them here, they hadn't had a choice: they'd had to cross the country, enter Hell, and rescue her father from Lucifer himself. It hadn't been a place for children. But now, she couldn't help feeling guilty for abandoning them. She knew exactly what it felt like, being left behind. God knew she'd been abandoned over and over again by her various caretakers. She couldn't bear being the one doing the abandoning now. Lyla took a deep breath to quiet the seething rage inside of her, and calmly replied, "They've known you for all of five minutes. They've lived on Hermes' island their entire lives. It's their home. It's where they belong, and it's where they're going to be returned."

"And who exactly will raise them?" he replied, unfazed. "The handful of angels left from the attack, who are too busy rebuilding their entire home?"

How much more had his sight revealed to him?

"At least they'll be safe there," Lyla spat out, full well knowing she was twisting the knife. "You've had them in your care for a few months, and, if it weren't for us, one of them would already be dead by now. You can't take care of your own. They aren't safe here, and you know it."

The old lost shrieked away as if she'd slapped him across the face. He had no response for that. She knew she'd hit him below the belt, but he'd provoked her first. And yet, she felt no satisfaction in hurting the old male. As he stared at her, readying himself for his next retort, Jeremy interrupted.

"Maybe we should let them choose for themselves, before you make them listen to any more of your vitriol."

That was the judgiest Jeremy had ever sounded to her, and Lyla felt a wave of shame pass over her, as she turned around and saw Cassiel and Raziel standing outside the nearest trailer, holding hands, and staring at them with big eyes.

"I think that's enough from you two," Jeremy continued, in a quietly menacing tone she'd never heard from him before. "The fledglings shouldn't be influenced by you in their decision. So I suggest you both go cool off, while Marcus and I talk to them."

Lyla hadn't taken her eyes off the Eldest and barely heard Jeremy's words.

"You're dismissed," he added, harshly. "Get out of here. Both of you."

10

It took Lyla the better part of an hour to cool off. She felt like a hamster in a wheel, chewing through her conversation with the Eldest over and over again, as she walked up the side of the forested hill in the shadow of which the tribe lived, dead leaves crunching under her feet. She knew what she'd just done was stupid. Angels and the lost may not have had an alliance, but the lost were neutral. Pissing one off who had information about her nature as well as her whereabouts was unwise to say the least. And yet she hadn't been able to help herself. She wanted to think it was because of the children. That she'd felt protective of them, that she wanted to spare them the kind of pain she'd been through herself. That she was taking them out of an environment in which they'd been endangered. But she knew that wasn't the full truth. The ugly little reality she didn't want to admit to herself was that she was constantly angry. She'd been angry at the world for as long as she could remember. But it had gotten so much worse since she'd found out about Max's betrayal. And she kept pushing. It. Down. She was enraged at him. At the Fallen for having used him that way. At Azrael for leading her on and rejecting her. All of her life, all she'd tried to do was to protect herself from hurt. And yet, it kept coming. How much angrier and more violent did she have to get until it stopped and she was finally safe from pain?

She felt like she could explode at any time, and the old man had pulled the pin out of that grenade with his comments. She should apologize to him. But she wouldn't. She wouldn't because she knew she'd been right too. The children were not safe here. Cassiel had nearly died in his care.

Kicking the leaves on the ground until she accidentally stubbed her toes on a hidden rock, Lyla turned around with an exasperated sigh and returned to the camp, plastering a fake smile to her face she knew no one would mistake for the real thing.

She didn't apologize, ignoring the uncomfortable feeling in her stomach telling her that she'd come to regret it later. She remained silent while Jeremy informed them that the fledglings had decided to come home with them. She remained silent as they collectively walked through a portal that brought them back to the island. And she remained silent while Azrael, with the love and care he could no longer show her, took the little ones to a corner of the infirmary he had prepared for them, decked out with plush toys he must have found at the orphanage and wooden figurines she knew he'd carved himself. The fledglings hadn't even looked in her direction, accepting only Jeremy's hands as they'd left the encampment, and Lyla didn't feel like receiving another rejection as Azrael carefully tucked them into two beds he'd pushed together for them. Weary and exhausted, she lay down in her own bed in the opposite corner of the large room, turned toward the wall, and prayed for dreamless sleep.

What was left of Lyla's anger dissipated the next morning

at the sight that greeted her in the kitchens. While she and Jeremy were getting the fledglings back, Azrael had successfully convinced Julien, Jeremy's husband, and his four best friends to come join their cause. They'd apparently come over from Paris, alongside the Hermes refugees who'd stayed with them these past few months. How he'd done it that quickly was a mystery to her. Julien and his friends were all mixed children like Azrael. Their grey wings attested to the fact that they were neither angels nor lost, neither descended from the Gods only nor solely from the Fallen, which is why they tended to be welcome on neither side and kept mostly to themselves. Azrael was an exception in that he'd chosen to live with his Hermes relatives and to fight for the God. But the color of his wings caused constant strife and struggle. Everywhere he went, he got dirty looks from angels who believed him to be inferior, while also respecting his immense magical power and strength. Maybe the mixed angels had been convinced by the fact that there were only a few handfuls of angels left anyhow, most of which owed them big for housing and feeding them for months. Or maybe Julien was simply tired of being separated from his husband and his friends loved him too much to let him leave on his own.

All forty or so angels enjoying an early breakfast together was a wonderful sight. The last time she'd seen them, they'd been beaten down from the attack on Hermes' island and the rescue mission into Hell. They'd all lost family members, friends, their loved ones as well as their tribe as a whole. They'd clearly bonded with one another in the months they'd spent in the Paris warehouse. They'd formed a new family. It warmed Lyla's heart to see such a display of community after the many months she'd spent in isolation, but she equally felt something twist inside of her. She wasn't a part of this community. She didn't belong with them.

Looking around the room and its many wooden communal tables and benches, she saw two isolated groups. To the left, in a corner, sat Jeremy, his head on Julien's shoulder, a look of absolute relief on his face. He looked tired, the kind of tired one only feels when, after a period of life and death survival, they're finally allowed to shed the stress and let their guard down.

And to her right, at the end of a long table, sat Cassiel and Raziel with Azrael, hatchling Sarathiel safely swaddled in his arms. She stood in the entry arch, unseen by anyone for several minutes, watching the large angel feed the hatchling and entertain the fledglings. Raziel was playing with a wooden toy angel Azrael must have carved for him, making it fight and fly like a priest of Hermes' would in battle. Cassiel looked more serious, but she smiled at her little siblings with so much pride and love.

Lyla felt it again then. That twisting in her heart, that longing for something. She'd never wanted children, nor did she imagine she ever would. But something about seeing Azrael with the fledglings – how sweet they looked, appearing like a little family – made her yearn to be a part of it. She'd experienced his softer edges herself. She remembered that angel now that she was looking at him with the little ones. And she realized how much she'd missed him. She'd been focusing on her anger so much these last few days that she'd forgotten that she was furious because she had feelings for him and craved his company. That she longed for him to look at her again the way he was currently looking at the fledglings, with care and tenderness, with that softness and sweetness that was so very underrated in this world.

A familiar face pulled her out of her reverie before she could decide where to take her breakfast. Artiya had been a bartender at the local tavern, which had been owned by her, her twin sister, and their father. She'd lost both of them in the attack, but she didn't seem to blame Lyla for it, which was a relief. The young angel rushed toward her, crying out her name, and wrapped her arms around her. Before she knew it, she'd been turned away from the little family portrait she'd been staring at and was walking toward a larger gathering of angels, where Artiya immediately grabbed a plate and filled it up for her.

An hour later, Lyla met with her father, who informed her that she was to keep a strict schedule, similar to her first few months at the compound, but busier. In the morning, she'd train with her father, while Azrael and the other five surviving priests of Hermes' would teach the civilian angels how to fight. In the early afternoon, she and Azrael would train the seventeen surviving fledglings in magic and hand-to-hand combat. And in the evening, she'd train alternately with Azrael and with Jeremy.

With that, another period of nothing but work started for her.

11

She arrived early for her first lesson with the fledglings. Not only had she not been able to eat much after spending four hours with her father trying to forcibly make her have visions, but she wanted to check in on Cassiel and Raziel. The little ones were standing in a corner of one of the fighting rings, apart from the other fledglings, leaning against the ropes, visibly uncomfortable with yet again being on unfamiliar grounds.

As Lyla approached them, Raziel ever so slightly huddled closer to his sister. It broke her heart that she had frightened them so. Kneeling down in the snow to be at their eye level, she said "Hi. I know I scared you yesterday. I'm really sorry. I was worried about you, but I shouldn't have raised my voice the way I did. Can you please forgive me?"

It was Raziel who spoke first. "Will you ever yell at us like that?"

"Never," Lyla responded, her heart breaking a little. How had she become one of the scary monsters, when all she'd wanted was to protect them?

"We liked it there, you know?" Cassiel interjected. "It wasn't all bad. We were happy. The old male took good care of us."

"Good," Lyla replied with a sigh of relief. "Good. I'm glad. And I'm sorry we had to take you away. But Cassiel, you were very sick. We can take better care of you here if that happens to any of you again."

"I know," the fierce little angel answered. "I just don't want you to think badly of the Eldest."

"I don't, Cass."

"It's Cassiel," the young female corrected her.

"Cassiel. I'm sorry. And I'm very sorry for how I spoke to the Eldest. Sometimes adults get into fights that don't make sense to fledglings. But, please believe me, we all only want the best for the three of you."

"I hope I never turn into an adult," Raziel replied and ran off as he spotted Azrael entering the ring.

As for Cassiel, she crossed her arms and gave Lyla a look that made it very clear that she was not forgiven.

Azrael began the training session with endurance exercises for the children, making them run around the yard, do jumping jacks, jump squats... everything he'd have done with a group of adults, short of pushups – except that he was significantly kinder and less demanding on the little ones than he could have been. Some of Lyla's physical education teachers had been harsher than the gruff angel, but she imagined that he didn't want to turn them off the idea of training. Not after everything these fledglings had been through, not after they'd witnessed firsthand what happened to untrained angels under attack. Besides, resisting the cold of the outdoors alone was an exercise in resilience, one she was certain Azrael had not left up to chance.

When it finally came time for the little ones to pair up, there was an odd number, and Cassiel found herself stuck with Lyla.

"I want you to sit down crossed-legged in front of each other, knees touching, hands up to guard your face," Azrael said, walking through the pairs of fledglings. "One of you is going to try to touch the other one's forehead. The other one's only job is to not let themselves be touched."

And so, Lyla began trying to touch Cassiel's forehead. Batting a hundred at first, she could sense the mounting frustration in the girl.

"Don't just slap my hands away," she calmly advised her. "Remember that you can move your upper body. Dodge me by leaning back or to the side."

Begrudgingly, Cassiel took Lyla's advice and soon improved significantly, leaning back and away from Lyla's reach almost every single time.

When they switched places, Lyla slowed down her movements so as to let Cassiel win every other try... right up until it really pissed off the fledgling.

"Stop it! Stop letting me win!"

"I'm not—"

"You are too. How's that supposed to help me?" she exclaimed, jumping up.

"I was just trying to—"

"To what? Make me feel better about myself? Make me feel like I can take on a grown angel? Like I can actually defend myself?" the young female yelled down at Lyla, who raised her hands in defeat and stared at the ground. "That's going to be real helpful when we get attacked again! I'm sure that'll keep me alive when a demon is biting through my neck, or a Fallen breaks me in two like a twig! All they had to do was point at the fledglings and they fell from the sky and impaled themselves on the trees!"

She'd seen all of that with her own eyes, Lyla realized. She knew all too well what it felt like to see something horrific, and realize in the next instant that you'd never be able to un-see it, that you'd have to live with the memory forever. She re-membered the day she'd realized that a memory could actually change you.

"Aaaand we're done for the day!" Azrael interjected, just as the young girl stormed off, every little eye in the courtyard fol-lowing her exit. "Remember, dodge and weave before counter-ing with a swat. You're little, use it to your advantage! Tomor-row, we'll teach you how to throw a punch!"

Lyla remained seated, her forehead in one hand, while the fledglings filed away and into the warmth of the compound. Cassiel had looked so fierce and yet so scared and angry in her righteous rage. She knew that look. She'd seen it in the mirror for most of her life. The little angel was traumatized, probably couldn't get those bloody images out of her mind, probably saw them every time she closed her eyes at night. And she herself was nothing but another antagonist to her, another adult who didn't understand her, couldn't help her. If it weren't for her own display of fury yesterday, she could have won her over, she could have been her friend and helped her. But instead, she'd ruined every chance to get through to the young angel. Lyla fisted her hands in her own hair, wanting to pull it out with frustration.

"I heard that your audience with the Eldest didn't go well, but it must have been quite something to leave Cassiel hating you that much..." Azrael teased. She hadn't heard him approach, but he was standing outside the ring, his arms casually leaning on the ropes, looking at her through them.

"I let my temper get away with itself," she meekly replied.

"Well, there's a surprise, Miss 'I'll drop all plans and risk the lives of all my friends by attacking Lucifer himself,'" he retorted, his voice an impossible mixture of humor and resentment.

"You still haven't forgiven me for that?" she asked, getting up and awkwardly standing across the ropes from him.

"As opposed to popular belief, Lyla, forgiveness isn't something people can just grant at will. It happens with time. And no, I certainly haven't forgotten the little stunt you pulled in Hell, and what an unreliable soldier it makes you."

"Well, get in line," she retorted, pulling out her wings and protectively wrapping them around herself.

At the sight of her feathery cocoon, Azrael's eyes softened a bit. "It'll get better. She's a fledgling, all she wants is to feel safe. And she doesn't feel safe around you right now. But she'll learn as she gets to know you."

"What makes you so sure?" Lyla asked, fighting the tears making their way up her throat.

"Because your charm is absolutely irresistible," he replied rather sarcastically. And in a gesture that was uncharacteristic of him, he pulled a small flask out of the inside pocket of his jacket and handed it to her.

"I grabbed it from the tavern. It's no use to anyone there," he explained when she raised an eyebrow. "Take a swig, it'll warm you up."

They weren't friends anymore, but it was somewhat of a peace offering. She drank the disgusting, burning, whiskey-like concoction, and he added in a reprimanding tone reminiscent of the old days, "And you better eat something before our session. I don't need you passing out on me."

12

After that, the frigidity between Azrael and Lyla thawed somewhat. They never spoke outside of their training sessions and were all business within them, but she kept the snark to a minimum and he stopped giving her grief about his resentment toward her.

The refugees had all been given lodging on the side of the compound Lyla never visited; the side she knew had apartments so families could live a more regular lifestyle. And after a week, Hermes decided that it was time for Jeremy, Julien, Lyla, Azrael, Cassiel, and her siblings to leave the infirmary and move into individual cells as well. Sarathiel, the hatchling, moved into Azrael's, while her siblings got cells right next to his, though Lyla suspected that they slept in one room each night just like Max and she had done all those years ago when they'd needed each other's comfort in a strange new home. Azrael had turned out to have quite the nurturing instinct and to be the only angel Sarathiel accepted as a surrogate parent, and he seemed more than happy to oblige. Which left Lyla feeling even more isolated and envious of the connections everyone else around her seemed to be making.

The moment she opened the door to her cell, Lyla's mind was flooded with memories. She remembered standing in the middle of the room, her father saying goodbye to her, ordering her to hide from the attack, showing her affection for the first time. She remembered Jeremy, sitting on the floor talking to her through every one of her study breaks when she'd first arrived on the island. She remembered going to bed missing Max, imagining him with her, crying herself to sleep. But she also remembered restless nights, fantasizing about Azrael's wings and the powerful pecs she'd felt every time they'd sparred and wrestled.

But something smelled different tonight. There was a sweet and somewhat acrid smell in the air. And a noise. Coming from under the bed. The shuffling claws of a small rodent. Maybe a mouse? The place had been abandoned for the better part of six months after all. Carefully, Lyla got on her belly and crawled under the bed, where she saw... what could only be two teenage rats. One white, one grey, their tails wrapped around each other, they stared at her with huge black eyes. White rats didn't exist in nature. They'd been bred as lab rats and sometimes domesticated, someone had once told her. How on Earth pet rats had made it onto the island was a mystery for another day. For now, she needed to figure out what to do with these two tiny residents.

They'd made a nest under the bed by ripping apart her sheets, and from the looks of it, they'd been living there for quite a while. Lyla had always loved animals, and rodents in particular. She'd read that rats were very empathic and social. Tearing them away from their nest and releasing them in the wild could kill them – unless one adopted them and took care of them. She really wanted to keep them, raise them, and finally feel a little less alone. She wished she could come home to their tiny paws and ever-moving whiskers every night. But she could think of someone who was more in need of a pet than herself. And if it won her points with the fledglings, it would be worth the sacrifice. It was a bit of a dirty win. Truly, it was emotional manipulation. A bribe. And Lyla didn't care one bit if her decision was morally ambiguous.

Instead of getting the much-needed and earned sleep after an exhausting healing lesson with Jeremy, she ran down to the kitchen to collect the items she'd need: a metal crate even a rat couldn't chew through – hopefully – some vegetable peels from dinner she fished out of the compost, a water bowl, and some pieces of wood for the little ones to chew on.

Excited about her discovery, and worried the rats may have run off, she made her way back upstairs only to find them sleeping in the corner under her bed. She stripped it of its torn sheets and used them for the bottom of the crate, adding in the other elements as carefully as possible. Finally, she crawled under the bed and grabbed each rat to place them into their new home. She'd been worried about getting bitten and scratched, but it turned out that these critters, having been born into the empty compound, did not know to be afraid of someone as large as her.

Proud of the new little nest she had made them, Lyla picked up the crate and made her way to Cassiel's cell, where she found Azrael sitting on the single bed, one fledgling leaning on each of his shoulders, reading them a book from the library about the mythical tales of the Ten in ancient Greece.

"What do you want?" Cassiel opened.

Lyla took a deep breath before responding. "I have a gift for you. It's for both of you, but you're older, Cassiel, so you'll have to be in charge."

When no one responded, she turned around, picked up the crate, and carefully placed it on the edge of the bed. Reluctantly

Cassiel took a peak... and melted. All her rage, all her resentment was gone the moment she saw the sweet little rodents on their hind legs, looking up at her, sniffing all the new scents in the room, their whiskers whirling around at a million miles an hour. Raziel climbed right over Azrael's lap to join his sister in the discovery of their new pets, and both fledglings cautiously reached toward the animals, petting them with one finger each.

Lyla crouched at the foot of the bed, and explained, "If you want them, they're your responsibility now. You have to make sure they always have water and something to chew on. You can feed them food scraps from the kitchen. They'll eat almost anything. And it's your job to clean their crate every day. Can you handle that?"

"Yes," Cassiel answered, in a much more mellow tone than she'd used toward Lyla all week. She carefully picked up the white rat and held it to her chest.

"What will you call them?" Lyla asked.

"Easy," answered little Raziel. "The white one is Jeremy. And the grey one is Azrael!"

At that, the big angel chuckled. "However did you come up with those names?"

Lyla didn't want to intrude on what strongly felt like a family moment, so she got up and headed to the door without a word.

"Thank you, Lyla," Cassiel interrupted her exit.

She turned around. "You're very welcome."

The sweet and intimate smile Azrael threw her behind the fledglings' backs was not lost on her.

Her heart fuller than it had been in a while, Lyla skipped back to her room to clean it of the rats' feces and make her bed. This had been more than just a win. It was a double win.

13

The next morning, however, Lyla's joy dissipated when she got news that the first case of the virus had emerged overnight. Jeremy had been trying to convince Hermes to isolate the refugees for a couple of weeks since they'd had contact with the outside world in Paris. But the God had refused, stating that their sense of community needed solidifying. They'd left the island in ravages and he worried their mental health might not take it well if they came back and were separated. But what had seemed like one or two cases of the sniffles all week, had turned into five grown angels running out of air overnight.

What made it worse was that Jeremy was the only official healer on the grounds. He'd spent all night running from one patient to another, but, while he'd stabilized three, two of them were in critical condition, and he was now spent.

Azrael, wearing a bandana over his mouth and nose, had woken her from her sleep, obnoxiously knocking on her door to deliver the news that the compound was going into emergency mode. Each angel was to move into their own separate cell, food rations would be brought to their doors by Hermes himself, since he was immune to disease, and all training sessions except for Lyla's were canceled until further notice.

"Did they separate Cassiel and Raziel?" were the first words out of her mouth.

"No, we made an exception. They are isolated together, with their new friends. Thank the Ten for those rats, Lyla," he stated, seriously. "Sarathiel is staying with me."

"What about Jeremy?"

"He's resting in his old cell. He's sad about being separated from Julien right after being reunited. But you know him. He'll do what needs to be done no matter what."

"I need to heal him," she replied, jumping up and down on one foot while trying to get the other into her pant leg.

"Lyla, are you delirious? You're not a healer."

She'd forgotten that he had no idea what she was.

"I healed Zadkiel, didn't I?" she started.

"Lucky coincidence. Jeremy had been working on her for weeks. You were probably just in the right place at the right time," he responded, clearly oblivious.

"We can't leave him like that!" she exclaimed, finally pulling the training pants all the way on, and getting to work on a button-down shirt.

"Lyla, I am not letting you expose yourself to the disease Jeremy probably carried back to his cell last night," he thundered. "He carries Aphrodite's mantle. He isn't sick, just exhausted. He will be fine."

He did carry the mantle, which meant that most of their mother's power had transferred to him in the moment of her death, leaving him the most powerful priest of Aphrodite's alive – not that there were many left. It occurred to Lyla that the mantle was supposed to carry on to Aphrodite's youngest child, which was technically her. But maybe it hadn't because Lyla wasn't an angel?

"Now get dressed, find something to cover your face with, and come meet me in the yard."

Begrudgingly, she obeyed the big guy.

One good thing, at least, came from this situation: Azrael and Lyla were to no longer train in hand to hand, as they had to stay six feet apart; they exclusively trained in magic, which went at a much more interesting pace for her. Not only was magical fighting what she'd wanted to practice for weeks, but she also preferred having a little distance from the stern angel these days. Physical proximity should be reserved for those she trusted emotionally and, as much as their banter was returning, that was no longer him.

Instead, they flew ten feet off the ground, and Azrael started throwing magic her way to destabilize her. She'd always been amazed by how nearly invisible those exertions of effort were for him. She'd trained her eye to see the lightning fast shimmer of magic ripple through the air between an attacker's wings and their target. But most of the priests she'd watched spar, train, and fight put a lot of energy into their strikes. Azrael did not. He'd effortlessly float in the air and a hit would knock into her with inexplicable force caused only by the slightest flap of a feather in her direction.

At first her job was to simply dodge his attacks using her physical training. No magic allowed. She'd dodge and weave in the air, fold her wings to the side... Failing more often than not, yet getting a good workout out of it. Finally, they switched and he became the target, which didn't go much better for her. She might have been a Goddess, but nothing beat decades of experience.

They kept on training all day, with only a short break for lunch. What Azrael didn't realize though, was how much Lyla had been holding back in the effort department. She'd fought him fair and square using Hermes' magic only. But her father's training had taught her to use several magics at once. She was still a novice in all of them and could only really wield Aphrodite's healing powers, some of Ares' raw strength, and force the occasional useless Apollo vision of what she'd be served at dinner. But she was now used to making much greater magical efforts as she'd begun to combine her powers. Which meant that, while Azrael thought she was knocked out for the night, she still had plenty of energy left.

Lyla ate her dinner, showered, and waited in bed, staring at the ceiling for two interminable hours, before she snuck out. The halls were empty, illuminated only by those Hermes-enhanced sconces that gave off more light than regular fire would or could have. His magic was such a part of the very fabric of the temple and of the island itself that she wondered sometimes whether it wasn't just a physical manifestation and extension of him. As quietly as possible, she made her way down the hall toward the stairs and to Jeremy's room. It was adjacent to Azrael's, so she made a particular effort to open the door quietly.

Jeremy was awake, and he looked even more exhausted than she'd expected.

"What are you doing? Lyla, go back to bed..." he whispered.

"Don't even," she replied. "I'm going to heal you."

"No one can know that I've been healed. Go back to bed. I'll be fine, I just need to sleep it off."

"They don't need to know. I'll heal you, and you can stay locked away for the appropriate amount of time, but at least you won't have to suffer."

"I'm not suffering. I'm just sleeping," he retorted in his most authoritative voice. It sounded like a kitten in comparison to the orders she was used to from Azrael and her father. So, she promptly ignored him, and pulled up a chair to the head of his bed.

"And you won't be useful out there if you're knocked out in here. I'm putting everyone out of their misery with this," she argued.

But before she could lay her hands on him, the door slammed open, and an infuriated Azrael, holding a shirt up to his face, rushed in. He didn't even bother to speak to them. He simply marched to Lyla, grabbed her in a bear hug, picked her up, and carried her out of the room.

Putting her down in the hallway, he shut the door behind them and said, "Outside. Now."

"What the fuck, Azrael?"

"I said, outside now," he answered in a low and threatening tone of voice, pulling the shirt he'd been holding over his head. "I can't yell at you in here, because people are sleeping."

"We're outside of training. I don't need to listen to you. I'm going back to bed," she replied petulantly, at which point, he grabbed her by the wrist and pulled her toward the stairs.

"You are making this so much worse on yourself!"

"Okay, okay, I'm coming. Jesus!" she answered, trying to pull away from him, but he wouldn't let go.

"Azrael, you're hurting me, please let go!" she added, when he kept pulling and squeezing her wrist with a force he was clearly not in control of at the moment. The instant the words came out of her mouth, he let go and mumbled a quick, "Sorry," before continuing toward the exit.

When they arrived in the training ring, Azrael turned away, taking a few steps in a circle, and ran his hand through his hair in frustration. Finally, he turned around, took a deep breath, and calmly said, "You better have a really good explanation as to why you're defying your father's orders."

She wanted to tell him the truth, to tell him that she too was immune to the virus, and that she could in fact have secretly healed Jeremy. But that would have defied even more of her father's orders, wouldn't it? Besides, Azrael didn't deserve to know her secret. He hadn't done much to earn her trust back since their falling out and it felt violating to have to tell him a truth she wasn't ready for anyone other than Hermes and Jeremy to know. So she remained silent.

"Lyla. Say something. Don't just give me this childish silence of yours."

She looked at him, lifting her chin defiantly.

"Fine. If you have nothing to say, I'll let Hermes know that I'll stop training you for the time being."

"No," she began, but stopped herself. She wanted to continue training with him. She craved his company more than ever. She wanted to believe it was because she'd missed him and wanted to repair their relationship. But there was an uglier, more selfish truth underneath all of that. She dreaded this new isolation. She was frightened at the thought of being alone in her cell all day. She feared the loneliness that might arise. She feared feeling trapped. And most of all, she feared the bad thoughts that would come up if she was left in her own company all day. But she wouldn't admit to that.

"No, what?" he asked.

"Nothing."

"I can't continue training an angel who consistently ignores my commands. Not when that disobedience might mean you could infect me with a deadly disease. This is about more than the fact you piss me off. You're a liability," he said and turned on his heel.

"Wait," she called him back. Swallowing her pride, she timidly added, "I thought I could help him. He's just one angel. And he's now repeatedly been exposed to something that's deadly to angels. I'm scared it's going to take him too..."

It wasn't the full truth, but it was the truth. And just as she said it, she realized just how true it was. She'd lost so much, and she'd just found her brother. She couldn't lose him too. Azrael's shoulders sagged before he turned back around.

"He's immune–"

"You don't know that. This virus is new, what if it's stronger than the mantle?" she interrupted, realizing just how much she feared that might be true.

"That's highly unlikely. But even if he wasn't immune, the last thing he'd want would be for you to be exposed as well."

Lyla opened and closed her mouth, barely refraining from telling him that she was most definitely immune.

"I know you love him," he continued. "Maybe even a bit more than you should..."

"What?"

"I see the way you've been looking at him these last couple of weeks," he explained.

"No, no, it's not like that. You are so far off the trail right now–"

"It's fine, Lyla," he interrupted her. "I don't care. I'm not jealous."

Ouch.

"Julien might not appreciate it though, if he realizes."

"It's not–" she started. She didn't even know where to begin. Did Azrael really think she was in love with a gay, married male? But on the plus side... Was that another note of jealousy she detected in his voice? She decided to let it go. She couldn't tell him that she and Jeremy were siblings without revealing too much. And if he was jealous, well, it served him well. Territorial troll.

"Whatever you say, fledgling," he concluded, using the address that had started as an insult and turned into a term of endearment between them. "Walk with me," he added, stepping out of the training ring and toward the exit that led to the village. She followed him in silence, wondering where they were going, when he finally stopped outside the tavern.

They'd spent many, many afternoons here. At the time, it had been bustling with angels, some priests, some civilians. She'd loved watching Hermes' descendants who hadn't chosen priesthood for their lives. For generations and generations, since the beginning of their species, they'd lived on the island, never knowing war or hunger. There was a serenity and a complete innocence to them that made them the most beautiful people Lyla had ever seen. They'd have lunch at the tavern, served by the twin bartenders, Jegudiel and Artiyah, only one of which had survived the attack. This is where Azrael and she had become friends.

Now the door stood askew, torn off its hinges by a demon, no doubt. Bracing herself for the horrible sight, she followed Azrael inside. The large room was just as she'd expected it: broken tables and chairs piled up on the ground, and a whole lot of dried blood covering every surface. Except for the bar. The bar had been cleaned by someone. When Azrael jumped up onto it, she realized it had been cleaned by him.

He tapped the surface next to him, inviting her to sit, and Lyla hesitantly climbed up. Why was he subjecting her to this sight, this smell? She could scent the lingering iron in the air, or at least she thought she could. Were her senses getting sharper than an angel's? Could he not feel the texture of the blood-soaked wood and smell the stench of angel guts hanging in the air? Oblivious, Azrael reached behind him for an unbroken bottle of liquor and took a swig before passing it to her.

"We've all lost a lot, Lyla. In the last few months in particular," he began. "We're all scared of losing more. You came to this island in more pain than anyone else on it. But you're no longer the exception. Every single soul on this rock has lost loved ones. Every single one has seen atrocious sights of violence and death. I come here every night, to remind myself not of what I've lost, but of what is still worth fighting for. I sit here, and drink, and list every single thing I am grateful for. My job is one of those things. And right now, my main job is your safety. I won't have you run off to expose yourself to the virus. Even if that means I need to sleep outside your cell every night."

Lyla took another swig, unsure what to say.

"So tell me Lyla," he said, grabbing the bottle. "What's something worth fighting for?"

"The fledglings," she answered, without thinking.

"I'll drink to that," he replied, taking a sip. Raising the bottle, he added, "Hermes' vision for a better world."

He drank, and so they kept going into the night.

14

"I don't understand why I can't secretly heal Jeremy," Lyla argued in her father's office the next morning.

"I don't want anyone asking questions I'm not ready to answer," the latter replied, having none of it.

"The Fallen know what I am. The Gods know what I am. Apparently, random lost know what I am. I thought the people on this island were our allies. What's wrong with them knowing?" she continued pushing.

Hermes sighed. "Angels, much like humans, are easily frightened by powerful things they don't understand."

"But I'm barely as powerful as them," she chortled.

"For now, yes, you're in your infancy. But someday, you'll be more powerful than anything they've ever witnessed, including myself. I don't want to risk a panic. Not when you'd be defenseless against a group of them," he explained.

"What you're saying is that I need to be looking over my shoulder in my own home?" she asked.

"I'm saying that that's exactly what I don't want you to have to do. So, will you please let Jeremy rest, close your eyes, and find my brother," he replied.

They were in the middle of one of their lessons, and her job was to find Apollo, a God she'd only met once at the most humiliating dinner party of her life and who had scared the living shit out of her. Apollo didn't share the Gods' animal features beyond sporting down on the top of his head instead of hair. In fact, he looked like a seven-foot-tall, gorgeous specimen of a man. But he had a second pair of eyelids that would close from the outside in, and on them were a second pair of eyes, purple with red pupils. Those eyes were the ones that could see the future, her father had explained. And their lids could close at any time, without warning, whenever the God had a vision. Which made him even more unsettling than the rest of his siblings with their fangs, claws, hooves, talons, and antlers. She pictured the fast-moving purple eyes, but nothing happened. Maybe she didn't know him well enough to locate him.

Or maybe she was too distracted by the idea that someday, her angel relatives would "other" her again. That she'd become different from them. That she already was different from anyone she knew. After all, even her father only had a vague memory of what his power had once been.

"Focus, please."

Right. Apollo. This was mostly an exercise. Hermes didn't really need her to find the seer God. He just wanted her to practice on a person she had met, albeit briefly. She wasn't sure she wanted to find him, if she was being honest. She knew Hermes needed to play his alliances at this moment, that the remaining Gods needed to band together. She knew he'd already contacted Apollo since their return. He'd explained to her that they'd always been the tightest of allies, even in the old days, when the Ten had all been alive. But since then, the Fallen had been picking them off one by one. Aphrodite and Poseidon had been destroyed in the last few decades, alongside most of their descendants – with the exception of a handful of priests, who, like Jeremy, had not been present during the Fallen's attack. Artemis and her people had fallen last year, with only three survivors. And their numerous enemies had attacked this island and butchered most of its inhabitants too.

The remaining gods were Apollo, Demeter, Hades, Haphaestus, Ares, and Athena. And of course, her father. Seven Gods, to fight the Fallen. She had asked him whether they were safe from them for the time being, and he'd responded that Lucifer would do anything to get to her now that she'd escaped him once in Hell, but that his best guess was that the Fallen were also struggling with a depletion of their numbers from the virus and that, for the time being, they'd be at a standstill. They needed to use that time as efficiently as possible to get her skills up.

Jeremy had gotten up in the morning to go back to healing a handful of patients before he needed to rest again, some of which were in worse condition than Cassiel had been weeks prior. Lyla couldn't help the wish to sneak out at night and heal them herself. But her father would likely lock her up if she attempted anything that daring. He didn't fully trust his own descendants, and rightly so. Last year, it had been one of his priests who'd sold them out to the Fallen. Michael, who was still alive somewhere, had given Lucifer the location of their hidden-away island and helped organize a fake mission for Ares which Azrael, Zadkiel, and three other of the strongest priests of Hermes' had blindly joined. Instead, they'd been abducted, injected with a serum that made them docile to the Fallen's wishes and sent back to destroy the island themselves. That made her wonder about Ares. Was it possible that he and his people had joined Lucifer's cause?

"Open your eyes and turn around," Hermes commanded.

"What?" she replied, returning to the room at once.

"You've been so distracted with your thoughts that you didn't even hear him arrive…"

She turned around and looked toward the other end of the room: Apollo casually leaned against Hermes' office door, looking straight at her with his regular set of eyes. Even those were disconcerting. They never seemed to blink. Lyla almost shrieked. Trying to keep her breathing under control, she jumped up and stepped back toward her father. "Hello there," she said, timidly.

"Hello."

His reply echoed in the room, just sitting there awkwardly, not followed up by anything.

Finally, he added, "You've been practicing my power."

"Not very successfully," she mumbled, intimidated by his unblinking direct eye contact.

"It'll come. In time. Everything always does."

"Is that what this power is supposed to teach me? That things happen as they're meant to?" she asked with less sarcasm than she'd intended.

"Maybe," he replied, unfazed. "I have seen millions of versions of the future. Thousands of versions of your future, Lailah. But I have yet to understand the why."

Finally, he looked to Hermes and said, "Brother, we need to palaver."

"We do," Hermes answered. "I expected your arrival any day now. I would like my daughter, Lailah, as well as Azrael and Jeremy, to join us in this war council. The better informed they are, the more equipped they'll be to fight back."

"As you wish," Apollo answered in that same echoey voice she had gotten so used to from her father, walking past her to embrace his brother. Every sound, every syllable reverberated just a little too long when the Gods spoke.

An hour later, she sat in an armchair in the back corner of Hermes' office. Her father was at his desk, Apollo across from him. Azrael was leaning against the wall equidistant from the two Gods, and Jeremy was lounging on the couch near the door, wrapped in a warm blanket. He looked as if he'd fall asleep at any moment, just sitting there. But she knew it was so much worse for him than simply being worn out. He was in pain over the suffering he'd been witnessing these past few days. He'd once explained to her that Aphrodite's gift was pure unadulterated compassion, that her descendants felt love even for their enemies. It must have been destroying him internally to witness the angels' anguish over this new disease, to witness the pain of their isolation and to not be able to find any comfort in his fellows.

"What are your numbers these days?" Hermes asked his brother.

"We have a couple hundred priests, and maybe three thousand civilians," Apollo answered.

She'd read in her history books last year that angels did not procreate nearly as much as humans. They were long lived, some of them reaching two or three centuries, but they lived in larger communities, not having such a strong need to have their own children. Oftentimes, a couple would only have one hatchling, or none at all, keeping the species alive but not ever increasing it to any degree.

"There are only forty-two of my children left," Hermes explained, his eyes lowered.

"I'm sorry, brother."

Hermes' shared sorrow echoed in the silence following Apollo's words.

"So am I. The three priests of Artemis' who survived the

attack on her island did not make it out alive when they came for our home, and by Jeremy's calculations, a couple handfuls of Aphrodite's priests still roam the earth, most of them hiding as healers among the humans. As for Poseidon's descendants who might still be alive, they are scattered to the wind."

Poseidon had been the most powerful of the Gods in a way. He and his priests possessed the power to change time itself. But Lyla had yet to learn of a historic instance of its use. She figured that it was just the way the movies represented time travel: too many potentially disastrous consequences in trying to change the course of history. Besides, nature had given them an inordinate amount of power but had balanced the scales by making them sterile: each descendant of Poseidon's was his direct offspring. There had never been many of them to begin with, and now that he was gone, they were dying out.

"Which of our siblings have you spoken with?" her father inquired.

"Only Hades," the double-eyed God replied. "I'm unsure if we can still trust the others. My priests have been trying to scry their whereabouts, but they're all hidden under a veil."

"One of them might have sold out Artemis..." Azrael mused.

"That's one of the things we need to talk about..." Apollo started. "I believe her island was never attacked."

"What do you mean?" Lyla interjected, before thinking the better of questioning a God. "I saw the three survivors, they didn't attack themselves."

"No, young one, they did not."

"Do you mean to say what I think you do?" Hermes asked, cryptically.

"I do. My priests visited her island... They studied the bodies, they scoured every inch of the place for evidence of the attack.... They couldn't find any trace of demons or Fallen. Not a single scale, not one black feather..."

What else could have wiped out an entire island of angels and a Goddess? Did he mean to say it was another one of the Gods? Or maybe monsters? She knew that vampires, were-wolves, and pretty much every other creature humans had stories about existed. But they were being managed by the Gods. None of them were allowed to ever draw blood, or they'd get wiped out immediately. That was a large part of Hermes' priests' job: to keep the monster population under control, though the M-word was frowned upon.

"It has begun then," Hermes replied, clearly knowing something she didn't. "It won't be long before the rest of us fall prey to it as well."

Lyla looked for understanding in Azrael's eyes, then turned toward Jeremy, but they both seemed as lost as she was.

"What am I missing?" she loudly said, not being as polite as her friends.

Both Gods snapped their attention toward her, which was a rather terrifying sight, and made her, ever so slightly, shrink back into her chair. Especially when those inner eyelids of Apollo's closed and he looked straight at her with the purple set of eyes. In a blink, they were replaced by his human looking ones, as Hermes sighed, looked around the room at Azrael and Jeremy, and explained, "What my brother is saying is that Artemis killed her own people."

"What now?" Lyla exclaimed.

"Hermes!" Apollo cautioned. "You cannot—"

"I have to. They need to know what is going to happen eventually."

"It might not," Apollo growled.

"Brother, you're the one with the sight. You know it will. Whether it's in a year or a hundred years. It will eventually come about. They need to be able to survive it."

Lyla shot Azrael a look, but the latter was staring at the God, a frown on his face.

"Survive what?" he asked.

"Us," Hermes replied simply. "Survive us."

Hermes picked at the down on his head with his clawed hands for a moment, an uncharacteristically human gesture for him. Finally, he addressed them with the same depleted expression she'd seen on him in moments of mourning.

"When we were a part of the hive, we were all interconnected. We felt each other at all times, as if we were one being, standing still in time. But when we fell to Earth, we separated from the hive and became individuals."

"We know all that. What do you mean 'Survive you?'" she interrupted.

"I'm getting there," Hermes responded, wearily. "As you know, we are still connected to all our descendants. We feel their joys, their pain, their suffering, their fears, and eventually their deaths as if they were our own. But it's a one-way street and we no longer have any buffers against that connection. We aren't one. Our minds and our hearts get overloaded with emotions that aren't ours. It eventually drives us mad. As mad as the Fallen already are. Artemis slaughtered her own people and destroyed herself in the process. And, if Apollo's guess is correct, Demeter, Ares, Athena, and Hephaestus might have given in to the madness too."

A silent tear fell out of Hermes' hawk-like eyes. And Lyla felt her heart rate go through the roof. The Gods and the Fallen were so powerful that they used angels and demons to fight their battles for them. Because if they duked it out on their own, they would wipe the Earth of every last living thing. That's what she'd learned when she'd first arrived here. The Fallen wanted to keep their evil playground, and the Gods were trying to save humanity. So both sides kept their power in check and sat back, sending others onto the battlefield. If Hermes lost his mind, they'd all get annihilated. They were in the presence of two nuclear bombs that could go off at any minute.

"Lyla. Lyla!" she heard through the roaring in her ears. Snapping back to attention, she looked at her father who calmly said, "I will destroy myself before this happens to me."

"You've been feeling it too, then?" Apollo inquired, oblivious or not caring about everybody's reactions to the news. "The onset of madness."

"At times," Hermes admitted. "You know that my love kept me sane for the longest time. But, without her, it's been much harder not to give in to it. We can only hope that the Fallen's numbers are being depleted by this plague."

"I doubt that," Apollo stated. "My suspicion is that our sister Demeter joined them and created the virus."

"Why aren't they taking us out if we're so outnumbered?" Jeremy sluggishly asked from the other side of the room.

"Our dark brothers and sisters deal in fear and torture. They'd rather watch us slowly die out, then to give us a mercy killing. Or perhaps they're biding their time for some other irrational reason" Apollo explained.

Hermes slowly nodded, a world-weary expression on his animalistic features. "We must band together. Round up your people and Hades' as well as however many priests of Aphrodite's you can find, and bring them to this island."

"In the midst of a plague? I fear our numbers will get weakened too quickly," the other God argued.

"We will put safety measures in place. We cannot afford to be isolated from each other in these trying times."

"Doesn't bringing everyone onto one island triple the risk of one of you going berserk on the rest of us?" Azrael asked what she was thinking.

"As I said," Hermes replied. "I would destroy myself before that happened. And I am certain Hades and Apollo would do the same. In the meantime, you will be three times safer."

15

Internal destruction aside, the island could house about four thousand angels, who, since they were being quarantined, had to clean up the rubbled lodgings they were given themselves. The priests of Apollo's, Hades', as well as a handful of Aphrodite's that the Gods had managed to round up came to live in the compound, while families were sent to the village. The remaining couple of thousands of civilians were temporarily housed in tents and makeshift shelters that popped up across the island overnight. Every store in the village was turned into a home. And, just like that, life was brought back to Hermes' haven.

But with it came a new wave of the disease. Hades and Apollo had a few sick amongst their refugees, and in the process of moving everyone to the island, the virus spread like wildfire. By the end of the week, even Hermes agreed to let Jeremy use his glamour magic on Lyla to disguise her as one of the priestesses of Aphrodite and allowed her to go into the village to practice her healing skills on the sick.

Jeremy had only used his glamour on Lyla once before to

hide the fact she'd been crying her eyes out. This time, he used it to slightly distort her features, so no one would recognize her. She wasn't sure if the magic actually affected her face, or if it simply affected how people saw her. But it was surprisingly effective and lasted several hours at a time. Luckily, with all the new faces and sudden changes on the island, chaos prevailed and no one kept track of where she was, how she looked, or where this new healer she pretended to be had come from.

The tents were not a long-term solution, and isolation made it impossible for anyone to help build any homes. But there was a mind-blowing answer for that too: Hades, wielder of all things dead, enlisted dead souls, people – human and angel alike – who had passed but not moved on – whatever that meant – to build small, efficient homes. Every evening, when Lyla and Jeremy flew home from a long day of healing the sick, they'd see them: dead working machines, cutting and lifting lumber, digging trenches in the moonlight. Most of them were ghosts that bare-ly manifested. In the movies, ghosts were translucent human-oids that looked the way they had in the moment of their death. But this was different: they still had the shape of humans and angels, but they flickered in and out of sight, depending on how well they could manifest on this plane. Sometimes only a part of the specters would be visible: the wing that allowed them to fly from one spot to another, the arm that lifted a pane of wood, the hand that grabbed a tool. And some of them were actual zombies, decaying corpses that the Fallen had brought back to life in one of their long-past failed experiments and abandoned to roam the earth forever, finding peace only when guided by a priest of Hades'. Both ghosts and zombies single-mindedly went to work on serving the God's mission of building a second village on the island – laboring day in and day out without a break. It was a truly eerie sight.

Days passed like that. Azrael, now isolated too, was nowhere to be seen. Lyla, Jeremy and a dozen other Aphrodite priests would silently go to work, healing one patient after another, trying to stop this plague that seemed to keep on spreading, that they themselves might have been spreading from one house to the next. She'd visit these isolated angels and families who still lived in the debris of the attack and put all their hopes for the survival of their loved ones on her, who expected her to undo fate itself. Lyla might have healed Cassiel and Zadkiel in one sitting, but that had been when she'd been well rested and hadn't been going from one patient to the next, exerting her magic all day long. Now, the same amount of magic had to be divided between dozens of patients every day.

And then came the first deaths. The first was a middle-aged priest, who'd made it to ninety-eight years of age. They had over two hundred cases at this point and each could only visit three or four per day. They tried to do triage and visit the sickest first, but the angel had slipped through the cracks. He'd been barely sick the day before. By the time Benoît, a descendant of Aphrodite's and one of Julien's mixed friends, had gotten to him, the priest had been on his deathbed.

Every night, they would meet at the tavern, sit far apart from each other, and debrief on the various cases of the virus. Who had been healed, who was a priority, who had shown fresh symptoms. The numbers would end up on Hermes' desk, who was barely to be seen these days, too busy strategizing with his brothers. If she was entirely honest, it was a relief, focusing on and perfecting one of her skills, rather than having to bounce around between lessons with Azrael, Hermes, and Jeremy.

But tonight, she felt nothing but existential dread. Someone had died. Someone they hadn't been able to save. If only they'd been there in time. If only... How many more would they lose before they got control of this plague?

Silently, they toasted to the dead. And thanked the dead at large. The irony wasn't lost on her, as she looked out the window and watched one of Hades' zombies erect the walls of a small cabin. They were trying to stave off death, while death itself was helping them rebuild their home.

Every time she saw them, she thought of Max. Would she one day be able to summon him? Would he have "moved on" or was he still roaming the Earth? What would she tell him? What would he say?

"Raphaella, how many did you heal today?" Benoît interrupted her nightly reverie, using the fake name they'd introduced her under.

"Five," she responded, absent-mindedly.

"Five?!" he exclaimed. "Your numbers never cease to amaze me."

She liked Benoît, and she didn't mind one bit how much his compliments warmed something in the pit of her stomach, and sometimes a little lower. He was tan, with short blond hair, and beautiful green eyes. He didn't have the muscular warrior build she usually craved in men, but he made up for it with the most dazzling, white-toothed smile. And he liked her. That much she knew. It felt nice, being wanted again.

"How are you so much better at this than the rest of us?" he asked the much-dreaded question.

"And how are you so much prettier than anyone else in this room?" she flirtatiously responded, trying to throw him off the trail.

"A little respect, please?" interjected Jeremy.

"Sorry," she mumbled, and suppressed a giggle. She couldn't help it. All of this felt absurd. They were being beaten by a virus that had not existed months ago, while alien creatures powerful enough to annihilate them all were plotting their destruction. The alien creatures in charge of them could go ka-boom at any time and slaughter them all themselves. And unless either of them got to her, she would outlive anyone she knew so that, someday, she could become the most powerful being on the planet. Meanwhile, a bunch of ghosts were building tiny houses in the woods. They had left normal and respectful a long time ago...

That night, Jeremy walked her to her cell.

"I know we're not supposed to touch, but may I hug you, Lyla?" he asked. She understood what he meant. She would never have believed it, but just a few weeks without touching another person who wasn't diseased with a violent virus had left her isolated, depressed, and apparently on the brink of delirium. She needed some affection. Without a word, she rushed toward him, and grabbed him around the chest, squeezing tight. They stayed like that for a while, until he kissed the top of her head, said, "Goodnight, little sis'," and left.

16

The deaths piled up over the next couple of weeks. Lyla suspected that some angels were breaking quarantine and covertly visiting each other. But she couldn't blame them. Isolation was wearing on everyone. She'd gotten used to the constant contact with Hermes, Jeremy, and Azrael over the last six months, and not being able to see anyone but Jeremy – and even him only for their gloom-and-doom, end-of-day meetings – weighed on her immensely. She never would have guessed how quickly she'd miss another's touch. How lonely she'd feel going weeks without a hug.

But apparently, others were affected even worse by their pandemic protocol.

One night, after losing two patients in a row – a young female priestess of Hades' who'd spent her dying breath promising to return and help rebuild the island, and a hatchling who'd never even gotten a shot at life – Lyla skipped the healers' evening meeting, and went for a walk instead. Aimlessly, she stumbled through the fields, right past the army of dead souls building tiny homes. They seemed completely oblivious to her, solely focused on the task at hand. As creeped out as she usually was by the apparitions that looked so very human, Lyla no longer cared. Not after what she'd seen today. So, she got right up into their faces, trying to get their attention. But they kept toiling away like good little soldiers. She'd have to find something else on which to let out her frustration.

The fields were illuminated by the existing tiny cabins, the bright windows of the few angels that were awake, isolating, hopefully as couples or families, hopefully having a less excruciating time of it. But past the fields, it was pure darkness. With zero light pollution, nothing illuminated the path to the Sacred Mountain she instinctively took. She crunched her way through the snow until she made it to the foot of the impressive mesa.

It stood alone on this rather flat island, surrounded by jagged cliffs. She knew that her father's power was anchored on this mountain, lest he explode with it. And it created a ripple effect, of constant wind tunnels darting through the cliff edges and canyons. She could almost see the shimmer of his magic catching purple and green lights in the darkness. Only one angel had ever flown up the mountain without getting impaled on one of its many sharp rocks: Azrael. He'd practiced as a child, when his wingspan had been much smaller, and he'd perfected the flight up and down as an adult. So much so, that he'd built a cabin atop the mountain.

She'd been too preoccupied with survival when she'd seen it, but she remembered how homey it was, and at the same time, how sad. It was perfectly set up for a cozy, warm, lovely family life. But its tragedy was that Azrael was the only one who could fly up to it and so it stood empty and cold.

Lyla stood at the foot of the mountain. She was tempted to fly up some of its dangerous canyons. She knew she couldn't make it to the top and she wasn't feeling suicidal, but she wanted to get hurt a little. Maybe the pain of being thrown against a rock wall would silence that of what she hadn't been able to fix today.

But as she walked around the base of the mountain, looking for the best flight path up, she almost bumped into someone hurting even more than her. Rounding a corner, she saw Azrael, sitting cross-legged, a bottle of liquor in his lap. He was already so drunk that he didn't hear her approach. Nor did he notice her as she swiftly slipped behind a rock. That was one hell of a bad sign for a warrior who was constantly relying on his senses.

The healers had been taking up the tavern every evening. Was this where he'd moved his nightly drinking ritual to? And had that ritual taken a dark turn? He'd told her that he drank to all the things worth fighting for, but he no longer looked like he had much fight in him. For a moment, Lyla closed her eyes and tried to send those tendrils of empathic Hermes magic his way, to see if she could feel what had him so twisted up inside. She came up empty. Frustrated, Lyla closed her eyes again and pictured her own feelings for Azrael as a bright colorful ball in the palm of her hand. She opened her hand and released those feelings, cleared her mind of them, so she could see him better. There he sat, in her mind's eye, hunched over himself, a grey cloud emanating from him. As she let the heavy silver substance float toward her, reaching out to touch it with the tip of a finger, she recognized it. Guilt. One of her long-term travel companions.

Lyla opened her eyes again and leaned against the rock hiding her from sight. Whatever it was Azrael felt guilty about, it was suffocating him. And there was nothing she could do about it. Not when he looked barely conscious. At least he wasn't drinking atop the mountain and flying down drunk. Though, he might have been avoiding the mountain for other reasons. Punishing himself perhaps for whatever was eating him up inside?

She wanted to tell him everything would be all right. To put that big head of his in her lap and soothe him to sleep. But she couldn't risk infecting him with the virus. Besides, she didn't want to lie. Everything would most likely not be all right. She knew all too well that guilt was not something the person we hurt could just lift with their forgiveness. Regret was how we ourselves felt about our own actions. The entire island could have told her she wasn't responsible for the two deaths she'd just witnessed, and it wouldn't ease her own remorse and shame one bit. Guilt was a hook you put yourself on, and only you could take yourself back off.

And whatever specific hook he'd put himself on, he had much too much time on his hands these days to let it sink into his skin. He'd dedicated his entire life to Hermes' fight. When he wasn't on a mission, he was training other priests or strategizing with the God. But now, they were being taken down by an invisible enemy, and Azrael had nothing but time while he watched things go to hell, not being able to do a single thing about it.

17

She didn't see Azrael for the rest of the lockdown. She knew she would have probably found him at the foot of the Sacred Mountain every single night, but she didn't want to intrude on someone who had no space for anything other than his own misery. She knew all too well that it was nearly impossible to care for others when one was in too much pain themselves.

She did, however, befriend Benoît in those long, harsh weeks. The flirtations stopped, as they were collectively in mourning, but he would silently walk her back to her cell every night, past dozens of black banners hanging from dark windows, ever-so-slightly easing the suffering from the day.

Angels took grief very seriously. Not that humans didn't, but humans no longer had such obvious societal norms around it. The angels, on the other hand, would hang said banners from their windows. The color black hadn't been chosen to evoke death – it was the color of their enemies' wings. And for each death, they would spend sixteen days not working, not training, not flying, and not speaking unless absolutely necessary. She didn't need to use her powers of foresight to know that there'd be a whole lot of silence in the future of the island.

She'd seen enough horror films to know that things would get worse before they got better. But she could never have imagined how much worse. New cases of the virus popped up faster than they could cure them, and she was the only one who could heal a dying patient in one sitting. The truly dark days, however, didn't start until the healers themselves began to get infected.

They'd been working themselves into the ground, stopping only to catch a mere five hours of sleep each night. The first to catch the virus was Gabriel. Gabriel was an angel in his fifties, like Jeremy. Also like Jeremy, he had been working in the human world when Aphrodite's island had been attacked twenty-five years ago. He had found work as a healer on Hades' island. But unlike Jeremy, who'd been healing Hermes' priests on a daily basis for over two decades, Gabriel wasn't as used to the workload, and wasn't as resistant to the exhaustion. Despite their best efforts to protect themselves, he sent them word one morning that he'd woken up with a fever, unable to stop coughing.

Jeremy had immediately rushed to his side to heal him. He'd missed all his other patients that day. When the healers met at the tavern for their nightly check-in, he was nowhere to be seen. Worried, Lyla left Benoît behind, and flew back to the compound as soon as their meeting was over. She flew right up to his balcony where he was sitting on the ground, staring at the floor. He didn't even react to her arrival.

"Jeremy... May I sit with you?" she asked, ignoring her body's need to rush toward him and hug him.

Wordlessly, he nodded. They sat in silence, looking out at the illuminated fields and at the dead toiling away at more and more shelters.

Finally, Jeremy spoke.

"Gabriel died in my arms this afternoon. I did everything I

could. I tried so hard. But I couldn't save him."

"I'm so sorry," Lyla responded. She wasn't sure if Jeremy and Gabriel had known each other prior to this plague or if he was simply distressed over losing one of the few healers they had. But she understood when he opened his mouth to speak again.

"There are only thirteen of us left. There may be more, hiding out. But officially, there are only thirteen of our bloodline left... Thirteen."

Jeremy had been born on Aphrodite's island, a place similar to this one but bustling with angels whose very magic was that of unconditional love. It was all he'd known for the first few years of his life, until he and his father had moved to Hermes' island where his father had been a healer. Aphrodite and her entire island had been destroyed while Jeremy was out working in the human world for a year, around his twenty-fifth birthday. In one fell swoop, he had lost his mother and every one of his tribe. And then, shortly after, his father had died of grief. The world he had been born into had been slowly chipped away at until none of it was left.

Lyla quietly reached her arm toward Jeremy's shoulders and at the first touch, he crumbled down into her lap, where he started weeping like a child.

They sat together, in silence, until dawn.

And then there were the funerals. Hades, Hermes, and Apollo would pick up the dead and give them their rites on a secluded beach, too far for the living to smell the ashes... almost every single night.

Lyla had been too busy healing patients and living under a false identity to think much about them. Besides, the Gods had kept them a closed affair. But she convinced Jeremy to take a few hours off to attend Gabriel's. At sunrise, she woke up her brother and pointed toward the beach they both knew the funerals were taking place on. His balcony wasn't high enough for them to actually see much on the horizon, but he immediately knew what she meant. Jeremy, his eyes puffy from all of last night's tears, quietly nodded as he stood and briefly disappeared into his cell. Lyla took the opportunity to stretch her limbs and breathe out as much of the pent-up anxiety in her lungs as possible.

Breaking mourning protocol, they flew toward the rising sun until they reached a beach Lyla had once associated with her newfound trust in Azrael and with the freedom of knowing someone would catch her. Now, the entire beach was covered in the remains of several weeks of funeral pyres. Fresh wood, tinder, and angel bodies piled up on old, burnt wood and ash.

Lyla and Jeremy stopped short of the beach and, their wings trailing behind them, sat on a cliff overlooking it instead. Instinct told them to leave the burning of the bodies to the Gods, to not intrude on the three brothers as they spoke the rites of a time only they remembered. The three of them stood, each seven feet tall, in front of a dozen bodies they effortlessly lifted onto the wooden construction. They left Gabriel for last. When it came time to pick up Jeremy and Lyla's fellow healer, Apollo and Hades shared a look and Hermes let them pick him up and place him aside the other corpses. But it was he who then stepped forward and carefully wrapped the angel's wings around his body. Lyla was much too far to hear the words he spoke as he placed both hands on Gabriel's feathers, as he touched his forehead to the dead angel's. But, as if she'd suddenly borrowed her father's raptor eyes, she saw the glistening tear that fell from his eyes onto the deceased's face, the tear that burst into a flame as it touched Gabriel and lit up the entire pyre.

Sobbing, Jeremy grabbed her hand, as they both watched the fire consume one of Aphrodite's last descendants and as

Apollo and Hades caught a stumbling Hermes down below. They watched him fall to his knees, his brothers, each an arm around his shoulders, extending their wings to create a sphere around him. They watched as he faced the sky, roaring in grief, and unleashed a ripple of rainbow-colored magic only his siblings' wings could absorb and stop from annihilating everything around them. And they watched as the three Gods took to the skies. There one moment, gone a nanosecond later, they shook the earth in their wake, collapsing the funeral pyre into a sudden pile of ashes and leaving a shimmering crater where they had knelt.

No wonder her father didn't want the angels to know how powerful she was. The Ten themselves never showed what they were truly capable of. Watching them as they believed themselves to be unseen, she realized that they were constantly slowing down and holding back their preternatural senses because the reality of what they were was too formidable and dread-inspiring to be witnessed by anyone, even their own people. Someday, she too would be too fast, too strong, too everything to ever be stopped by anyone other than a God or a Fallen.

The unease must have shown on her face, because Jeremy broke the silence, asking, "Are you all right?"

"I didn't know they were that..." she trailed off.

"...beyond comprehension?" he finished her sentence.

"That's one way to put it. I knew in theory. But seeing them take off like that. They are... We are..."

Her breathing picked up as the reality hit her. That she would be just like them some day. That her senses were already waking up and beginning to surpass an angel's. That the dormant magic in her hands would someday give her power and responsibility far beyond her comfort zone.

Jeremy wrapped a gentle wing around her shoulders. Looking at the horizon over the ocean, he asked, "How are you doing with... all of that?"

Lyla let out a shaky breath. "Most days, I just try to be present with what's right in front of me. Or I remind myself that I fought the devil himself and I may not have won, but I didn't exactly lose either..."

He chuckled. "You sure didn't."

"But... I don't know. It's too much, you know?" she continued turning to look into his blue eyes. "A year ago, I was human. And now, I'm... whatever that was down there..."

"You're also my little sister," he responded, tightening his wing hold on her shoulders. "And I've got your back. Always."

She didn't want to point out by how much she'd outlive him. She couldn't think of that. That someday soon, she'd truly be the last of Aphrodite's descendants. If she survived long enough to see the day.

"He really loved her, didn't he?" she asked instead, remembering her father breaking down with the burden of saying goodbye to Gabriel.

"He really did. And she him," Jeremy told her. "She loved my father too. But Hermes and her... It was different. It was deeper and yet lighter than anything I've ever seen. I don't think they had any idea but they seemed almost... human together. I wasn't around much the year she was pregnant with you. And of course I believed your father was one of her angels. But I noticed that there was something different about her. She'd always had so much faith in everyone else, but at the end there, there was this giddiness about her, this hope she'd found for herself somehow. I asked her about it the last time I saw her. She and I had gone for a walk on her eternally green island. I don't know if my mind twisted the memory to have perfect weather or if that truly was the case. But I remember sitting on this grassy hill with her and asking her about the secret I could see in her eyes."

Jeremy was absent-mindedly staring out at the ocean, as if he could still feel the grass under his hands, and the warm sun on his skin. "She looked down and touched her own stomach. And then she said, 'This little one – she's the answer to a riddle my kind has long since forgotten.'"

Jeremy finally turned to look Lyla in the eyes. With a smile, he added, "She made me promise to enjoy every little moment of happiness I'd get with you."

With that, Jeremy squeezed her hand and indicated it was time to return to their duties. Lyla quietly got up and started walking back. Her mother hadn't made him promise to be a protective big brother, to love her, to watch out for her... Instead, she'd only wished for them to be mindful of the happy moments they shared.

18

It took another month before the numbers started slowing down, another two hundred and something dead angels, two of them priests of Aphrodite's. They were down to eleven healers when they finally got back to manageable numbers.

Lyla's final patient was Sophie, one of Julien's friends, a mixed angel. When Lyla arrived, she was delusional with a fever, struggling to breathe. It took her all day to beat the virus, an entire day in Sophie's mind, fighting a constantly replicating virus. By the time she was done, she was so exhausted that she fell asleep, kneeling by the bed, her head in her arms.

She didn't wake up until the next morning.

"Lyla," she heard a French accent through the fog of her sleep. "Lyla, what are you doing here?"

Shit. Jeremy's glamour had worn off. How was she going to explain herself? Sophie knew her from last fall, when they'd strategized together and attacked Hell itself alongside Azrael, Jeremy, and the rest of Julien's friends.

"You're the one who healed me, aren't you?" the blonde angel asked.

"No... No, I just..."

She sat up, blinking the last remnants of sleep out of her eyes. Sophie was sitting up in bed, staring down at her, wide-eyed.

"You're a healer? I thought you were Hermes' daughter..." she mused.

"I'm not. I—" she tried to deny it.

"Lyla, I am a hundred and twenty-six years old, please don't sell me for a fool. I remember you falling asleep in exactly this position last night. I wasn't delirious anymore."

"Fuck," Lyla replied, trying to shake off the grogginess.

"Do I want to ask follow up questions?" Sophie asked, a smirk on her face.

"You really don't. Look, I'm not actually Hermes' daughter. I'm Aphrodite's," Lyla lied, thinking on her feet.

"You're her heir, aren't you?" the other female continued. "And Hermes is hiding you, because your people are gone."

"Something like that," she replied, glad she was thrown off the trail.

"But I thought Jeremy carried the mantle?" Sophie inquired.

Gods, she was stubborn. How would Lyla explain that one away?

"He does. We're not really sure why... Maybe because I wasn't technically born when Aphrodite died...?" she tried.

"I see. They cut you out of her after the fact, so Jeremy was the heir in the moment of her death," the grey-winged angel mused. "That's so very Macbeth..."

Lyla didn't really remember her English lit classes, or which of the Shakespeare plays she'd been made to read, so she wasn't sure what Sophie meant, but as long as it made sense to her, all was well.

"Can you please not tell anyone? Only Hermes and Jeremy

know," she begged her.

"Cross my heart," the French angel replied with a smile. "Aphrodite's numbers are depleted enough as it is. I'm not going to contribute to that by blabbing about a descendant of hers who's going under the radar."

"Thank you," Lyla replied, truly relieved.

"Besides," her new friend added. "We fought together in the bowels of Hell. We're bonded. And that is sacred to me."

Lyla smiled at her. It should be sacred. But after Max's betrayal nothing seemed to be anymore.

"So," Sophie asked. "How's it going out there? Every morning we receive supplies for the day and a piece of paper with the names of the dead written on it. But how has it really been? Are we being beaten by this thing?"

She could tell the older angel was trying to keep her composure, but, in reality, she was so very anxious to hear the answer to the question she hadn't been able to ask anyone in weeks. So much so that she ignored their mourning protocol, and grabbed the opportunity to find out all the information she so desperately sought.

"Not anymore. The numbers have been steadily decreasing. As long as people aren't secretly meeting up, which I'm pretty sure they did for a while, we should actually be able to get control of the disease," she reported.

"Thank the Ten!" Sophie exclaimed, with so much relief in her voice it broke Lyla's heart. It must have been such a burden on solitary angels, to be stuck in isolation for months with no one to talk to.

"I should go," she said, standing up and feeling equally guilty about staying when she shouldn't have and leaving now that Sophie had found companionship.

"Sophie," she asked, turning around at the door. "Who are

you descended from? I don't remember you using any magic in Hell."

"Ah, non," the female replied. "My father was Poseidon. Our magic is reserved for one purpose only. Changing time. Outside of that one trick, we don't possess any magic to speak of. That is why I fight extra hard with my fists and elbows."

What a weird existence, she thought to herself. To be a magical creature, one with functional wings, to live separate from humanity because of it, and yet to have almost no magic at all.

"What about your mother's side?" she asked.

"My mother was a lost child living down on the Atlantic Coast. I received some magic from her. But it is very specific, earth-based magic. Mostly good for domestic tasks and growing plants. Back in Paris, I was our group's chef and pharmacist. Well, and... how do you say... drug dealer. It's ironic that my peaceful magic is what came from the blood of the Fallen..."

"Do you ever go back in time for small things? Like undoing your drinking when you wake up with a hangover?" Lyla asked, fascinated by these new types of magic she herself would someday possess.

"Ha!" Sophie laughed. "If only it were that simple. No... I have never gone back in time."

Lyla wasn't sure what to make of that. Did Poseidon's people not actually use their power? Were they effectively impotent because going back in time wasn't actually possible? Something told her those were questions for another day. She had enough on her plate with the various magics she'd been practicing this year.

"Get some rest," she told the recently healed female as she opened the door and left.

19

When she went to work that morning, walking into the tavern to get her assignments, she was surprised to find the other healers calmly sipping coffee. Usually, there was a nervous energy in the air; the rush to get back into the trenches would be as palpable as the dread to actually do so. But today, they all sat back, their feet kicked up on the proverbial table, as if they had nowhere to be.

And it turned out... they didn't have anywhere to be. They'd healed the last of the active cases of the virus overnight.

She couldn't believe it. At this very moment, not a single angel on the island was actively sick. They estimated that the virus took about two to five days to incubate. So, they'd have to wait a week or two to be extra safe before declaring it beat. But even if a few cases still popped up, they could probably fight it back at this point.

Lyla plopped down into a chair, incredulous. She hadn't realized it at the time, but the last two months had felt endless. Not only had they felt longer than they were, but she'd lost sight of the future. The disease had been their entire reality; there hadn't seemed to be a life past it. It was and it would always be. This new normal, the quarantine, the isolation, the fear, the death of any future goals because only the present bleak truth existed, had become such a stark reality that she'd almost forgotten life had been different once upon a time and that it surely would be again, because this "normal" was in fact entirely abnormal. She wanted to be happy and to celebrate, but she was too empty, too worn out to feel any joy. They'd lost so much in the last few months, it was nothing but a pyrrhic victory. And from the looks on her fellow healers' faces, they all felt the same way.

Benoît walked her home that morning, as was their daily habit. But this time, he broke the mourning guidelines to ask, "Lyla, I haven't used my wings in what feels like forever. Would you want to go on a flight with me after the mourning period is over? If this virus is in fact gone."

She looked at him, certain of only one thing. She needed some joy in her life. Some light-heartedness. She might miss and want Azrael, she might be confused over Max, and life, and her entire existence as a God being. But a date with an angel? That sounded like exactly what she needed.

"I'd love to," she replied, grinning behind her face covering.

And then she went to sleep for a week. No one woke her up all day, nor the following day, nor the next. It seemed as if they'd finally beaten back the plague, and no new cases were popping up. So, she rested at last, spending hour after hour, dozing or sleeping, wanting for nothing but the occasional bite of food that appeared at her door, no doubt dropped off by her father.

And then one day, after what must have been a couple of weeks of rest, she sensed it: life in the compound. It was hesitant at first, but, as she fought off the drowsiness, she heard the most heartwarming of sounds: fledglings running in the hallways. Their lockdown was finally over. They had no more cases of the virus and it wouldn't return, as long as no one entered or left the island. Lyla leaned right back into her pillow, smiling and delighting in the sounds of joy reverberating through the temple.

A knock finally got her out of bed. Sore from doing nothing for two weeks, she made her way to the door, which flung open the second she cracked it even a little. In came Azrael, Sarathiel strapped to his chest, followed by Raziel and Cassiel, each carrying a now significantly larger rat on their shoulders.

They barged in with the energy of a family on Christmas morning, excited to be alive, excited for the day. In fact, they were a little too excited. Like people who'd been in so much pain, they were artificially putting on a joyful face. But it wasn't truly happy. It was manic.

"Gods, open the window once in a while," Azrael exclaimed, striding toward the little balcony to open the doors himself.

"What's going on?" she sluggishly asked.

"We're going for a walk. And Cassiel here suggested we invite you," the large angel responded.

"Is that so?" Lyla inquired, turning toward the young girl.

"Well," the fledgling replied, staring at her shoes. "Azrael said you fought a lot of demons in the Winter. So I guess you can't be that bad."

"You know what?" Lyla said, getting somewhat infected with the mania in the room. "I'll take it. I will take 'not that bad.' Now. A little privacy perhaps?"

But they were all so excited that she couldn't for the life of her kick them out. So, she let them sit on her bed while she slipped into the bathroom. She heard the fledglings tripping over each other's words to catch Azrael up on every single development their new pets had gone through while they'd been locked away, as she stepped into the shower and got ready for a walk in the last bits of melting snow.

PART TWO

20

In the fashion of children, Cassiel and Raziel didn't just for-give, but all but forgot their grievances against Lyla after their walk. Building a very basic hut in the woods together and telling scary stories that everyone listened to with bated breath, including the two rodents who were warming up in Cassiel's pockets, had been enough to regain their trust. Or maybe that was just what forgiveness was. Maybe Azrael was right, and it wasn't something that could be granted, but simply something that happened one day: enough time made you forget why you were so angry in the first place.

Beyond wanting to keep them safe, Lyla grew to love the little ones. They'd been through so much, as much as she had at their age and then some. And she cherished the moments in which they forgot their fear and just acted like fledglings. But even their nightmares – even their trauma – were gifts to her. Because she was able to be there for them. She was able to soothe them and to remind them that they were now safe, that someone cared. She was able to give them what she had so desperately needed as a child. By some magic that had nothing to do with the blood coursing through her veins, that's how she started being able to forget and to let go as well. If the horrors she herself had endured had made her into the person who could now show up for Cassiel and Raziel, if her own pain had taught her everything she needed to know in order to soothe theirs, hadn't it all been worth it? She'd have welcomed twice as much trauma if it meant being able to help the fledglings and she definitely wouldn't have traded one piece of her own childhood – not even the darkest parts.

She didn't apply any of her Aphrodite magic to them. Instead, she just met them with an open heart. She knew that that would eventually heal them. That they stood a chance to one day be complete again. And that they'd each make one hell of a grown angel when they were.

While almost no one knew of her secret identity as a healer, the other priests of Aphrodite's were hailed as dark heroes of a time no one dared speak about. It was strange. Every single angel on the island simultaneously acted as if they owed them their lives and shunned their company if they got too close. As if they were walking reminders of the death that had plagued them for months.

So, outside her lessons, she mainly enjoyed the company of Azrael, the fledglings, Jeremy, and Sophie. After all, the other healers only knew her as Raphaella and had no idea of the part she'd played in healing their tribe.

Hermes had welcomed her to his office the night the lockdown was over, to let her know how proud he was of her and that her Aphrodite powers were clearly fully unlocked. She hadn't mentioned that she'd attended Gabriel's funeral and seen his display of grief and power. Nor had she mentioned that her ample free time was now beginning to carve a pit of anxiety about the future in her core. She'd hoped it would disappear again, since her father had instructed her to begin daily training with Apollo.

How wrong she'd been. Training with Apollo mostly meant sitting in awkward silence waiting for visions of who knew what to appear in her mind who knew how. Needless to say that it did nothing to abate her fears.

Gods, she needed a distraction.

Which came in the form of Benoît. Benoît was a ray of sunshine in this new world she was trying to navigate. He didn't know her as Lyla but he always had a smile for everyone, and when she had finally recovered from the exhaustion of the pandemic, she had Jeremy glamour her back into Raphaella so she could ask him if he was ready to take to the skies with her.

They met at night in the courtyard since that was the only time she was free from her lessons, and he greeted her with that warm smile of his, admitting, "I know I asked you to come fly with me, but I realize that you know this island better than I do. Would you like to take the lead?"

"Sure thing," she replied, unfolding her wings, and took to the skies. She hadn't flown in what felt like years, and the wind in her feathers was pure bliss. She didn't know if it was because she hadn't known she could fly for most of her life or if this was innate to all angels, but soaring through the skies always caused her an inordinate amount of joy and giddiness. She flew up, up, up, until she could see the entire extent of the fields behind the temple. They were now populated with one tiny home next to another, all illuminating the darkness with their brightly lit windows and fireplaces. She could see the village to the left, with its one main road and few windy little side roads. The orphanage at the very end of the village looked like a tiny castle that would have made any Disney attraction envious.

She kept gaining elevation until she could see the vast forests surrounding the meadows and the agricultural fields beyond that. Finally, she took a sharp right, flew straight over the temple with Benoît in tow, and flapped her wings all the way to the coast. She herself had never flown the width of the island. She'd seen it from the air during her lessons with Azrael, but she'd never actually explored it in its entirety. But today she would. Today she would fly once around the island, the way Max and she had ridden a motorcycle once all around Manhattan what felt like a lifetime ago.

By the time they'd flown over all of the island's dangerous cliff edges and Lyla had flirtatiously brushed her wings against Benoît's more than once, she'd almost forgotten about the harrowing year she'd had. They landed on a rocky beach, sat down near the water, and let the spray wet their wings.

"So," he said. "I haven't seen you around these last few weeks. Where have you been?"

Right. Raphaella had only made an appearance to ask him out, but otherwise, she had completely vanished along with the disease. That's when Lyla realized this relationship was dead in the water. Not that she wanted much from Benoît other than appreciating the ego boost and the occasional company.

Was she deceiving him? Was it unfair to him that he didn't really know, could never know, who he was dealing with? She figured that, while the name was made up, Raphaella was real. She was the alter ego she had lived under for the entirety of the pandemic. After all, didn't we all put on different masks depending on who we were dealing with? Was there really such a thing as one's true self, as soon as societal norms and expectations came into play?

"I've been keeping to myself," she lied.

And so, the lies continued. Every single thing she said to him about herself that night was fiction.

As for him, he was surprisingly... normal. He'd grown up in his mother's tribe in Normandy, but had resented living in the human world and yet hiding from humans. He'd resented the liminal state of the lost. Never quite an angel, and yet never quite human either. He'd fought for the right to go to high school and get a diploma. He'd subsequently gotten a medical degree from University College London, which explained his good English and his somewhat pretentious British accent. And in his thirties, after he'd returned to France, he'd finally found his home when he'd met Julien at the Paris hospital where he was working. He'd moved in with him and Sophie and their other friends, a merry band of misfits who'd carved out their place in a world they didn't belong in.

His story was straightforward. He'd never been through any major hardship other than not knowing his father. He'd always been loved. And because of it, he said what he meant and meant what he said. He was straightforward and to the point. He knew what he wanted. Which in this case was that he liked Lyla – or Raphaella – and wanted to get to know her better. He was everything Lyla should want in a guy. And yet, she found him so very boring. She hated thinking that. She knew he was lovely – he was one of the best-looking males she'd met and he wore his heart on his sleeve. But something was missing.

What was wrong with her for not wanting easy and simple? What was wrong with her for not wanting available? Ok, that wasn't entirely true. Max had been available and she'd wanted him. It had just taken her forever to figure it out. Until it had been too late. Could she grow to be attracted to someone like Benoît? Or did he miss the canvas of pain that usually attracted her to someone?

"Where did you go?" he interrupted her thought process.

"I just remembered I have to be up early," she mumbled and

stumbled back to her cell with a quick "Goodnight," wondering if she was just too broken to be with anyone healthy.

21

S he did indeed have to be up early the next morning for a meeting with Hermes.

"I've decided to tell you more about the Fallen," he started, pushing a cup of peppermint tea across the desk between them. "You need to know what you are up against."

"Okay. Lay it on me."

"The most important thing for you to remember is that the Fallen are fundamentally the same as the Gods. And we share one flaw: we weren't made to fall to Earth. Something snapped in each of us when we arrived here. We processed it differently. The Fallen wear their madness proudly, while the Gods keep it at bay for as long as possible. But make no mistake, Lyla, we are equally as broken and equally as dangerous. The only difference is that the Ten chose to invest everything they were into protecting mankind, while the Fallen embraced chaos. But the void of chaos gets all of us in the end. It always does."

Lyla took a deep breath, wishing away the memory of him kneeling on the beach, howling in pain and rage and his magic bouncing up against his brothers' wings. She didn't want to ever see what would happen if he snapped. And she didn't want to lose him. She didn't want to think about the expiration date on their relationship.

"What I don't understand," she asked, inhaling the fresh scent of peppermint to ground herself in the moment, "is, if the Fallen want to destroy earth, why haven't they done so already? They have greater numbers than you. They could do so much more damage than they have been."

"Correct. But they don't want to be kings and queens of a wasteland. Humanity is their toy. If they break it, they won't have anything to play with anymore. And they are nigh-immortal. Eternity is a long time to be bored. But more importantly... What is the most evil thing one can do to another?"

Lyla thought about that for a while. She thought about causing pain, torture, raping, killing, the obvious evil deeds one thinks of. But then she thought of another. The Fallen had done none of the above to Max. They had done something so much worse. They'd broken his integrity, they'd compromised his morals.

"Making them do something dark," she responded without hesitation.

"Precisely," Hermes exclaimed. "They don't want to destroy humanity, they want to break its spirit, make it destroy itself from the inside. They want to cripple the human species so that it will never evolve into anything as powerful as we are."

"What do they need me for?" she asked the much dreaded question.

"You would be their nuclear weapon. A being capable of annihilating the world in a dozen different ways at once. You'd be a symbolic threat to keep everyone else – Gods, angels, and humans alike – in line. With you at their side, the fight would be over. But only once you unlock."

"So the Gods and the Fallen are playing nuclear arms race with me?" she asked, appalled.

Hermes hesitated. Then, putting down his own mug, he walked around the desk and came to sit in an armchair next to hers. "My intention was never to use you as a weapon or a threat. I hope you believe me."

"But I am a weapon by nature..." she finished his thought for him. "What if I don't want to join the fight?"

Hermes grabbed her hands in a paternal gesture, his claws poking at her skin. "That would be your own decision. No one will be able to stop you from doing anything once you unlock."

Lyla had a flash vision of Dr. Manhattan in Watchmen. She'd always thought him to be such a sorrowful character, entirely alone in his plight, so connected to everything that he could never fully connect to anything.

"But I won't make you do anything until then either," the God continued, letting go of her hands. "I've been training you for your safety and your safety alone. I promise."

"If some of the Ten joined the Fallen, what happened to their angels?" she changed the topic, lest her head start spinning.

"Most of them will have followed their God. It is all they know. They aren't priests of good or evil. They are priests of a certain God. Whoever dared rebel will have been executed by now. Unless they succeeded in fleeing, in which case they will be hiding in the human world."

"With all their resources, why haven't they gotten me yet?" she asked, shaking her head. "I understand that I was of no use to them as a child, but they could have come for me at any point in the last few months, and they would have succeeded."

"They tried. They successfully lured you into Hell, didn't they? That was all about you. I was just the bait... But you outsmarted them."

"What about since? They know the location of this island now. Why haven't they come back?"

"Because Lucifer miscalculated and he knows it." Hermes sighed, leaning forward to reach for his cup of tea.

"I don't understand."

"He waited for you to be an adult. But he still wanted you unformed. Prone to chaos but not in touch with your magic. You learned faster than he bargained for. And he saw it in Hell last winter. He saw how strong you already are and it scared him."

Lyla scoffed. Her? Scaring the Prince of Darkness himself? Please...

"You did," Hermes replied, a glint in his eyes. "And you are so much more powerful now than you were even then. See, Gods unlock fully from one moment to the next. We train, we practice, we grow, and then one day we come into our own. Lucifer fears that you might unlock at any moment. If he kidnapped you and you came into your power without warning, you would destroy everything and everyone around you. You'd destroy them all. He missed the boat on getting to you at a weak point. So instead, he's going to have to use every persuasion tool in his arsenal. He needs to make you come to him willingly."

"But I'd never—" she exclaimed.

"Don't underestimate my brother's capacity to persuade you that his cause is worthy..." he interrupted her with an inexplicable finality.

Lyla had the distinct feeling that there was something he wasn't telling her but, whatever it was, she wasn't sure she wanted to know.

"You make unlocking sound like an explosion..." she asked without really asking.

"It would be best... for everyone else... if I or one of my brothers was around when it happens," her father cryptically replied.

"What you're saying," she continued, her hands shaking so much she spilled burning hot tea all over her skin, "is that I could kill people, a lot of people, if it happens at the wrong time."

"Lailah," Hermes said, taking her mug and setting it down. "Listen to me. You cannot stop living because you live in fear. You cannot stop living because of all the ways this could go wrong. Trust me and let me do the worrying. Let me shoulder this burden for you. Please."

22

It took Lyla the rest of the day to digest everything Hermes had told her. She was leverage to the powers at play. Pure and simple. Not to him. She believed that. But she understood now why he'd kept her progress a secret from his siblings when he hadn't been sure of their allegiances. She was the atom bomb and the Gods and the Fallen were racing toward being the first ones to get her. She couldn't think of any convincing arguments Lucifer could possibly make to convert her to his cause. But she couldn't shake the creepy feeling that had come over her when her father had warned her against his brother's powers of persuasion. Maybe he was aptly named after the devil himself...

And much like a bomb, she could be a guarantee of peace, or she could be the end of it all. How was she to wrap her head around that one?

The truth was that she didn't want to unlock. What did that even mean? She'd be coming into her own as the only being of a long-extinct species. That sounded terribly lonely. She thought of creatures in science-fiction books, superheroes in the movies... They all had their isolation in common. The fact that no one quite understood them. She wanted no part in that.

Taken by a sudden urge to forget her predicament, Lyla considered walking to the tavern, which Artiya had reopened and was running again, this time on her own. But then she vividly remembered the night she'd stumbled upon Azrael slowly drinking himself to death. Alcohol wouldn't make her problems go away, it would only exacerbate them. And yet, she already felt the burden of loneliness like a big black hole inside her core. One she desperately wanted to fill with any pleasurable activity she could grab for. Alcohol. Food. Sex. Drugs. She felt it like an itch in that spot in the center of her back she couldn't quite reach. One she could scratch around, but would never satisfy. And she knew that the more she scratched around it, the more the spot itself would itch. Alcohol wouldn't fill this black hole.

Neither would exercising, but at least it would exhaust her enough to send her to sleep for a few hours. So, Lyla turned on her heel and made her way to the gym.

She was drenched in sweat, her knuckles scraped from the heavy bag she'd been hitting when Benoît entered the room.

"What did that bag do to you?" he asked.

Lyla turned around and almost made up some explanation about how hard the pandemic had been on them, before she remembered that she wasn't glamoured. She looked like herself, Lyla, the girl he'd sometimes smile at in the halls but had never had a conversation with.

"Excess energy," she simply replied. "Want to spar?"

"Okay," he said and stepped onto the mat in the center of the gym.

"No magic allowed. Wings stay in," she told him.

And so they went at it, for an entire hour. Benoît was a priest of Aphrodite's; he was not a fighter. In fact he'd barely ever had a training session until the end of the virus, when

Hermes had insisted that everyone on the island get lessons in self-defense. So, this mostly consisted of him trying to hit her, her blocking or evading every single time, and her getting a hit in on him. Sometimes beginners were the worst people to spar with, because they'd accidentally hurt you, so she had to be extra careful to parry or evade. By the time they were done, she was exhausted.

"Thank you," he said between two heavy exhales, sitting down on a bench. "I needed that."

"Rough day?" she answered, joining him. Whatever he had to complain about, it surely wouldn't beat being a super being that could "unlock" at any time...

"I went on a bad date last night," he confessed.

Oops.

"Why was it bad?" she carefully asked.

"She was clearly not into me. Couldn't get out of there fast enough." He leaned his head back, his breath still heaving from the exercise.

He had a point...

"I'm sorry," she said, meaning it more than he'd ever know.

"I think I've just been lonely," he admitted. "I don't even know this female well at all. But the last few months have been hard on everyone. The isolation really wore on me."

"It was horrible," she agreed. "I never thought I'd miss physical intimacy that quickly."

"Gods, I can't even remember the last time I was intimate with someone!" He laughed.

"It's been a while for me too," she sympathized.

"How long?" he asked, turning his head toward her.

"Nine months."

"Longer for me."

"That sounds truly terrible," she teased him. "However do

you survive?"

"Didn't you notice the unnaturally large muscles in my right arm?" he chuckled.

This was a whole new side to Benoît she'd never seen before. When he'd been courting her as Raphaella, he'd been so very serious and proper. He'd probably acted the way he assumed she wanted him to, rather than just being himself. But Lyla had never been into serious and proper. She much preferred irreverent, and she strongly believed that a raunchy sense of humor was a sign of intelligence. Maybe he wasn't that boring after all.

"Care for a walk?" she asked.

So, they took a walk around the village, which had now been expanded all the way into the green pastures, and was inhabited by a few thousand angels who celebrated their luck every night, having survived a plague that had threatened to eradicate them all. Everywhere she looked, angels were gathering in the streets, catching up on much-needed social time. The skies were full of them most nights, going on flights to the beach or soaring over the forest. And the edge of the woods was populated with little campfires angels were gathering around.

Benoît and Lyla walked around for a couple of hours, enjoying the hustle and bustle of the island before making their way to the tavern. They kept talking about their need for intimacy, slowly feeling out their chances with one another. It became clearer and clearer that they both wanted to remedy their loneliness – just for tonight. Azrael popped into Lyla's mind a few times, but she decided that sleeping with an angel who was being open and honest with her was better than holding out for one who played games and never told her the full truth.

When they were finally ready to order at the tavern, Lyla asked, "Are you drinking tonight?"

"It depends where the night takes us," Benoît answered suggestively.

"Are you asking me if you're getting laid tonight?" she responded crassly.

"I'm just saying that if I were, I'd prefer to be sober for it."

"Then, don't drink."

With that they'd sealed their fate for the evening. They continued talking, some of it serious, some of it the cheekiest jokes they could think of.

Lyla insisted on taking a shower before meeting him in his cell, since she'd been sweating like a pig in the gym. But she also wanted to buy herself time in case she changed her mind. She thought about it under the hot water stream and could not come up with a good reason not to have a casual night of hot sex with the handsome healer. Not only had she never seen anything wrong with casual encounters, but more importantly, she needed to feel physically close to someone right in this moment. She needed to remember the joy of intimacy, she needed to remember what it felt like to be held by someone and to connect and share a moment.

Benoît's cell looked like a hotel room. After all, he'd only been on the island for a few months and probably considered the arrangement temporary.

"Are you sure about this?" he asked as he let her in.

She nodded and he added, "We don't know each other well so please know that we can stop at any moment, all right?"

"Thank you for saying that," she responded and wrapped her arms around his neck.

The second she touched him, he ravaged her mouth, pushing her up against the wall.

And then, they were off to the races.

Lyla usually liked her sex mindful and kinky, long and thought out. She had always loved foreplay, a slow drawing out of things, being made to really, really want someone before getting them. But right now, she needed the opposite. Fast, sweaty, and maybe a tad sloppy. She wrapped her legs around his waist and started humping him, moaning into his mouth.

"I can't wait," she said. "I need you inside me right now."

The rest was a messy tearing off of clothes, stumbling toward the bed, and falling over right on top of each other.

As she spread her legs, he asked one last time, "Are you sure?"

She nodded frantically and he replied, "Thank fuck," before getting inside of her.

And then they slowed down at last. Both of them highly aware that they may not know each other or have a special bond, and yet that they were lucky to have found each other tonight. That they were fortunate to share a semblance of connection. And that they might not get another for a long time after this.

There was nothing particularly special about their sexual encounter. No bells or whistles. Just two angels, hanging on tight to each other while finding comfort together, riding each other in a frantic attempt to forget their loneliness, their pain. She sighed in relief after orgasming for the first time in months in the presence of another living being. But it wasn't about that. It was about forgetting, for the briefest of moments, that the weight of the world had just been put upon her shoulders. It was about feeling normal and ordinary for just one night.

The kinkiest thing that happened that night was him biting down on one of her nipples as he pulled out and came. But Lyla hadn't needed special and unique that night. She'd just needed someone to look at her and want to connect with her.

They lay in each other's arms in silence for most of the night. There was nothing to be said. After all, they didn't know each other. Nor would they ever repeat what had just happened.

They'd both gotten exactly what they needed and could easily part ways again.

When she finally left his cell to go sleep in her own single bed, an unexpected wave of sadness overcame her. She knew that feeling all too well, the drop that followed a dopamine rush. She went to sleep ultra-aware of the fact that, while Benoît had offered her exactly what she'd asked for in the moment, it wasn't what she really wanted. What she really wanted was to connect with someone who knew her and cared about her, someone she'd want to wake up to the following morning, and possibly even the mornings thereafter.

23

Lyla woke up with an emotional hangover the next day. Sleeping with Benoît had left her feeling inordinately empty. She wasn't exactly new to casual sex. At one point in her life, it was all she'd done. Except for Max, it was really all she'd ever done. But something had changed. Ever since the day she'd realized she was in love with Max and had then lost him forever within the next hour, she'd been craving more. She'd been craving meaning and closeness. And as good as the sex last night had been in theory, it hadn't been meaningful. Benoît was honest and present in the moment perhaps, but he didn't really know her well enough to care about her. Nor she him. Which left her feeling hollow, like the void inside of her, that itch she'd been so desperate to scratch, had grown larger rather than being relieved.

It was July seventeenth, her birthday, and the last thing she wanted to do was spend it alone with her thoughts. She'd always loved her birthdays. Max had ridiculed her for calling herself the "Birthday Queen" and making him be at her beck-and-call for twenty-four hours straight. But he'd always been the very best birthday buddy, tending to her every whim and desire. Even when she'd made him watch Young Frankenstein for the twentieth time since it was her birthday breakfast tradition.

Today, she realized that the person she wanted to spend the day with was Azrael. After her intimate night with Benoît, he was who she wanted to see. Someone who knew her, and cared about her. Someone she had true feelings for, even if she still needed to move on from them.

She knocked on his door and asked him to train with her. She had different plans for the rest of the day, but she needed to butter him up first, and she knew that the fighting ring always put him in a good mood.

He opened the door wearing nothing but his underwear, unkempt hair, and sexy two-day stubble. "It's my day off," he grumpily answered her request.

"Maybe," she replied. "But it's also my birthday, so you have to do what I want today."

"Is that so?"

"Yep. Them's the rules!"

"All right, all right," he begrudgingly agreed. "Give me a minute to get myself together."

She met him in the fighting ring half an hour later. It wasn't as warm as the summer days she was used to, but the island finally had perfect training weather. It was warm enough that her teeth weren't chattering whenever she stopped moving, yet it was cool enough that the exercise wouldn't make her overheat.

"All right, little birthday shit, let's see what you've got today," Azrael exclaimed, as he flew up into the air.

And he wasn't kidding. He immediately threw a magical attack her way. She saw the ripple burst through the air as if in slow-motion and dodged. And then another. She ducked and weaved and flapped her wings his way. He easily dismissed her attack, shielding himself with one wing, but he hadn't expected her to be as agile as she was. She wasn't as lucky with his third attack though.

They kept going like this, back and forth, the big angel always ultimately beating her. But she gave it her best and that best was far beyond the skills she'd demonstrated even just a few months prior. Finally, she landed on the ground, needing to catch her breath.

"Water break," she heaved, exhausted.

As she bent down to grab her canteen, Lyla got dizzy, closed her eyes, and felt the usual rush in her ears that, these days, preceded one of her visions.

She saw Azrael dropping height in the air and attacking from below. She saw him soaring up behind her to shoot his power straight at her wings. And she saw him rush toward her to knock her down with a roundhouse kick.

It couldn't be... Could it?

Lyla took back to the skies, squared off on Azrael, her wings splayed out behind her... He dropped all of a sudden and shot his will power in her direction from underneath. It hit her in the shins like a cannonball and almost dropped her. But she was ready for the next strike. As he flew up behind her, she rolled forward, laying down on her belly in the middle of the air, her wings pointing upward into the sky, and vocally hissed her power toward the angel who was trying to ambush her from behind. She wouldn't give him the satisfaction to hit her with that roundhouse kick either. As she straightened back out, she lifted her knee, to block his kick. In a daring move, she grabbed his leg and flipped him in the air. Losing control of his flight, Azrael lost his balance and dropped down into the ring, barely slowing down his fall with a flutter of his wings.

"I'm impressed," Azrael chuckled, picking himself up.

"Yeah, me too..." Lyla slowly replied.

She'd seen his attacks coming. She'd known what they'd be before they'd even been back in the ring. She couldn't rely on her very hit-or-miss Apollo foresight in a fight. But did that mean, when she unlocked, she'd be able to predict an opponent's every move before it happened and counter it with the force of an Ares priest, the precision of a Hermes fighter, and buff herself like one of Artemis' people?

No wonder the Fallen were scared of her.

Foreseeably, the rest of the training session was a fair fight. One she lost over and over again.

When they finally sat in the kitchens for lunch, Lyla suggested, "So... you owe me a birthday present..."

"Oh do I now?"

She was taken aback for a moment. "Wait, do angels not give each other presents on their birthdays?"

"Actually, no. We share experiences. But Jeremy told me all about human birthday traditions. Do I owe you cake too?" he asked, clearly very satisfied with himself.

"Nah, never mind the cake. I'm not a cake girl," she replied. "What do you mean, experiences?"

"We take angels out on adventures on their birthday. Could be a shopping spree in the village, a flight around the island, or a day on the beach. That way, their birthdays can last days, depending on how many loved ones want to gift them with an experience."

"Wow, I kind of love that..." Lyla replied, awed.

Shared time was a love language she'd always appreciated much more than gifts. Gifts were easy. But getting to spend hours with those you loved? That was truly special.

And it was her opening.

"All right. Can I pick my shared experience?"

"Perhaps..." he mused, guessing that she was up to no good.

"But you have to promise to say yes," she said in her sweetest voice.

"Hmmm, I don't like where this is going."

"Pleeeease?" she asked, making big doe eyes. "It's my birthday after all."

"All right. You're a pain in my ass, but all right," he conceded.

"I want to go to the Sacred Mountain."

Azrael immediately shrunk into himself.

"You promised..." she insisted.

"That was before I knew what you'd ask," he replied harshly. "I don't want to go, Lyla. I haven't been since California."

"And I say, you need to go back."

"Come on... I'll give you anything else," he bargained.

She was tempted to tell him not to make promises he couldn't keep, but flirtation would get her nowhere with him.

"You promised. Please, do this for me," she tried once more.

Those last words seemed to pull him over the edge.

"Fine," he grunted. "But don't expect anything good up there."

"That's ok," she conceded.

They flew out of the second floor of the compound. At the foot of the Sacred Mountain, he drew her into his arms and took them up to the top, landing in the patch of grass where he'd once shared his story with her.

At first, they just stood near the tree under which they'd had their first deep conversation. She had no idea what kind of tree it was, but it was in full bloom, majestically standing at the edge of a cliff, sprouting massive red flowers that occasionally dropped their petals into the lush green grass. No one ever came here. No one could ever come here, other than Azrael and anyone he chose to carry up. She wished she could soak it all in, just sit here and meditate in the untouched green. But the longer they waited, the more apprehensive Azrael would grow. Instead, Lyla started walking toward the cabin. He dragged his feet, but slowly followed. Outside the house, she could see and sense his internal struggle. Knowing he wouldn't reject her, she grabbed his hand, said, "It's ok. I'm with you," and entered the cabin.

Lyla looked around the room, she herself feeling a wave of relief wash through her. The last time she'd been here, she'd been traumatized and scared. Her father had taken down the currents for her to fly up in the middle of the attack, where she'd helplessly watched the massacre from the top of the mountain. She'd been lost up here, not knowing what to do next, until Azrael had arrived and immediately attacked her, scaring the living shit out of her. And then, they'd slowly made preparations to leave the island and head to California. She hadn't known whether she could trust him, only that she didn't really have a choice. It had been a grueling twenty-four hours that she'd avoided thinking about ever since.

But now that she stood in the cabin, all she saw was a home. A warm and welcoming home. There were no remnants of the trauma, no remnants of the fear, the helplessness. And yet, the cabin hadn't changed. It was exactly as they'd left it on that gruesome December morning. She, on the other hand, had changed. She wasn't helpless anymore, was she? She wasn't a lost angel who'd been hurt by the human world. She was a God who was coming into her own. She was more powerful than any of the people around her. She had a father who loved her. She had a place in this world. And she'd proven it in their fight against the virus.

Looking at the logs near the fireplace, the cozy couch she'd forced herself to have a meal on the last time she was here, the paintings on the wall, the strategically placed weapons around the room, she felt her power. She realized she was no longer the woman who had first arrived on this island almost a year ago.

Turning around, she noted that Azrael did not feel as self-assured. He was standing in the entrance, helplessly staring at the wall he'd pushed her up against months ago. She'd never seen him like that, his arms hanging by his sides looking too long, too awkward, his eyes wide like those of a spooked horse.

"Azrael?" she quietly asked, walking right up into his field of vision. "Azrael, I'm right here. You're not alone."

He didn't react, barely even looked at her. So she walked into his space, wrapped her arms around his torso, and let just the smallest wisp of her Aphrodite power course through her hands and into his back.

Azrael let his head hang over her shoulder and sighed.

"I'm so sorry," he said after an eternity. "I'm so sorry, Lyla. I was supposed to protect you... I never wanted to turn into one of the people who terrorized you... I never wanted to be one of your nightmares..."

"You aren't. Azrael, look at me," she said, pulling back to look him straight in the eyes. "I have not been scared of you once since that day. Not once have I remembered it and resented you. Other people populate my nightmares. You aren't one of them. I promise."

He looked somewhat relieved at that. But not entirely.

"Az," she added, grabbing his hand and pulling him further into the room. "You fought the serum."

"What are you talking about?" he argued.

"You had me pinned against the wall. I was so scared, it almost choked my airways. I had no way to use my magic on you. I didn't make you stop. You made yourself stop."

He looked at her with skepticism.

"I don't remember that."

"You've been beating yourself up over nothing. You fought a serum that everyone else fully succumbed to. You're not the bad guy here."

Azrael didn't respond. He just walked toward the wall against which their interaction had taken place, and put his head against it. She'd said what she needed to. It was up to him to forgive himself now. Slowly he placed both his hands on the wall, and his shoulders sagged. She heard a small sob escape his throat, before he turned around, put his back against the wall and slowly sunk down to the ground.

Lyla chose to let him have his moment. Quietly she tiptoed past him and toward the kitchen, where she looked for something for them to snack on. She found an unopened tin can of cookies. Wait, she'd seen these cookies before. She read the label: "Lebkuchen." These were traditional German cookies sold at holiday markets in New York. She would visit the three big markets with Max every year: Bryant Park, Columbus Circle, and Union Square. And she would ravenously eat these very cookies, while sipping spiked mulled wine. Angels were self-sufficient. They didn't import anything from the human world. Interesting... That meant that Azrael had liked these cookies enough to bring them back. And it also meant that he had spent enough downtime there to discover the tasty cookies in the first place.

Lyla grabbed the tin can and put on a kettle, looking for tea. It turned out Azrael's tastes weren't quite as refined there: he only had what smelled like very strong black tea.

When she returned with two mugs and some cookies, she found him sitting on the couch, more relaxed than he'd been in months.

"Are you all right?" she asked.

"I think I am actually, yes," he responded.

She sat down and passed him one of the mugs. The tea was too hot to drink, but it felt like a safety blanket, holding the warm concoction in her hands while she waited for Azrael to speak.

When he finally did, the words that came out of his mouth were the last she'd expected.

"I'm sorry if I led you on, Lyla," he said.

"What?" she responded, baffled.

"The kiss..." he explained. "I got carried away. But I didn't mean to lead you to believe that it meant anything more than it did."

"Um, ok," she retorted, taken aback. "What did it mean?"

"We had a moment. But we were in survival mode, and we'd just spent two weeks traveling together. It was just something that happened. I didn't plan it or want anything to come of it. And I'm sorry if you and I weren't on the same page about that."

That was as unexpected as it was actually on brand. Should she call him on his bullshit? Should she tell him that she wouldn't give him the satisfaction to make him the bad guy in this inter-action? Should she tell him she felt sorry that he hated himself so much he couldn't open up to anyone else?

That was what her more self-assured side thought.

And yet, another little part of her believed him. Maybe he really hadn't meant anything by it. Maybe the way he'd called her "little fledgling" when he'd slept in her bed hadn't sounded as romantic to his ears as it had hers. Maybe he really had just opportunistically grabbed the moment without caring about her feelings.

Regardless, it didn't matter whether he reciprocated said feelings or not. He clearly wasn't ready for anything other than a friendship. So, friendship would have to be the way forward for them.

"Thank you for being honest," she replied. "It's ok, really. Tensions were high at the time. And, if anyone else had been there instead of you, I probably would have cathected to the first person around after everything that happened that fall."

She wasn't sure if that was the truth or a lie. She cared about Azrael a lot more now than she had then. Then she'd been all hormonal and rosy-eyed. But now, she actually knew him. And she loved him for what she knew. And because she cared about him so deeply, even if romance was an impossibility, she wanted to safeguard whatever was possible between them. He may not love himself, but she loved him too much to lose him entirely.

"You're not mad at me?" he asked, true concern in his voice.

"No, I'm really not."

As she said it, she realized it was true.

"So what's wrong with you today then?" he inquired.

"What do you mean?'

"Something is off about you. You look upset somehow..." he mused.

"I just had a rough night," she evaded his question.

"Hmmm... You slept with someone last night, didn't you?" he coaxed her.

How did he know? Maybe he knew her better than she realized.

"It's ok. You can tell me," he added.

"I mayyyy have," she admitted.

"Ha, I knew it. So, what's the problem? Wasn't it good?"

"No, it was great... In theory," she stalled. "I don't know, it just didn't feel right, you know?"

"Yeah, I've had my fair share of those. So, who was it?" he inquired.

What was this, an interrogation?

"Why does it matter?" she rebuked, trying to put him back in his lane.

"Because we're friends. Come on. I'm not judging."

Ugh, he was really good at getting information out of people. Part of the job description as a priest of Hermes', she assumed.

"Benoît. Julien's friend," she admitted.

"Ha! Look at you getting dicked by the grey-winged peacock!"

Was that a trifle of jealousy she sensed? He'd coaxed the truth out of her by playing the friendship card, but somehow this didn't feel entirely friendly...

"Peacock? How so?" she asked.

"He may be a priest of Aphrodite's and full of love and what-not, but he's also pretty in love with himself. You haven't noticed how he struts down the halls like he's the single hero of the pandemic?" he exclaimed.

No, she hadn't. But maybe he wasn't entirely wrong. Maybe Benoît's arrogance was the thing in him that simultaneously attracted and repulsed her.

"So, what did you two get up to?" the big angel asked, a gossipy touch in his voice that most certainly didn't have a place in their friendship.

"Sex, Azrael. We had sex. Stop fishing for details," she retorted, fed up.

"All right, all right. I'll stop digging. But why aren't you feeling good about it? Was he disrespectful?" he continued to pry, some concern now seeping into his voice.

"No. He was fine. I guess I just don't care for casual so much anymore..."

Sometimes admitting something out loud made it easier to

bear. And sometimes it made a harsh reality much truer than she wanted it to be.

"Ah. I see."

But he didn't explain further as to what it was, he saw. Though she couldn't help reading some self-satisfaction in his features as he leaned back, a slight smile on his face.

"Sounds to me like you needed to try it to figure out what you really want."

24

After another half hour of small talk that thankfully did not revolve around her sex life, they got ready to fly back off the mountain. Azrael's rock-solid abs were not lost on Lyla when he swooped her up and took off into the skies. He was definitely holding her closer than he had before finding out about Benoît.

And he also seemed somewhat distracted. Twice he got too close to a rock formation and scraped his wing on the stone. Could he have gotten out of practice so quickly?

"Hey, what's on your mind?" she asked.

"I was just thinking that I hope you took a shower after sleeping with that buzzard..." he answered grumpily.

"Are you jealous?" she simply asked.

"I'm not. I'm not jealous of a vulture," he replied and sped up, flying straight down the side of the mountain. Just as he did, he glanced off the side of a sharp rock. Lyla barely had time to see blood in his grey feathers when Azrael lost control. He instinctively wrapped his large wings around her to protect her, and they got pummeled down the side of the mountain, back and forth, back and forth through the canyon they'd been descending. Until they crashed at the foot of the mountain, his wings unfolding and letting her softly fall out of their protective cocoon.

It took Lyla a moment to understand what had happened as she rolled onto the grass and away from Azrael's warm feathers. It must have been a twenty-foot drop. She didn't have a scrape on her, thanks to him, but she immediately kneeled in the grass and retched up the cookies and tea along with their lunch.

When her head finally stopped spinning, she turned around to check on Azrael.

He lay in the grass, his wings splayed out to the side, covered in blood, one of them at an angle that was so very wrong she immediately realized that it must be broken. A sharp piece of rock stuck out from his thigh – oh Gods, that might be the femoral artery it was blocking. She'd seen this before. If she pulled out that rock, he could bleed to death in minutes. And his face was covered in scratches, a long gash in his forehead bleeding steadily into his long dark hair.

"Lyla," he whispered. "Lyla, get Jeremy."

She didn't have time for that. He couldn't see the damage, but his wings were bleeding much too fast, his thigh was barely kept together by the piece of jagged rock that he'd impaled himself on. He was slowly but steadily dying, the grass around him dyed red. By the time she found Jeremy and brought him back, he might not make it.

Lyla panicked. She'd healed Zadkiel's mind, and she'd healed hundreds of patients from the virus, but she'd never mended a bone or stopped bleeding. Okay, okay, she thought to herself, same principle. Use your magic.

What was the most pressing wound to heal? The cut artery could kill him at any moment, but his left wing was now surrounded by a six-inch radius of blood seeping into the grass.

Triage said that she should start there and hope for the best on his thigh.

With trembling hands, she removed a waist belt she was wearing around her shirt, carefully laced it around Azrael's thigh, and tied it off as snugly as possible. Unfortunately, the motion pushed the sharp piece of rock out of his artery, and blood came spraying upward out of his thigh.

"Oh shit!"

"Lyla," Azrael murmured. "Lyla, please, get help."

"I need you to be quiet for a moment, okay? There's no time to get help. You're stuck with me. Just, please let me try to fix you up," she hastily replied, as she pressed both her hands down onto the wound.

Lyla unfolded her wings and started humming, willing the wound to close, but nothing happened. Bright red blood flowed up between her fingers and down the sides of her hands and Azrael's head suddenly lolled to the side. He'd passed out, she hoped. But she feared the worst. With that thought, tears of panic closed off her throat and her hum. She was losing. Her magic wasn't making its way into his body.

What was different between him and her other patients? She knew the answer immediately: she was emotionally invested. She'd wanted to save everyone else, but it had been impersonal. This was deeply personal. And that was why she couldn't focus enough to apply her healing powers.

Taking a deep breath, and pressing down on Azrael's leg with all her might, she tried her best to concentrate. To remember her meditation lessons with him. To block out everything except him, his need for healing, and herself. She took a few conscious breaths in and out of her mouth, and closed her eyes. Slowly, too slowly, the world around her disappeared, and she was in the dark chamber in her mind, in which nothing but her and her patient existed. In that space, Lyla took her hands off his thigh, and assessed the damage. He was bleeding out, but he was still alive. As if she did this every day, she summoned an imaginary needle and thread out of thin air, pressed the edges of the wound together with trembling fingers, and started suturing him up. She'd watched some videos on how to do proper medical stitches in case she and Max ever needed to patch each other up, but at this moment, she couldn't remember any of what she'd learned. She simply stitched away until the wound was shut tight. Then she summoned up some super glue and glued it together, just to make sure. Carefully, she removed the belt tourniquet she'd made in the real world and watched as his wound closed up on its own.

With a sigh of relief, Lyla left the chamber in her mind, opened her eyes, and returned to the real world, to see that the only sign of damage left on Azrael's leg was a whole lot of drying blood. She removed the real tourniquet and nearly collapsed with exhaustion.

That's when she realized his upper body was laying in too large a pool of blood. Crap, he was bleeding out from his wing. In a moment of panic, she checked his pulse, leaving a bloody mark on the side of his neck. He was alive, barely, but he was alive. Thank the Ten.

Crawling around to kneel at his head, she searched his wings, examining each square inch, pulling feathers to the side to get to the membrane underneath them, looking for the wound. He had scrapes all over them, but she finally found a large gash in his left wing. Gods, was that another artery? How was he still alive?

Lyla pressed her hands onto the wound in his wing, his soft feathers matted with wet blood underneath them, and tried to focus again. Oh Gods, what if she didn't get it right this time?

What if sewing up wings was more difficult than skin? It had to be.

When she finally made it into the void in her mind, Lyla carefully ripped out the feathers surrounding the wound. She knew she wasn't tearing out any feathers in reality, but it hurt her soul to even think about harming Azrael that way. Their wings carried their magic. Losing feathers was the most excruciating pain an angel could suffer. And just as she thought it, the Azrael in her mind started reacting. He curled himself up into a ball in pain, effectively pushing her off his bleeding wing and giving her no room to work.

Lyla knew it wasn't real. *Focus, focus.* Shit, he was bleeding out in the real world. How could she– suddenly she had an idea. If she could summon up a needle and thread, she could surely conjure an anesthetic. Swiftly, she grabbed a large syringe out of thin air and popped it into Azrael's neck. The latter went to sleep and she went to work getting feathers out of the way of the wound. When she finally had a clean surface to work with, she started stitching up his wing, careful not to tear any holes in the membrane – though of course, just as she thought that, she realized she was causing small gashes in the skin.

Breathe, she told herself, *just breathe and keep working.*

When she finished the job and returned to the real world, Lyla was shocked to see that Azrael's feathers had been plucked out in reality too. As for the rest of him, he lay in the grass, pale as a sheet, breathing shallowly.

Lyla took a deep breath. He was going to be fine. She'd just patched up the lethal wounds. As long as he didn't have any internal bleeding, or brain swelling, or– he was going to be fine, he had to be. Before tackling the gash in his forehead, Lyla looked at his body, inch by inch, and took stock of his other injuries. It looked like a ton of scrapes, but only scrapes. Those could wait.

His head injury was easy to mend, but Lyla was running out of steam, and she had no idea how to set a broken bone. His wings were paramount to his work, hell, to his very identity. If she set the bone wrong, he could lose his magic and his ability to fly. She couldn't risk it.

Instead, she healed every cut, every bruise she could find, unsure whether that was actually helpful. But it was helpful to her, to see him slowly come back to life. By the time she was done, he was still covered in blood, but he wasn't turning blue anymore.

Finally, as Lyla readied herself to tackle his brain, to somehow go in there and make sure everything was as it should be – not that she had any idea how to do that – Azrael opened his eyes.

"Lyla? What happened?" he asked, trying to sit up, using his broken wing for leverage. He screamed at the pain in the appendage and fell back into the blood-soaked grass.

"Don't move," she calmly replied. "Your wing is broken, but you're otherwise fine."

"Where's Jeremy?"

"I need to go get him, so he can set your broken bone. That means I have to leave you alone for a bit…"

"Wait. Who healed me?"

"I did," she responded, too tired to continue keeping secrets.

Wearily, she took off her jacket and laid it across his chest. It wasn't even large enough to cover the big guy's torso.

"What? I don't understand…" he replied, grabbing her by the wrist and not letting go.

She knew this state of mind. She'd seen it on Max a couple of times after an accident. His brain was so jumbled, he'd hyperfocus on this Lyla-healing-him thing until he got answers. But they didn't have time for that. She had no idea how long she'd been here healing him, but at some point the sun had set and the stars had come out to play. It was high time Jeremy set his bone.

"Azrael, look at me," she replied, taking her wrist back and grabbing both his hands in hers. "I promise that I'll tell you everything. But I need to go get Jeremy, so he can heal your wing now. I will be back as quickly as possible. I need you to wait here and not move. Can you do that for me, please?"

"Okay," he responded, sluggishly, and passed out again. It seemed that he'd blown all his energy on their short interaction.

Lyla flew back to the temple as fast as she could. She landed straight on Jeremy's balcony and started banging on the window. Thank God he went to bed early. He opened the door, Julien in tow.

"Lyla, what the..." he started, sleepily. "Lyla, what the hell?!" he repeated, getting a good look at her.

She'd forgotten she was covered in blood.

"Jeremy, I need your help," she exclaimed. The sight of him was such a relief after the stressful hours she'd had, she almost collapsed into his arms. "Azrael's hurt. I think I mostly healed him. But his wing is broken and I don't know how to set bones..."

"Where is he?" Jeremy immediately jumped into action, ignoring the fact she'd just blown her cover in front of Julien.

"At the foot of the Sacred Mountain."

Without a word, Jeremy stepped out onto the balcony, and they both flew away toward the mountain.

"How did this happen?" he shouted, mid-flight.

"He was flying me off the mountain. He got distracted and we got caught in a wind tunnel that pummeled us all the way to the ground."

"How come you aren't hurt?" he inquired.

"Azrael wrapped his wings around me and took all the damage."

"Of course he did..." Jeremy simply replied and remained quiet for the rest of the flight.

When they arrived, Azrael's teeth were chattering. He was conscious, but didn't make much noise other than the occasional moan or grunt. Lyla sat down by his side and grabbed his clammy hand, while Jeremy set to work on the broken wing.

The moment Jeremy set the bone, much like a human doctor would have, Lyla regretted holding Azrael's hand. He crushed hers so hard, she might need to get some bones of her own set.

But that was the worst of it. Jeremy laid his hands on Azrael's wing and closed his eyes in concentration. She had no idea what exactly the healer was doing, but warmth slowly returned to Azrael's skin. Sitting back against a rock, she put her other hand on his head and started soothingly caressing his blood-soaked hair. She wanted to tell him that everything would be fine, but she didn't want to disturb Jeremy's concentration. So, she sat in silence, while Jeremy finished healing the wing and then proceeded to take Azrael's head between his hands, presumably to check on his brain.

By the time all was said and done, a sliver of the moon was high up in the sky. Jeremy helped Azrael up and instructed him to lean on them. It took them a felt eternity to get him back to his cell, one agonizing step at a time. He was fully healed, but his body had undergone such a terrible ordeal, he'd still need several days in bed to return to full function. And the more Lyla thought about her own lack of wounds, the more she suspected part of the reason he'd let himself fall rather than to attempt escaping the wind tunnel, was that he'd exhausted all of his power on keeping her safe. He'd need time to recover from that too.

Lyla couldn't leave after bringing him to his cell. Azrael could barely stand, he was caked in blood and dirt, and she found it physically impossible to leave him alone in that state.

Jeremy helped him sit on his bed, looked back at Lyla in the corner, and, when he realized that she wasn't leaving, quietly excused himself. Much like the cabin on the Sacred Mountain, Azrael had turned this tiny room into a true home. He'd carved figures and stories into every inch of his chair, table, and bed frame, and covered the walls in paintings she was fairly certain were his. They stood in stark contrast to each other. Some were depicting epic battle scenes, while others were of quiet lives of simplicity. She knew him well enough to realize that those were the warring sides of Azrael that constantly fought for his attention.

"What do you need?" she asked him, turning around to look at his exhausted face.

"A shower... But I don't think I can handle it on my own, so it's really up to your comfort level," he replied with zero humor.

Under any other circumstances, it would have been awkward seeing the big guy naked. But there was nothing sexual about this situation. So, Lyla slowly helped him out of his shoes and socks. Jeremy had mentioned that he should not pull his wings back into his body for a couple of days. They needed to stay out while they healed. Not wanting to hurt the sore appendages, she grabbed for one of his many knives and carefully cut his shirt off his body. Angels' shirts and tops all had slits in the back for them to fold and unfold their wings at will. So, she simply cut along the slits, to the collar and bottom of the shirt, until it was in three pieces and falling off his torso.

"Can I please lean on you?" he asked, standing up.

She nodded, and he leaned his body against her while undoing his pants. As he tried to bend down to pull them off his legs, he almost doubled over. It took all she had to push him in the opposite direction and gracelessly drop him back onto the bed. Wincing as his recently broken wing hit the mattress, Azrael started chuckling but stopped himself, putting a hand to his midsection as if feeling sick.

"Gods, look at us..." he started.

"Yeah," she replied, taken by a sudden fit of the giggles and dropping onto the bed herself. "Happy birthday to me..."

Lying there next to him, she turned to look at his profile. "I'm really glad you're okay," she said.

"Me too. About that..." He turned his head toward her. "You still owe me an explanation..."

So he hadn't been too delirious to remember.

"Fair enough," she said, getting up to crouch on the ground and pull on his pants. "May I take your pants off and get you in the tub first? I'm kind of struggling over here."

Five minutes later, he was hunched over in the tub, naked, his wings wrapped around him, while Lyla, sitting on the edge, carefully soaped up his feathers and showered the blood off of them.

"I'm sorry I had to tear out some of your feathers," she said, soaping up the naked membrane from which he'd been bleeding out mere hours ago. "You had a gash there through – what I think was – an artery. I couldn't heal it back up with the feathers in the way. I mean, I'm sure Jeremy would have known how. But it was my first time healing life-threatening wounds."

"Does that mean you've healed people before?" he carefully asked.

"I have..." she replied, holding the shower head over his wings and watching the pink water go down the drain.

"How many?"

"I lost count," she said cryptically, then explained, "I was one of the healers who helped fight the virus. Jeremy glamoured me up every morning, and I went by the name 'Raphaella' so no one would ask questions."

"How? I don't understand," he admitted, looking at her, a disturbed expression on his face.

"My parents are Hermes... and Aphrodite."

"That's impossible!" he exclaimed weakly.

"It shouldn't be possible. But it's the truth."

He remained silent as she began to rinse the blood out of his long black hair.

"That explains your sonic attacks..." he finally mused.

"...and the fact I sucked at magic for the longest time. Apparently, for what I am, I'm pretty young. Hermes called me a 'hatchling' when he told me," she added sheepishly.

"You... you're a Goddess," he said, creasing his forehead.

"I am. Apparently, I have the powers of all Ten Gods. But I only really know how to wield Hermes' and Aphrodite's. Everything else is very unreliable."

"Earlier today... You predicted my attacks, didn't you? You were too fast in your responses, I didn't understand how you did it. I thought it was luck, but that was Apollo's power, wasn't it?" he asked.

"It was."

"Gods... that makes you..." he drifted off.

"Potentially the most powerful being on the planet? Yeah..." she finished his sentence.

He stared at her in silence.

Wanting to break the discomfort of the moment, she added, "On a funnier note, I can't believe you thought I was crushing on Jeremy!"

At that, Azrael laughed, a roaring laughter she hadn't heard from him in months.

"Lyla... I just realized I kissed you, and I fucked your brother. A lot."

"That's... a little weird," she admitted and handed him the soap. "Your wings are clean. Think you can manage the rest?"

He grabbed the soap and started cleaning the blood off his skin. Cleaning his wings had felt oddly intimate, but she was grateful to not have to take it further. She held the shower nozzle over him to keep him warm, but looked away, giving him as much privacy as possible.

Thirty minutes later, he was laying on his belly in bed, wearing only underwear he had painstakingly taken minutes to pull up his own legs. She pulled the covers to just under the base of his wings, and he was asleep before she could say "Goodnight."

She carefully tiptoed out of the room, grabbed a pillow and some blankets from her own cell, and returned to sleep on his floor.

25

I n spite of the exhaustion of the day, Lyla barely slept a wink that first night by Azrael's side.

She stared at the grey wing hanging off the side of his bed, realizing, only as the shock wore off, that she'd almost lost him tonight. Being in the bathroom with him, after being sure he would die... It wasn't the nudity that stayed on her mind. She'd imagined him naked plenty of times before – still did on the rare occasion. But it was the fact that her heart had been burstingly full while she'd cleaned his feathers that kept her awake. The fact that, after having touched him more intimately than she'd thought she ever would, she didn't want anything from him.

She lay awake, staring at the ceiling and rolling that thought around in her head. She still had feelings for him, she knew that. Even now, she was resisting the urge to reach out and touch the soft feathers draping down toward her. But she no longer had any hopes or expectations. Twice now he'd used his jealousy to keep her at bay. Nothing good would come of pushing him into something he wasn't ready for. And yet, she was happy listening to his quiet breathing. Happy looking at his peaceful face, the stubble around his relaxed lips, the lashes fluttering about as he dreamt. Happy he existed. No, she didn't want anything from him. But she wanted everything for him. If she never saw him again, she wanted him to have all the happiness in the world. She wanted him to be safe and taken care of, but she didn't need to be the person providing those things.

Lyla tossed and turned as the stars shifted outside the window. When she finally fell into a fitful sleep, she dreamt of Azrael with a faceless female and fledglings of his own. She saw him teaching them how to fly, sitting with his wife, watching them grow up. He was happy, fulfilled. She watched from afar and realized that all she wanted was for that picture to last forever, until he was old and wrinkled, playing with grandchildren and great-grandchildren. After everything they'd been through, after falling for him and being rejected, after living around him for the better part of a year, after sharing moments of deep connection and intimacy, all that mattered to her was his safety and happiness. In the dream, she turned around and walked away into a dark forest. The path, broken up by knobbly roots and difficult to navigate without tripping, was covered in something soft... brown, black, and white hair... moving... legs... there were clusters of eyes in those moving balls of hair. Lyla almost shrieked when she felt a furry creature pass across the back of her thigh.

She woke up to a sliver of light outside the window and realized that no spider was crawling across her leg – Azrael had stretched his wing in his sleep, scraping the back of her naked thigh with its edge. What had felt creepy and foreboding in the dream, felt intimate and sensual in the moment. She was tempted to caress those feathers in kind, though she knew she shouldn't consciously answer an unconscious gesture – no matter how much she wished to make it last.

Instead, Lyla shifted her leg away from under him and turned to her side to look at the wall that was lightening with sunrise. She thought of her dream, of how it had felt to see Azrael in love with someone else. His happiness had been her happiness. In that moment she realized: she was capable of unconditional love. She'd learned how to love unconditionally from him.

She loved him. Truly, fully loved him. And not just him. She realized that that love extended to... well, everyone. She couldn't pick and choose who to love. She loved Azrael, because she knew him. Truly knew him to the core of his being. But the reason she felt connected to him was that he mirrored her and the rest of the world, that he was a microcosm of life itself. What made her love him was his – for lack of a better word – humanity. The fact he was alive and loving and caring, that he had a beating heart with hopes, dreams, and desires... even when his desires did not include her... made him this perfect example of what it meant to be alive, to exist in this crazy world, to believe in its beautiful moments in spite of how painful it could be. That was what attracted her to him. That was what had opened her heart. But that "humanity" mirrored her and it mirrored the world. Every single human, angel, and even God shared those universal traits. Which made them all loveable.

Her heart ached with the realization.

Love was empathy. Love was compassion. Love for another, was love for life itself. And now that she wasn't living in her own pain and fear, she could see it. She loved him, because she trusted him and felt safe enough that she could love him, as well as every other living being...

Even... Max.

Lyla sat up, her chest bursting with an energy she needed to expel. She quietly opened the door to Azrael's balcony, where she stood, looking at the rising sun on the horizon, and deeply breathing in this new day.

She'd been so focused on her righteous rage, she'd forgotten that Max was just another human trying to navigate life to the best of his ability. He'd morally failed. Greatly so. But that didn't take away from the fierce, protective little boy he'd been. He'd sold her out to the monsters that had threatened his own life, but he'd protected her from everyone else. Even when it had cost him greatly.

Max had never had a chance. He'd never been safe. All things considered, he'd done a pretty great job at being loving and caring. After all, he'd always put her first wherever the Fallen were not concerned.

Her heart now wide open, Lyla was overcome with shame for how much she'd disowned Max in the last six months. He'd harmed her greatly, but he'd also kept her alive. His example of how to treat someone with care was probably the reason her heart hadn't fully shriveled up by the time she'd met Jeremy.

Lyla closed her eyes and let the tears flow freely down her face. She cried not for herself, but for the scared little boy who had been stuck between a rock and a hard place. Finally, returning to her makeshift bed, she curled up and fell into a long, dreamless sleep.

Three nights went by like that. Azrael sleeping, and Lyla watching him and rethinking the way she'd looked at the world. It felt like, sometime in the last year, she'd taken the smallest step to the left and suddenly the entire world had tilted into place. Everything that had always felt uncomfortable and uneasy about being a person in the world had dissipated and been replaced with this strange, inexplicable understanding that things were just as they needed to be.

By the end of the third day, Azrael woke up, fully healed.

Lyla insisted he not get up yet, brought him breakfast in bed, and quietly sat with him.

When she finally left his room, he broke the silence.

"Lyla?" he called as she opened the door.

"Yes?" she asked, turning around.

"I'm so sorry."

"About what?"

"I'm sorry I've been such an idiot about this thing between us," he replied, looking away.

Surprised, Lyla just stared at him.

"Just give me a little time to wrap my brain around it. Please?" he asked, looking at her with the kind of sincerity she was only used to from her brother.

"Okay," she simply responded. "Get some rest in the meantime."

She left and closed the door with a smile. Maybe there was hope for them after all.

26

Her newfound peace soothed Lyla into another entire day of dreamless sleep. But she had plans for that night. After checking in with Azrael and making sure he was truly and fully healed and could painlessly summon and disappear his wings, she walked out of the compound, through the fields, and into the woods. She'd walked these woods many times before during her early training sessions with Azrael. This was where she'd taken her first baby steps in trust and vulnerability when her post-traumatic stress disorder had been so present that she couldn't use her wings without going into survival mode and leaking out every last drop of her magic. Azrael had taught her how to control her fear, how to acknowledge it without letting it run the show. He'd taught her how to put the traumatized little girl that lived inside of her in the backseat of the car so she, Lyla, could be the one making decisions. There was an entire ecosystem in these woods, animals the angels let live in the wild and that Hermes would hunt to feed the village every so often. But the forest was quiet tonight. As if it knew what she was about to do. She stopped in a clearing she and Azrael had trained in what felt like eons ago, sat down, and meditated for an hour, clearing her head of every drifting thought. Then, she focused on Max. She had no idea how Hades' powers worked. Her father had never even begun to discuss the raising of the dead with her. But she was hell-bent on summoning her old friend and lover.

Her vague understanding was that the dead could move on or not, though she didn't know where to or for what reasons. But if popular human culture had gotten it even remotely right, souls didn't move on until they were at peace. And with the life Max had led, there was no way he was at peace.

Lyla focused on her memories of him for the longest time... to no avail. She didn't want to think of him as she'd last seen him – nothing more than a pile of bloody meat. Instead she recalled his smile, his laughter ringing out every time they'd watched their favorite comedies. She remembered how blond his hair had been when they'd first met. How years later, she'd admired the line of his profile against the blue California sky sitting on top of the halfpipe at their favorite skatepark. How nonchalantly he'd sat there, a cigarette loosely hanging from his lips, how comfortable she'd been, laying her head in his lap. How hesitant his touch had been later on that night, when she'd first discovered that sex could be something she chose and controlled. She remembered the triumphant glee with which he'd handed her the keys to their first shared apartment, and the desperation in his eyes when he'd asked her to run away with him, just hours before his death. When nothing happened, she called out his name, feeling only a little bit silly.

Finally, she gave up and strolled back home, wondering what it was she was missing. As she rounded the corner to enter the temple's courtyard, her body instinctively stopped. It took her brain a moment to catch up. There was – how could it be? – a tarantula sitting right in the middle of her path.

They were on the latitude of Greenland...

She took a step toward the creature to get a closer look. The spider was immobile. Just sitting there, possibly looking at her with its cluster of eyes. It looked... flawless. If she'd had any talent for painting, this was the perfect tarantula she would have painted. Black, with thin white stripes on each of its patellae.

She'd seen demons, she'd faced Lucifer himself, and yet something deep and instinctual in her reacted like it would rather face off on a two-legged Fallen than on the small, hairy creature.

But it was impossible for a tarantula to be this far north. Humans kept them as pets, yet there weren't any humans on the island. There was nowhere it could have escaped from. And she hadn't done any drugs in a long while now. So why was she seeing this apparition clear as day? Lyla was starting to panic that she might be hallucinating when she dropped to the ground and darkness enveloped her.

27

She found herself in the same dark void of her meditations, the same dark void she healed patients in. And the only other creature in it was the spider. Except that it was the size of a very large dog now. She could clearly see every single one of its milky eyes, its glistening fangs. It looked straight at her, but somehow, she knew it wouldn't attack.

"Hello, Lailah..." it purred, as Lyla's heart rate went through the roof.

Oh God, the thing spoke. Hearing monsters speak English somehow never got any less unsettling.

"What... What are you?" she asked in a trembling voice, slowly walking backwards to put more distance between her and the creature.

"Me?" the arachnid said in that silky voice that reminded her of the webs it would spin if it could. "I have been a steady companion to you your whole life. Don't you recognize me? I have walked in your shadow since you were born. But you no longer need me, do you?"

Lyla swallowed, looking around for an escape route. She had

no idea what any of it meant and frankly, she didn't feel like sticking around to figure it out.

"Max cannot come to the phone right now, I'm afraid," the hairy creature continued. "But I think there are a few things you need to see."

And then it walked toward her.

Everything in Lyla's body wanted to crawl away, but she fell down on her ass and felt an unfortunate wall appear at her back. The spider meanwhile closed the distance between them, like it had all the time in the world. Slowly shifting each of its many, many legs one at a time, it approached her, until Lyla could see her own reflection in its eyes, those very large downward facing fangs much, much too close to her head for comfort. As she felt her pulse jump into her throat and became lightheaded, Lyla stopped breathing. Then, the thing lifted its front leg and caressed her cheek. With surprising gentleness, its hairy appendage stroked once down Lyla's face, leaving behind the cool breeze that follows the touch of a slightly sticky palm.

Eyes wide in terror, Lyla could do nothing but listen, as the creature said, "Goodbye, sweet girl, it has been an honor."

And then it disappeared into thin air. Lyla exhaled and nearly collapsed in relief – just as a silhouette appeared in the distance. Unable to go anywhere, unable to wake up, Lyla waited, as it grew larger and larger. It was a little boy, bouncing a yo-yo in his hand, a cap shadowing half his face.

She knew that boy, she realized. That was Max. As she'd first met him.

"Max!" she called out to him, but he didn't respond. This was a memory, she realized. She wouldn't be able to interact with it.

Just as she had the thought, she saw a man walk up to the little boy. But it couldn't be human. Something was off about it. Its movements were just a little too sharp and ill-timed. It wore a trenchcoat, a hat, and sunglasses, as if it had something to hide. And much like its demon cousins, it spoke in an eerie voice. There was a scratchy tone in the back of its throat, as if talking was something it wasn't used to doing with its vocal cords.

"Hello, young man," it said, and Max dropped the yo-yo, which shattered on impact and rolled away into the darkness.

"There's a girl that's going to come live at your home in a few days. I need you to spy on her and report everything you see to me."

"What are..."

The creature lowered its sunglasses and revealed yellow eyes, with rectangular goat-like pupils. Max was too scared to finish the sentence.

"My siblings will be in touch. Your job going forward is to tell us everything about her," the creature said, putting its nose into Max's neck and inhaling deeply. "And if you don't, I'll take a bite out of you."

Max froze and squeezed his eyes shut as if he was hoping it would all be a dream when he reopened them.

The two figures disappeared, replaced by a slightly older Max and a different kind of demon, more akin to something Lyla had seen before in hell – a crab-goat monster straight out of a nightmare, with a flat face and red eyes.

Max was sitting in a chair, the demon circling around him.

"Tell me everything she said and did," it said, its face unnaturally close to Max's.

"That's it. I told you everything, I swear," the boy responded, trying to follow the circling creature. But Lyla knew he was lying. She knew his tell-tell signs, the balled up fists, the drawn up shoulders. He'd withheld things from the demon.

And it knew too. She watched, as it punched him, with one of its pincered legs. It drew its face as close as demonly possible to his, salivating at the thought of eating him, and yet unable to act on that instinct, since he was their spy. But Max remained silent, blood running out of his broken nose. Taking the pain, and still protecting Lyla. Despite the fear that he was currently wetting his pants with. Despite the fact this otherworldly creature threatened his very existence.

Time passed again, and a teenage Max appeared. But now it wasn't a demon facing him. It was a Fallen. She recognized it by its wings: jet black feathers on a seven-foot-tall humanoid creature with black, protruding bat eyes, horns like a deer, and the fangs of an old-fashioned vampire.

"What scared her the most about this last home?" it asked.

"The mind games," Max answered, voice trembling yet composed. "The gaslighting. The fact she thought she was going crazy."

She knew what home he was talking about. One of the few she hadn't gotten physically abused in. And yet the mental torture had been almost worse. She'd learned how to shut out physical pain, how to dissociate from it. But thinking she was losing her mind, that had been worse than anything she could have imagined.

"Are you speaking the truth, Max the Deceiver?" the Fallen asked in a silky voice.

"I am. I swear, I am." Max replied, shutting the eyes that tears of fear and shame were streaming out of. For a split second, Max reopened them and Lyla could have sworn that he looked straight at her, as if asking for forgiveness, begging to be seen as worthy despite his flaws.

Before she could fully lock eyes with him, the two figures disappeared again. This time nothing replaced them. Instead,

Lyla was hit by a cannon ball in the gut. Her senses were flooded with feelings. Feelings and thoughts that weren't hers.

A sense of sheer terror.

Fear for her life.

Fear for anything and everything she held dear.

A sense of deep shame and guilt. Not only that she was betraying her loved ones, but that she was betraying everything she believed in.

And a sense of absolute loss. The knowledge that she was entirely meaningless in a world ruled by monsters. That she was nothing but a speck of dust, floating about in a cruel universe that would destroy itself no matter whether she went left or right, chose right or wrong.

These feelings, so opposite to the emotions she'd carried into the forest mere hours earlier, were crushing. She knew they weren't hers. After all, wasn't the very definition of empathy the ability to feel another's feelings as if they were your own? These were Max's feelings, they were the relentless pain and fear he'd grown up with. Every time he'd put on a brave face with her, this is what he'd been covering up. Every time he'd taken a beating for her, this is what his reality had been. Every time he'd been seemingly joyful, free, sharing a happy moment with her, this is what he'd been covering up.

These feelings were what it meant to be Max.

Max had been stronger than she'd ever known. He'd tried his best to give her a childhood, to preserve her innocence in the face of insurmountable odds, in the face of existential terrors so large they'd have swallowed up anybody else.

Max had preserved most of his humanity, his heart, when anyone else would have caved entirely.

"Max..." she spoke into the void. "If you can hear me, please, move on. I'm going to be ok now. I am ok. And I'm moving on too. Thank you for everything you did to get me here. I love you."

28

Lyla was extremely distracted in her meeting with Hermes, Hades, and Apollo the next morning. She barely heard their status reports on the descendants of Aphrodite's they'd managed to round up and what they thought the Fallen were up to. Usually she was mildly on edge around the two less familiar Gods. As much as Hermes called them "brothers," they did not feel like family to her. They felt otherworldly, dangerous, and predatory. Being around them felt like sitting between a talking tiger and a smiling grizzly. She was always uneasy and paying attention to every single word and gesture. But today she was dead tired from staying up as Azrael healed and then spending a night trying to summon the dead. All that, after having worked herself to the point of exhaustion healing Azrael in ways she'd never healed anyone before. And it didn't help that the little bit of consciousness left in her brain kept drifting toward Azrael. He'd asked her for time to get used to the idea of... them. His near-death experience had pushed him to admit that he'd been a dumbass about their relationship. She agreed with him there.

But she couldn't help wondering how much more time he'd

need. She'd needed a day to figure out she was in love with Max. She could give him a day. Even a week, or a month. Would that be sufficient to overcome whatever self-sabotaging systems he had in place though? And had she really only needed a day to uncover her feelings for Max? No. She'd needed twenty years and a day...

Her ears perked up when the Gods mentioned the lost. They were bent over a map of the world showing the locations of all known tribes, scattered across every single continent. Tens of thousands of black-winged, ostracized angels hiding out in plain sight.

"They are dying in droves," Apollo reported, presumably returning from one of his many missions outside the bounds of the island. "Entire tribes swept away by the disease. Others halved in numbers."

"Should we help them?" Hades mused.

"How?" Hermes chimed in. "We have eleven healers left, and we can't risk their lives."

"Plus the half-dozen Aphrodite acolytes Apollo herded..." Hades argued.

"All right. We have maybe twenty. We barely made it out of this plague ourselves. Why risk them on a people who have consistently refused to fight for our cause?'

"Because they are our cousins," Hades continued his argument.

"That may very well be. And if we'd known the Fallen's plan ahead of time, when we still had numbers and support from our brothers and sisters, I'd happily have stopped it. But we don't."

The finality with which her father spoke the words didn't allow for argument. Yet, Hades warned, "If we leave them to die, we'll have to live with the implications."

"What implications?" Apollo snapped, taking Hermes' side.

"That we make sacrifices for the greater good? We have done so since the dawn of human times. The lost made their bed. We have tried to win them over numerous times. They chose to live away from us and to stay out of the fight. Let them live with the consequences."

Lyla tuned out the rest of the meeting. She'd seen the virus. She knew how easily it killed their kind. If left untreated, an angel was certain to die from it. How could they let an entire species be eradicated by the very disease that had caused them so much suffering? She didn't know how often her father had to make difficult choices for "the greater good," but leaving their closest cousins to this fate didn't feel like a rational decision. Could it be that he was beginning to lose his mind?

Lyla's brain was spinning so hard on her lunch break, while turning a corner into the courtyard, she almost bumped head-first into Azrael's shoulder.

"What's up with you today?" he asked, grinning.

He looked to be in particularly good spirits. Probably something about having a brush with death and being given "time..."

"I just heard something disturbing," she answered. "Actually, can we talk?"

"Sure," the large angel replied, setting aside the sparring pads he was carrying and sitting down in a low window frame in the corner of the yard.

He remained quiet while she reported on everything the Gods had said. And he remained quiet for a long while thereafter.

"Az?" she finally asked.

"I'm not sure I should voice my opinion on meetings I wasn't invited to..." he started, picking at his nails.

"Dude, come on," she replied. "Don't give me that good little soldier routine—"

"It's not that," Azrael interrupted. "I don't have a complete enough picture to know if there's any value in my opinion."

"But you do have an opinion. So, what is it?" she pushed.

"What you're reporting is alarming," he slowly explained. "The lost are just angels with black wings. It feels unethical to leave them to die. But if it is the call of the Gods, they must have good reason–"

"Their reasoning is that the lost refused to fight for them," Lyla interrupted. "That ain't good enough."

"Lyla, as distressing as this is, there is nothing we can do... The Ten are looking at a bigger picture than us."

"What bigger picture?" she shot back. "They're standing by, watching a genocide. That makes them complicit. It's not that complicated."

"Actually it is," Azrael argued, turning to look her straight in the eyes. "I've been doing this for a lot longer than you and believe me when I say that making snap judgment calls on partial information has always left me feeling and looking foolish. The Ten are flawed, but you're trying to play checkers on a chess board."

"But that's just the thing, isn't it?" she retorted. "It's no longer The Ten. It's three dudes fumbling around in the dark. Three dudes who might go crazy at any moment. What if they're making the wrong call?"

He bit his lip, clearly torn between his impulse and his duty to the Gods.

"Sooner or later this is all coming to a head," she continued. "Don't we want the lost on our side? From a purely self-serving standpoint, don't we want them to want to fight for us when the day comes?"

Azrael sighed and remained silent for a long while. She could almost hear the gears turning in his brain.

Finally he lifted his head toward the cloudy sky and asked, "What are you plotting?"

"Well," she mused. "We can't convince the other healers to go against the Gods' orders. That would undermine their authority and lead to chaos. And I can't single-handedly go cure the lost. But we could make all of this a moot point..."

"What do you mean?" he asked, frowning.

"What if the disease never existed? What if the pandemic never happened in the first place?' she suggested.

"I don't understand," he replied.

"Hermes said he'd have stepped in if he'd known before our numbers were depleted... It so happens," she explained, "that I saved one of Poseidon's descendants. She could help us go back in time, find Demeter, and stop the whole thing before it even began."

"Time travel isn't a real power. It's never used because of how dangerous it is," he retorted.

"Buddy, we are a small island of a few thousand and we lost hundreds to the virus. This disease is killing humans and angels alike in the hundreds of thousands, millions more likely. And we ourselves are only safe as long as we remain isolated, which we can't do for much longer. Doesn't that sound like a good reason to go back in time?"

"I hope you're not meaning to say that you yourself would go back in time," he warned.

"When was the last time I was that reckless? Nevermind, don't answer that. But come on, give me some credit..."

He just lifted an eyebrow in response.

"I'm going to suggest it to my father, like the good daughter I am," she explained.

"Best of luck," he replied as she walked away. Before entering the temple, she turned back around and suggestively added,

"Besides, I'm not time traveling backwards now that you've finally promised to think about... what did you call it? 'This thing between us...'"

29

She was on her way back upstairs, flying up the hollow center of the staircase when it hit her like a punch to everything right under her guts. The pain almost pummeled Lyla right back down the staircase, but she managed to grab the banister and haul herself over it. The highest level of the temple mostly housed Hermes' office and quarters and, thankfully, few angels had any reason to be up there. Not that Lyla would have noticed anyone's presence, as she crumbled at the top of the stairs, holding her shins to her chest, struggling to breathe. Gods, it hurt. Everywhere. There was a sharp pain, for lack of a better term, in her nether regions. And it radiated to the rest of her body. It was the same pain she experienced when seeing another person fall or get hit, amplified a thousandfold. Seeing black spots in her vision, Lyla grabbed the banister behind her and tried to pull herself up, only to slip as her legs folded underneath her. Shit. Her wings hung low, feeling too heavy to lift. She looked at the door to Hermes' office, not wanting to call out and attract attention, and began crawling on all fours toward it, the agony inside her not giving up one bit. After a couple of steps, she fell to her belly, weighed down by the torturous blaze of anguish inside her. As if moving through jello, Lyla dragged herself along the floor, one excruciating limb at a time. After what felt like hours, she reached the door and weakly lifted her hand to knock on it, only for her arm to drop and the black spots to fully take over her vision.

Lyla vaguely registered the door flying open and strong arms picking her up. Then came darkness, an infinite void she needed to resurface from and tried so hard to claw her way out of with each pained stroke toward the surface. The next moment of true clarity was the uncomfortable wet towel on her forehead dripping down the back of her neck and soaking the soft pillow underneath her. Her breathing was shallow, but the world was returning. The light blue ceiling in her father's office, and those black and yellow eyes she'd learned to associate with safety. The harrowing radiation inside her had ceased, leaving only the discomfort of loneliness behind.

She wanted to open her mouth, but her body had yet to obey her commands.

"Slow down, little hatchling," her father commanded.

"Hmmm," she responded, unable to form words.

"Deep breaths..."

"C- c- cold," she murmured, realizing it was true as she said it.

Hermes immediately grabbed a blanket off the back of the couch she realized she'd been deposited on, and covered her with it.

"I..." she began. "I felt them, dad."

"Who?" he inquired.

"The lost. I felt their pain. Their grief. The anguish... the desperation... the anger... all of it."

Hermes sighed, slowly removing the uncomfortable towel

from her forehead and removing wet strands of her hair from her face. He gently grabbed her right hand in his much larger ones.

"Breathe, Lailah. It's over for now. It won't happen again for weeks, maybe months. You're safe. It's just growing pains," he explained.

"Is this..." She couldn't finish the question.

"It gets easier, much easier," he assured her.

"They're in so much pain..."

"I can only imagine," he replied.

"You have to do something. Please." Unwilling, hot tears rolled down the sides of her face.

"I can't."

"Please! Dad, it was agony being in their shoes for just a few minutes," she pleaded with him.

But he only shook his head.

She'd planned on a much more self-assured entrance and an uncompromising presentation of her plan. Instead, she found herself begging.

"Dad, we could go back in time and stop this whole thing before it even begins. Sophie is one of Poseidon's children. She could take you back and you could confront Demeter or whoever else is behind this thing yourself. Please."

"No."

"You said, you'd have helped them before if you'd known..." she argued.

"That's not the same as going back. Lailah, this is not a conversation." She'd never heard him so unyielding. Even when she'd first met him and he'd been stern and authoritative, he hadn't been this... grim. There was something pained and sinister in his expression.

"We do not go back. Ever. Do you hear me?' he asked, his

voice rising, as he stood and stepped away from her.

"I don't understand," she sluggishly replied, pulling herself up into a seated position.

"You don't need to understand," he replied, turning away, his face haunted. "Rest. Stay as long as you need."

With that, he opened the door behind him and flew off into the skies without further explanation, leaving her shaking with the memory of her first empathic blood connection to her distant relatives.

30

"Lyla, it's not as simple as that," Azrael argued, when she returned to him, after her failed attempt at convincing her father. "First of all, time travel is unheard of. I've read about it in theory, but I haven't heard of a single case in my lifetime. And secondly, even if someone went back, how would they stop a virus of unknown origin?"

"Let me think..." she responded, buying herself time.

"There's nothing to think about. It's a terrible idea," he replied, standing up to return to his solo training session.

"First we find out when and where the first case of the virus appeared," she interjected.

"How could we possibly find that information?" he threw over his shoulder.

"The internet," she replied with a self-satisfied smile.

That stopped him dead in his tracks. "The intra– What?"

"The– Never mind. There's a good chance the first cases were human. The Fallen won't have wandered into a lost tribe and infected them. Besides, humans would spread it quickly through travel."

"Fair enough. So how do we find out who the first human case was?" he asked, turning back toward her and leaning against the wall.

"Can you just trust me that, if you take me to the human world, I can borrow a phone, do a search, and find out within a minute."

Azrael's forehead creased skeptically. He clearly didn't believe her, but she'd used too many human words for him to argue. Besides, his body language was easing up, which meant she had about a thirty-second window to sell him on her crazy plan.

"Once we find out when it started," she hurriedly continued, "we go back a month earlier and do some homework."

"Such as?" he asked.

"Such as me using my power of foresight to find where the virus was created."

"Your Apollo powers are shoddy at best. And you wouldn't have any anchor or anything specific to search for," he argued, crossing his arms.

"It has to be Demeter, don't you think?" she asked, losing confidence.

"Hermes suspects her of treason... And she is the expert of all things earth-based. She would be the obvious candidate to create a disease. But even if you found her – which I highly doubt you could – she might not be near the research. She could have ordered her acolytes to do the work for her."

"Is that really likely? The Gods are pretty overbearingly hands-on in my experience."

"Fair," he conceded. "If she betrayed us and if Lucifer tasked her with the creation of a virus, she would have overseen it herself. But, Lyla, those are too many 'ifs'. If you're wrong on any count..."

"Then we hide out, let history replay itself and come right

back to this moment. No harm done."

Azrael shook his head.

"It's too dangerous. We don't know the implications of time travel. It might not be as simple as staying away from the world and not changing the course of history."

"We can't just do nothing."

"That's exactly what we're going to do, Lyla, if you can't see the enormous holes in your lousy plan!" he replied, his voice rising.

"Then help me make a better plan!" she yelled back.

"I am not going to help you go against a direct order from Hermes. You asked him and he said no–"

"In this moment in time, he did," she interrupted. "Let's not give him a choice. If we bring him the information in the past, he'll have to do something about it."

"Strong-arm a God? Are you out of your mind?" Azrael exclaimed.

"They're hurting..." she began to plead.

"I'm sure they are..."

"I'm not speculating," she continued, her voice shaking with the memory. "I felt them. I felt what they're going through. The way Hermes feels his descendents. I felt them like their feelings were my feelings. And it literally brought me to my knees!"

Azrael looked at her wide-eyed.

"You *felt* them?"

"Yes! And they need help."

"Lyla, if you're developing that sort of empathic connection, how do you expect yourself to think rationally?" he retorted, speaking softly, as if scared to set her off.

"What's that supposed to mean?" she asked.

"You're not a neutral party coming to the rescue," he tried to explain. "You're too deeply emotionally involved to make reasonable calls. You need to step away from this right now. You can't help them if you can't think straight and separate yourself from the issue."

"Are you calling me hysterical?" she yelled.

"I'm not," he replied, calmly. "If that's what you choose to hear, that's on you. I'm just saying that you need some emotional distance."

"Emotional distance, eh?" she replied, hoping her next words would sting as much as she intended them too. "Well, you're the expert at emotional distance, aren't you?"

Feeling the short-lived satisfaction of pettiness, Lyla walked away with only one hope at an alliance remaining.

31

Sophie wasn't easy to convince. "No," was her immediate response. "Time travel is too dangerous."

"It's your power..."

"Exactly," she replied in the same uncompromising tone. "There is a reason it is never used."

"I understand that changing history is dangerous. A butterfly flaps its wings differently and blah blah blah. But millions are going to die from this disease. The lost might be eradicated entirely. The Fallen are massacring them. And there's only so long we'll be able to keep angels safe. Isn't that worth the risk? Is saving these angels, lost, and humans really that likely to lead to something worse?"

"It's not that..." Sophie said, elusively.

"What is it then?"

"We can't use our power—"

"Are you telling me you shoot blanks magically as well as physically?" Lyla mocked.

"That's offensive," Sophie replied. "And not entirely accurate. We can. But we mustn't use our power."

"Why?" Lyla insisted. "What's the problem?"

The older angel didn't reply. Lyla could tell she was struggling with something. She looked out the window, something like pain in her eyes.

Finally, she said, "Even if I brought you back, how would you find Demeter?"

"Would you trust me if I said that I have a way of finding her?" she replied, unsure if she could trust Sophie.

"No," the other female simply replied, in the same uncompromising tone Hermes had used earlier.

Lyla weighed it in her head. Her father would go berserk if he knew she'd revealed her identity to anyone. But without Sophie, her plan fell apart. And the female had a right to know if she was putting her own life on the line for Lyla's crazy plan... Throwing caution to the wind, Lyla decided to tell her the truth.

Sophie stayed silent for a while after the confession.

"You will usher in a new world," she finally mused, awe coloring her words.

"What do you mean?" Lyla asked.

"If you come into your power, the world will never be the same," Sophie explained. "No matter whether you choose a side or not, your mere existence will end the war as we have known it."

"Maybe," Lyla replied, uncomfortable with the idea of being that pivotal to anything of importance.

"You could unite angels with the lost. You could bring mixed children back into the fold. You could... You wouldn't be like the Ten..." she continued.

She was talking about her as a leader. As if she expected her not to align with the Gods, but to become their ruler. Lyla thought her new friend was giving her much too much credit, but if it played in her favor, she figured she might just let it slide...

"Lyla, I need you to make me a promise," Sophie said, suddenly perking up, her eyes glistening with moisture. "I need you to promise me that when you ascend you'll bring these alienated groups back together. That you'll welcome white, black, and grey wings alike and bring them all back into the fold."

It was one hell of a request. Lyla wasn't a leader. She wasn't a strategist. And she had no intention of becoming either. But if she did, she would want to bring them together. If she did, she'd want to fulfill this promise.

"I'll try my best," she meekly replied, looking away.

"That's not good enough, Lyla," the other female insisted. "If I take you back in time, that is my price."

Was it a promise she could make? She didn't think she'd ever want to rule, but if she did, it would be her first order of business to try to unite these factions...

"Okay. It's a deal," Lyla conceded, a heaviness settling in her chest as she offered Sophie her hand.

Instead of shaking it, the blonde angel pulled her into a tight embrace. After what felt like an eternity, she pulled away, grabbed Lyla's face in both her hands, and leaned her forehead against hers.

"Get to work, little Godling. We've got lives to save."

PART THREE

32

Lyla spent every waking minute practicing her powers of foresight. When she wasn't training with Apollo, she was playing a version of hide-and-go-seek with Sophie. The latter would go to some location on the island, and she'd have to find her in her mind. At first, they kept it to the ground floor of the temple, and it would take her forever to find her, if she would at all. But slowly but surely, she started finding it easier to quiet her mind and look for her new friend.

By the end of the month, she could find her anywhere on the island. Now came the hard part. Finding someone she'd only met once in passing. Last Halloween, there had been a meeting of the eight living Gods at which she had been introduced. She'd been so scared and angry at the time, she could barely remember any of them. So, she started visiting the library for the first time in almost a year and studying every book on Demeter she could find.

She found out that the Goddess' powers extended from making potions and remedies to causing natural disasters. If she applied herself she could cause a tsunami or an earthquake.

Which, as long as she was working with the Ten, she would never have done, but now it crossed Lyla's mind that that didn't bode so well. She found out that Demeter had been in a long-term relationship with Ares, the God of war, much like her father had with Aphrodite. Creation and destruction getting it on. How poetic. And she found out that Demeter was an eight-foot-tall Goddess with the eyes of a fawn, the antlers of an elk, and green vines growing in and out of her skin and covering her entire body, including her large white wings.

She learned every last detail she could about the terrifying Goddess of the Earth. And then she tried to find her. They'd agreed that, unless she could consistently find her five times a day for a week straight, they would not go back in time. And when she truly couldn't find her, presumably because she might be veiled in Hell, Lyla would look for other random people on the island and Sophie would confirm her findings.

She practiced, and practiced, and practiced.

She hated lying to her father as well as to Azrael, but she allowed the discomfort to give way to rage by remembering their dismissive words and attitudes toward the situation at hand. Luckily, Hermes was mostly absent, which saved her from lying to him, or getting silly notions about confronting and convincing him. She didn't really want to know his reasoning, nor did she want to spend too much time lingering on her disappointment that he wouldn't help her with this one thing she knew needed to happen. She couldn't stand by, not after what she'd felt. Not knowing that the empathic torment she'd endured would return in weeks' or months' time. Once was enough.

Meanwhile, Benoît gave her a sweet and knowing smile and head nod every time they crossed paths in the hallways. They seemed to be on the same page: grateful for the moment they'd shared and not interested in ever repeating it. The fledglings on the other hand spent ample time with Azrael, Jeremy, and, whenever she was too tired to practice, Lyla. Their pet rats had grown to be at least a pound each and would proudly ride everywhere on the little ones' shoulders, mischievously combing their hair with their four-fingered paws. Lyla would read the fledglings stories at night and take them out for flight practice. Little Raziel was indeed beginning to learn how to flap his wings and hover a few feet off the ground. As for Apollo and Hades, they were nowhere to be seen, no doubt gathering intel on the whereabouts of their remaining siblings.

After almost two months of practice, blissfully free of any empathy attacks, it was finally time to put their plan into action. It took a week of them taking turns spying on Hermes' office to get a relatively safe idea of his comings and goings. One thing he did like clockwork: every single evening at ten, he left his office to go on a hunt. He never returned until after one in the morning.

So, one September evening, Sophie and Lyla flew up to Hermes' office balcony and let themselves in, courtesy of Lyla's old lockpicking talents. The office wasn't secured particularly well. Being an apex predator, Hermes probably didn't think he needed to protect himself against much – an arrogant belief he'd bitterly paid for in recent months. Or maybe he simply kept all truly valuable information and objects locked in the many trunks lining the walls that Lyla would not have dared attempt to open, for fear of an unknown magic attacking her. Maybe the office itself was just a room and they weren't that clever for successfully breaking into it.

Without hesitation, the two angels stepped through the portal together, Lyla telling Sophie the exact coordinates to keep in mind on her way through. She had picked said coordinates ahead of time knowing they'd send them to New York

City, near Lyla's old house. The neighborhood had changed in the year since she'd been gone. Every restaurant had tables on the street now, many stores had closed down, people wore face coverings everywhere they went, and there were generally fewer people around, less traffic on the streets... For dinnertime, it was surprisingly dead.

"Wait here," she told her companion outside a small playground at the corner of twenty-second street and tenth avenue.

"If you need help or need someone more charming to convince the nice humans, let me know," Sophie replied as a way of acquiescing.

Lyla turned on her heel and walked around the corner and half a block down Tenth Avenue. Across the street was a cute little Italian restaurant with eight tables set up outside and people starting to have dinner. Maybe the virus wasn't the death sentence to humans that it was to angels? Judging from the face coverings and the fact all restaurants had "outdoor dining only" signs, they were still in the midst of it. Yet there were four couples and a family happily dining out at this place.

The family looked stressed and had a crying baby. That meant they were out. As for the couples, three of them fit perfectly into the wealthy neighborhood, which meant they were a little too uptight to easily ask for a favor. But the fourth couple didn't fit in. The man wore overalls, a lumberjack shirt and a farmer's hat. He vaguely reminded her of Azrael with his long dark hair, ethnically ambiguous features, and large upper body. Which brought a slight pang of guilt as well as disappointment that she'd now have to wait for at least a year before getting an answer from Azrael on "that thing between them." A pang of guilt and disappointment she promptly shoved down to unreachable parts of her psyche. Lyla checked out the woman who had short black hair and wore sweatpants and a hoodie. They'd do.

She crossed the street and meekly approached them.

"Hi," she said in her best New York debutante voice. "I'm so sorry to disturb you, but I'm looking for an address and my phone ran out of battery. Would it be ok if I borrowed yours to look up this place?"

The man didn't even hesitate. He pulled out his phone, unlocked it and handed it to her, demonstrating the privilege of someone who is simply too big to fear theft or violence.

Quickly Lyla opened up his internet application and ran a search for, "first case of pandemic virus."

There it was. This disease qualified as a coronavirus and its first known appearance had been near a virology lab in the Wuhan province of China in November of 2019.

She quickly erased the last hour of search history, closed the window, and returned the phone.

"Thank you so, so much. Have a fabulous evening!" she said and turned around to cross the street and join Sophie.

"I know where the first case of the virus appeared," she said, approaching the bench on which she'd left her friend, looking back toward the street to make sure the trees and bushes covered them from view.

"Oh, please, do tell," Azrael's most sardonic voice replied.

Lyla found herself face to face with him as she turned forward, Sophie grimacing an apology behind his back.

"How?" Lyla started.

"You're not as slick as you think at outthinking people who've been thwarting plans for decades. Besides, you gave up way too quickly. I figured you had a plan B and kept an eye on you. I was waiting in your father's office tonight. And you made it real easy, by saying your coordinates out loud. You're way out of your ken. Now, will you come back home, please?"

"First case of the virus was traced back to mid November 2019," she said to Sophie over his shoulder. "The faster we get out of here, the better."

Lyla was furious at him for babysitting her, but more than that, she was impatient to get their plan in motion. The sooner they made it to the past, the safer they'd be from being missed in the present. But the longer they waited in this timeline, the bigger the chance that their disappearance would be noticed. Sophie had explained to her that she could only travel one way. They'd agreed to go back two months earlier than the first case, so they could stop the making of the disease – which was a little less than exactly one year into the past. And they'd need to wait out the year before being able to reappear in the present. They'd have to hide out, away from their other selves, away from anyone who could find them – Fallen or Gods – which would be strange. But she figured she could use the time to practice her skills.

But now they had a whole other problem. And that problem was muscular and livid. Lyla looked around the empty playground, morose and gloomy-looking from the contrast between the cute seal statues and the absence of life and children's laughter, and reached her hand past him toward Sophie. What would he try next to stop them?

"Sophie!" he exclaimed, turning around toward the older angel. "You can't be seriously fucking considering this? You know what's going to happen to you if you go back!"

"I know," Sophie replied, grabbing Lyla's hand to pull them back in time. "And it's worth the sacrifice."

Sacrifice?

"Wait, what–?" Lyla exclaimed, trying to pull away.

But it was too late. Sophie held on to Lyla's hand, as Azrael, shock in his eyes, enveloped both in his. In the blink of an eye, she spread out her grey wings, and wrapped all three of them in the silky down. For a moment, everything went black and Lyla felt dizzy. There was a drop that felt like a rollercoaster catching up with gravity, as they fell into darkness for minutes of sheer terror, before she felt solid ground under her feet again.

They were standing in the same playground, but it was full of life now. Children on swings and going down slides. Parents chatting while watching their children. Everyone was so busy living their lives, they didn't notice the arrival of three people, one of whom quickly pulled her wings back into herself.

"What do you mean, 'sacrifice?'" Lyla finished her sentence as soon as the world stopped spinning.

"Let's find a safe space to spend the night. We can talk then," Sophie replied, ignoring her question. "You said you knew a place where the police won't stumble upon us and we won't be caught on camera. Where is it?"

"Hour up on the subway. Then a twenty-minute walk."

With that, she pulled two surgical masks and two cheap party masks that went around the eyes out of the same old backpack she'd carried to California and back. Sophie had agreed that – in combination with a hoodie – this would be the best way to remain anonymous on the subway. No one looked twice at weird in New York City.

Azrael, eyes closed, stood motionless between them.

"Look dude," Lyla preempted his fury. "You can come with, or you can get lost. But I don't have time for a lecture."

She'd expected just that. A scolding for her impetuous actions. What she saw in his eyes when he finally opened them and looked straight through her was so much worse. She'd never seen him truly angry, she realized. So wrathful that he had gone completely still, silently leashing his ire lest it destroy everything around him.

His voice entirely devoid of passion, he simply said, "You have no idea what you've done. And you," he continued, turning toward Sophie, "you are a real piece of work for not telling her."

Chin high and ignoring his veiled threats, Lyla began walking to the fourteenth street subway station, bought one-way tickets with the cash she was carrying, and spent an hour in uncomfortable silence with her two companions, going all the way up to the last stop on the A-train.

It had been a year since she'd spent significant time in the human world. Right around this time, in fact. And she'd forgotten how loud it was. How overwhelming. The smells, the sounds, close and far – everything was just a little bit too much now that she was accustomed to life on the island. She could hear music from a multitude of different people's earbuds; everyone absorbed in their own bubble, insulating themselves from the violence of all the stimuli.

In good old A-train fashion, they didn't get a seat until they got to 168th street station. And indeed, no one looked at them twice for appearing like they were going to a masquerade party. She'd used to love New York, its busyness, its diversity, the fact that anything could happen at any moment. And yet, she realized that she hadn't thought of it or missed it in months. In fact, it felt like another life, one she could no longer identify with. Another Lyla's life. Instead, in this very moment, she missed the cobbled, windy streets of the village, the makeshift paths in the fields between the newly constructed homes. And most of all, she missed the clean air.

She guided the other two angels out of the subway station, past a church and toward Inwood Hill Park. She and Max had haunted this park on many nocturnal occasions. She knew that the police would patrol it, but only on certain paths. Indeed, once one crossed the park, they came upon a wall of actual indigenous forest. The last bit of it, on Manhattan Island. It stood majestically right at the northern tip of the island, between the neighborhood and the Hudson River, a tiny sliver of the old magic, dividing two pieces of civilization.

They made it to the entrance of the woods and the little monument that claimed that Manhattan had been bought by the Dutch on this very spot, and Lyla pulled out a couple of flashlights and the knives she'd packed for them. She and Sophie strapped the latter to their belts, turned on the flashlights, and started walking toward the ravine, Azrael in tow. The path went steadily deeper into the forest, rock walls and boulders slowly appearing to their right, looming over anyone who dared walk into the night.

During the daytime, this park was full of families with children, lone hikers, and runners. But at nighttime, it changed. It turned into something old, haunted, seemingly busy with spirits and faeries alike. Even when she hadn't believed in magic, Lyla hadn't been able to stop the feeling that she was being watched in this part of the forest, that something "other" lived here. But it had always been welcoming to her. Much like it had been welcoming to the old man, Sabbas, who had lived in these woods for decades. She and Max would occasionally bump into him, and he himself, always wearing the same pristine red checkered pants and yellow boots, had seemed magical.

Fifteen minutes later, they made it to the steep hill that would take them past the glacial potholes and up to the ridge of the mountain. There was a boulder on the top, which the city had named "The Whale Back," but Max and Lyla had dubbed it "Faerie Rock." They'd sat here on so many occasions, sharing a beer and solving the world's problems long before she'd learned that the world didn't need her to solve anything. Lyla paused and looked at the now-bare standing boulder, hoping so very much that Max had heard her and forgiven himself.

They took a right, walked along the ridge, and then deeper into the woods, until they arrived at a small cliff overlooking the Hudson.

Lyla stopped and took a deep breath of the city she'd once missed so strongly and where she now felt like a stranger, before turning toward her morose companions. Azrael looked beyond words, so she silently handed him the tent and blanket and nodded toward the clearing on the other side of the path. He looked as if he'd bite for a moment, before grabbing the tent out of her hands and setting to work. Lyla decided to leave him alone, turning back toward Sophie and the cliff.

"Meanwhile, you can tell me what you meant by 'worth the sacrifice,'" she told the older female, with just about as much ice in her voice as she'd found in Azrael's eyes.

She sat down on the cliff and looked at the dark landscape across the water, waiting for whatever atrocious truth would come out of her friend's mouth.

"Well?" she asked.

Sophie shifted uncomfortably and sighed.

"There is a reason time travel is never used..." she began, slowly.

"Because it's too dangerous to change something in the timeline, yes, I know," Lyla replied.

"No," Sophie stopped her. "Because it kills the time traveler."

"What?"

"You will be fine. You and Azrael will merge with your old selves once you make it back to the future. But I won't. I will live out this year, and then I will disappear. The moment we left, is the moment I will die."

Lyla was speechless. She'd expected anything except that.

She heard a muffled curse behind them and ignored it.

"No," she said, unable to comprehend the words. "No, no, no, that's not possible. No."

"Yes. It is the reason heirs of Poseidon's are rare. Not only are we all descended from him directly, but we die if we ever use our powers. Poseidon himself was able to travel both ways, but we're not."

"Why didn't you tell me? We shouldn't have come here!" Lyla yelled, jumping up and realizing there was nowhere to go.

"This is why. You wouldn't have let me take you back," the angel calmly answered.

"Of course I wouldn't have!"

"But it was the right thing to do. You said it yourself, it'll save millions," Sophie replied, looking across the water at the steep New Jersey cliffs of the Palisades.

"At what cost?" Lyla argued.

"Only that of one life. What's one life against millions? What's one life against an entire species' extinction?"

With that, Sophie calmly lay back and looked up at the light-polluted New York City night sky.

"It's..." Lyla stuttered, sitting back down, deflated. "It's... everything."

"I had over two months to think about it, Lyla. I made my choice. Please believe me when I say that I'm at peace with it."

"How can you be at peace with sacrificing yourself for something that may or may not work?!"

In her powerlessness, Lyla felt her old rage resurface. She liked Sophie. She'd gotten to know her these last couple of months, and she couldn't bear the thought of losing her now. She'd thought she was making a life-long friend, not a passing acquaintance.

"Because of you," the female replied, serenely closing her

eyes. "When you told me what you are, I realized that you will bring about a new world. And the best thing I could do was to align myself with you, and help you become who you are meant to be."

"The promise you made me make..." she realized. "That was your dying wish."

Sophie turned her head, and looked into Lyla's eyes. "It was. And it's what makes this worth it. I've lived longer than any human ever has. I have had a life, Lyla. I have loved, I have felt alive, I've been happy, joyous, and free. Nothing brings me more peace than the thought of you uniting our people."

"What if I can't?"

"I know you will," Sophie replied and grabbed Lyla's hand.

There was nothing more to be said. The sacrifice had been made. Now Lyla had to make good on her promise. She had to succeed in order to make Sophie's death worthwhile.

Lyla held on to her new friend's hand, felt her chest cave in, and began quietly sobbing.

33

They'd discussed the fact that the virus would likely have appeared in a different place than it had been created. Demeter was who they needed to find. She would probably have perfected the disease in a hidden-away place, then unleashed it somewhere else. Lyla woke up at sunrise, unable to sleep anyhow, sandwiched between the two large angels. She slipped out of the tent and walked toward the cliff, damp with dew. Sitting down on the granite, she felt like her head was full and her heart was empty. She was trying to digest Sophie's news, but there was no way to process it. She tried to tell herself that Sophie had just told her she was terminally ill, that these things happened. But it wasn't the same. This was more akin to suicide. She'd chosen to die. If they failed, her sacrifice would be in vain. And Lyla would have had an unwitting hand in it.

But she couldn't think of that. She couldn't focus on it. She couldn't afford to waste any time. The longer they stayed in this place, the likelier they'd be discovered. During the day, the park turned much more lively and they didn't need anyone asking too many questions.

Besides, she'd trained for this. Back in January, when they'd sprung her father out of Hell, she'd still been an emotional fighter. Azrael had given her so much shit about it. But he'd been right. The last six months had changed that. The months spent fighting an invisible enemy and being unable to save countless lives, had made her less emotional. There was nothing stopping her now when she went into her meditation void to get to work.

So she did. She meditated for an hour, solely focused on everything she had learned about Demeter, picturing the terrifying, vine-covered Goddess. Until she finally got a clear picture, not only of where she was, but of what she was doing. She was indeed working in what looked like a lab of sorts, surrounded not by demons but by what seemed to be either angels or humans. Ever so slowly, Lyla zoomed out of the location. The surrounding rooms and corridors of the building were hazy, almost as if they were protected by a veil or spell – they probably were, she realized. Luckily, only the building itself was veiled. The more she zoomed out, the more she saw. She saw green pastures and mountains, a river and little chalets, and finally a sign, some miles away: "Pala di San Martino," with a number in kilometers.

It sounded like Italian or Spanish, but she didn't know either, so she committed the letters to memory.

When she finally made it out of her trance, she found Azrael and Sophie, sitting in the clearing, all packed up, looking like two regular day hikers. She updated them on Demeter's location and they made their way back down the hill and through the forest.

"Does that mean you're in?" she dared ask a grim Azrael along the way.

"I've been informed that I am outnumbered and have a choice between leaving you alone or coming with you," he replied, not taking his eyes off the steep path.

"Great. I wasn't looking forward to fighting you."

"You're out of your mind," he informed her. "I know I can't stop you. Not at this point. Not now that we've already traveled back. Not now that Sophie will die anyways. And definitely not without understanding what your God powers are."

She bit back a snarky response about how little she herself knew about her God powers. It could play to her advantage if he believed her more powerful and more in control than she really was.

"Besides," he continued. "I feel for you. Sophie duped you into this thing just as much as I was pulled in against my own will. You didn't really know what consequences you were signing up for, so I don't need to add to your plate of guilt by telling you that this entire enterprise is beyond ridiculous and bound to fail miserably."

"Except that you just did."

Azrael stopped in his tracks and sighed, demonstratively sticking his hands in his pockets.

"Look, fledgling," he said, a raw edge coloring the otherwise frustrated word. "My instinct is to hog tie you, drag you into one of the caves I saw on the side of the path, and keep you there until next year. So me telling you that you're a colossally frustrating, infuriating, irritating, aggravating, pesky little shit of a thorn in my side is showing an inordinate amount of restraint!"

Lyla held back a laugh.

"So you'll help me on my ridiculous enterprise then?" she asked, batting her eye lashes in his direction.

He stared at her like a deflated balloon.

"Don't make me say it," he huffed. "But yes, I'll try to mitigate the damage as much as I can now that you went and fucked things up again."

"It would be a lot nicer if you weren't so... cantankerous in the process, you know?" she continued, taking a step toward him.

"You're asking a lot," he growled.

"Maybe just smile pretty once in a while..." she added, closing the distance between them.

She was only met with his smoldering stare. Unfazed, Lyla braced herself on his shoulders and whispered into his ear, "I love watching you shove those protective cave angel instincts aside for the greater good. It makes me feel all gooey inside..."

Feeling daring, she planted a kiss right where his ear met his neck, and sauntered back down the path.

"Angels never lived in caves!" came the flustered response behind her, as he started following.

"Then why do you behave like you crawled out of one?" she threw over her shoulder, not turning around even though she knew she'd see him belligerently kicking rocks down the path.

Once they reached the little cafe at the entrance to the park, Lyla played her trick on the tourists again, politely claiming that her phone was broken and borrowing one in order to find the exact location she had seen in her vision. There it was: a mountain peak in the Italian Alps.

34

The travel to Italy would be the difficult part. They'd been hoping to find Demeter within driving distance, but they knew that was unlikely. The only way to travel across borders without being tracked in this timeline would be to use a portal. Which meant that they had to return to Hermes' island. New York City hadn't been the most practical choice for that purpose, but it had been the safe choice, the known entity, and a town in which they could easily rent a car under one of Lyla's false credit cards and get away with it. Besides, Azrael had a contact in a border town to Canada who could take them back to the island on a boat. There was a priestess of Hermes', specifically stationed there, whose job it was to ferry angels back from their missions if they were in no shape to fly. Lyla had heard of this individual in the past and had planned on using her services, but she was glad Azrael had ended up with them, for more than just the reason that he'd be their best bet at getting on that ferry without too many questions.

It took half a day of Sophie and Lyla alternately driving to make it to Azrael's friend. Her name was Eileen and she was used to his visits. That part was easy.

The harder part would be to infiltrate the island without being seen by anyone. They reached the beach shore after sunset the next evening and agreed to wait in a cove until Hermes' nightly hunt, lest they bump into him. The wait was awkward to say the least. Sophie leaned back and napped, looking serene and peaceful. Lyla wanted to shake her awake and berate her for throwing away her life and for making her complicit in that suicide, and Azrael paced back and forth like a caged tiger, probably battling similar feelings.

Once it was finally well after dark, they quietly took to the skies and flew over the woods, fields, and town, toward Hermes' balcony. It was wild, seeing the island as it had once been. Peaceful. Tranquil. Full of quiet life that would soon be snuffed out. They had gone back in time to stop one genocide, but what about this one? What about Hermes' people? A couple of months from now, they would all die horribly. If all went well, they'd return and Hermes would be able to confront Demeter on Halloween when the Ten all gathered on the island. Who knows what would ensue then? If Hermes was focused on the virus, he'd be even less ready for the attacks on Artemis' and his islands. It could all turn out even worse.

Lyla was still deep in thought when they landed on the large balcony. It took her a moment to realize that the light was on and that someone was inside the office. But before she could reveal their presence, Azrael grabbed her by the waist and pulled her against him, flattening himself against the wall to the side of the door. Sophie did the same on the other side.

And yet, not fast enough for Lyla not to recognize the intruder. There was only one angel on the island with that head of red hair. Michael. The traitor who was currently selling the island out to Lucifer. The very angel who was selling information to the Fallen so they could plan their attack with maximum efficiency. Maybe they could stop it? What if they just apprehended him right here, right now? What if they put an end to his betrayal before it was too late? Or was Lucifer's plan already in motion? They couldn't know. Maybe they should just come clean to Hermes about the time travel and warn him of everything that was to come... Lyla twisted around to look at Azrael's face. But the large angel just squeezed his lips together and shook his head. He was right, of course. They'd change too much if they put this new thing into motion. Things were bad in their own time, but they could always get worse. And yet, she could see it was killing him to stand down. He closed his eyes and held her tightly to his chest, his arms trembling with the desire to go after Michael.

In that moment, everything about the attack came back to her. The fear. The agony of watching the destruction and of being powerless to help. She had felt so lost in that moment. Abandoned by the world. Her old life, gone. Her new life, burning. She remembered her fear, as she'd waited for Azrael atop the Sacred Mountain, unsure if anyone had survived, unsure if he'd come or not. She hadn't noticed it at the time, because she'd been too busy moving on, but the weeks following the attack had been pure survival. Azrael had been the only safe constant through the trauma. And thank the Ten for him. She'd needed someone to cling on to, someone to be her compass.

Grief suddenly making its way up her throat to leave her body where it had been lodged, hidden for so many months, Lyla turned around in Azrael's arms and wrapped hers around his waist, holding on to him for dear life. He'd been there with her in those days. Those days in which they hadn't known how many had survived, or how her father was faring in Hell... it had only been him and her, adrift in the midst of the horrors. Lyla buried her head into his chest as the faces of those who were bound to die in upcoming months flashed across her memory.

Giving in to her absolute lack of control over the situation, she quietly sobbed into Azrael's jacket while they waited for Michael to finish his snooping mission.

The rest of the trip was easy enough: portal to the nearby village of Fiera di Primiero, find a hotel, and pay for three weeks in cash so they wouldn't be asked for passports. Between French and English they managed to make themselves understood, and – while Sophie went to buy a truckload of groceries so they wouldn't have to leave the hotel room unless necessary – Lyla was sleeping in one of the beds by eight in the morning.

35

Thankfully, the building was almost deserted in the off-season, so there wouldn't be too many eyeballs on them. Unfortunately, that meant they'd be sticking out more to the few humans present and had to get their information sooner rather than later. They woke up in the small room around nightfall. Sophie and Lyla had taken the two single beds, while Azrael had made a makeshift cot on the floor. In good grey-winged behemoth fashion, he did not complain an ounce. Indeed, he woke up first, and had already neatly rolled his blankets into a corner in the time it took Lyla to open her eyes.

They'd agreed on a plan ahead of time, making talking over breakfast unnecessary. Chewing on a tasteless bowl of oatmeal, Lyla peered out the window at the town. Night had fallen early in the valley and, in the shadow of the surrounding mountains, she couldn't see much more than the outlines of chalet-looking houses, their windows illuminated by electricity. She could hear the rush of a river running through town and a few drunken teens hollering up and down the cobblestone streets. Otherwise, the place was almost as quiet as the island had been, almost as isolated and protected.

The first step in their plan was a reconnaissance trip to the facility on the mountain peak Lyla had seen in her vision. Azrael would stay at the hotel, since Demeter could potentially recognize him. Naturally, he hated that and started pacing back and forth again as if that would bring them back faster.

"Read a book or something..." Lyla mumbled, getting dressed in yoga pants and a hoodie. Thankfully they'd brought a couple of sets of human clothes one could hike in as well as sturdy boots. Demeter and her people had never met either of them – not yet at least – and, with their wings tucked in, they looked perfectly human. However, on the off chance that any of the Fallen she was working with were present and capable of recognizing Lyla, she wore a baseball cap, and covered her face with a scarf as if she were cold.

She had a vague idea of the location of the mountain they were looking for and she'd spent half the day looking through hiking maps, discarding the trails that looked wrong. The peak in question lay northeast of them, on the other side of the river. That much she knew. But it could be at the end of three different trails, any one of which would take them half the night to hike. She had thought about trying to use her powers to mentally follow the entire path down from the mountain peak into the valley and concluded that it would take her more concentration and time than to just invest three nights of hiking into the enterprise. Besides, knowing their surroundings, in what was essentially enemy territory, could only be advantageous.

Unsure which one to start with, she gave the choice to Sophie.

"Path one, two, or three?"

"Three's a magical number. Let's start there," the other female replied.

So they took the easternmost path, which led them along the river and into the forested mountains. They remained quiet for the first leg of the journey. Lyla was unsure what to talk about, though her head was brimming with questions. But she didn't mind observing the sights. She was no stranger to mountains and nature, but these mountains were different. Their jagged outlines and snow-capped peaks lay in stark contrast against the night sky, illuminated by a full moon that made their footing a little easier to find. As much as the trails seemed well-worn and clearly demarcated, the Dolomites – as Sophie had informed her these mountains were called – towered over them like rocky, rugged teeth extending all the way into the sky, as if the valley were the maw of a giant that would close on them at any time and swallow them whole.

Finally, as they walked into the dark woods and turned on their flashlights, Lyla broke the silence.

"Should we be worried about wildlife?" she asked.

"This is Europe. There's barely any wildlife left. The chances of us bumping into anything dangerous are slim to none," Sophie replied as they passed the ruins to what might have been a small castle once upon a time.

"I didn't know that."

And with that they fell back into uncomfortable silence. All the way to the rocky peak, which did not turn out to be the correct one.

By the time they returned to the hotel, the sun was rising and even crotchety Azrael was asleep from boredom. Lyla fell into bed, disappointed and exhausted.

When they reached the other wrong peak halfway through their second night of silent hiking, Sophie and Lyla dropped their backpacks into the snow and sat down. Lyla sighed and leaned back onto the untouched, icy, white snow cover, looking up at the stars.

"Twice in a row," she said, "What are the chances?"

"Sixty-six point seven percent the first night, and fifty percent the second..." Sophie replied, sitting down next to her. "Pretty good odds that we'd choose wrong, I'd say."

Exhausted, Lyla started giggling. "Oh man, what are we even doing?"

"Saving the world?" Sophie suggested.

"That's not what I meant. Don't you feel weird, being the only three people in the wrong timeline, just bumbling about, knowing that if we bumble the wrong way the whole world will pay the price?"

"Actually," Sophie mused, pulling out a protein bar and taking a large bite, "I feel like I'm finally doing what I was always meant to do. It's weird, you know, having a power you can't really use. It makes a lot of us feel pretty purposeless. We can't ever do the thing we were born to do. We can't have kids. We're neither God, nor human, nor full angel. So I'm pretty good with bumbling through the past right now."

"Oh, wow," Lyla teased. "And here I thought I was the only one suffering from terminal uniqueness."

She wasn't sure what made her comfortable enough to poke at the other female's ego. Maybe it was just the relief of not being around a dude for once.

"Are you saying I'm having a pity party?" Sophie replied, gently jabbing Lyla with her shoulder.

"Your words, not mine!" the latter replied, playfully dodging the hit.

"You're right, I am. And I love it. I get to: I am dying, you know?"

"Loooow blow," Lyla exhaled, starting to snack on an apple.

"Speaking of blowing," Sophie asked, turning and throwing

a suggestive look in Lyla's direction. "What is up with all that pent-up sexual energy between you and Azrael?"

"Ugh," Lyla started, "I'm not sure. I don't know if I want to deal with the brooding and the self-loathing."

"You sure seem like you want to deal with it the second you're around him..." the other female retorted.

"Is it that obvious? Look. Yes, there is something there. I want him bad, ok? Does that make you happy?"

"Yes," Sophie replied. "Aaand?"

"And he's got some walls up I'm not sure it's worth trying to get past."

"I see. For what it's worth, I've never seen him as comfortable as he is around you... And I've known him... How long's it been since Julien and Jeremy's wedding? Over two decades?"

"What do you mean?" Lyla asked, her curiosity piqued.

"Azrael always looks mildly uncomfortable. Even amongst friends. He invariably looks like he's expecting to be thrown out of every room he's in and like he wants to crawl out of his own skin the moment he's perceived by another angel. But around you, he looks... peaceful, at ease. He looks like a male who's just come home and can leave his worries at the door..."

Before Lyla could ask any follow-up questions, Sophie jumped up and said, "Sun's rising, we should go back and get some sleep."

Without another word, they grabbed their backpacks and began the hike back down the mountain, illuminated by the first slivers of sunlight in the sky.

36

On the third night, Azrael was no longer willing to wait around.

"I'm going with Sophie," he declared, stomping into his hiking boots. "This one has to be it. So we might be a while. And by a while, I mean a couple of days."

"I'm coming with," Lyla insisted.

"No," he stopped her, pushing her away with a hand on her shoulder. "You are going to stay here and hold down the fort. And you're going to leave this to the stealthier angels. We'll have to hide out and observe their comings and goings. Three is too many people and I have way more experience than you. Expect us back in two or three days."

Lyla sat on the bed, watching him walk out the door.

"What am I supposed to do?" she yelled after him.

Popping his head back in, he smiled and said, "Read a book or something."

The next three days were torture. Lyla didn't dare leave the room for fear of missing their return. She ate, slept, and worried. The more time passed, the more horrific the scenarios she envisioned of what Azrael and Sophie might have encountered at the top of that mountain.

Maybe he had a point. Maybe it wasn't fair to make him wait around. Damn him. Goddess or no, she felt entirely powerless over this situation. Finally, she gave up, sat on the ground, and started counting her breaths for lack of anything more productive to do.

Finally the door opened and the two sleep-deprived angels returned. Lyla jumped up and immediately assaulted them with questions.

"What did you find? What's going on? Have you been made?"

Sophie sat at the little table with a sigh and began to fill her in as Azrael grouchily undressed in a corner. They'd spent the better part of three days watching the comings and goings of the lab. The operation was being run out of a nondescript chalet that blended right into the landscape. The tree coverage had played to Sophie and Azrael's advantage. They'd hid in the brush and memorized every single person walking in and out of the place. They'd noted everything in a book: the exact time anyone would walk in or out; what they'd carry in or out; when the guards switched up; how many people were in the lab at any given time; which routes they took down the mountain... They now had a reliable twenty-four hour schedule of the compound.

Demeter was clearly trying to keep a low profile, not wanting to be discovered by the locals. Why she hadn't set up her research center somewhere further away from civilization was a mystery. Unless this was one of the places where they would unleash the virus. They only had angels coming and going from the facility. Technically, the people they'd seen might have been human researchers, but Sophie and Azrael assumed that they were more likely angels given the fact they all shared their bronze skin and ethnically ambiguous traits. Ten of them came and went every day, at very specific times. The guards rotated: there were six total, with two of them outside the cottage at any given time. The only obvious human who came in for day shifts appeared to be a janitor, an older gentleman who seemed entirely oblivious to his employers' intentions. That man was their ticket into the place.

"It's a trap," Azrael finally chimed in from the corner.

"Excuse me?" the females replied in unison.

"It has to be a trap. I'm stealthy. But we spent three days up on that hill without being noticed. That's impossible. The Gods may underestimate us. But they're not that clueless," he explained.

"That's absurd. No one could have predicted us doing the most unpredictable of things, which was to break a God's edict and go back in time," Sophie challenged. "They don't have better security because they're going under the radar. Everybody believes Demeter is working for the Ten. No one has any reason to suspect her or look into her affairs at this moment in time. That's why everything is so low-key. Why have more heightened security, when all it would cause is questions and unwanted attention?"

"You think I'm being paranoid?" Azrael asked genuinely, sitting down onto the edge of one of the beds.

"Yeah, dude!" Lyla exclaimed. Then, turning her attention to the documents on the table, she asked Sophie, "What's the plan?"

"The human janitor will be the easiest to turn," her friend began.

"And how exactly do you propose we do that?" she replied, since this was a good time to admit that she was no strategist.

"We tell him the truth," the beefy angel said from behind

her, as he took off his pants and climbed under the covers. "I'm taking your bed. I need actual sleep. Can we continue this in the morning?"

"The truth?" Lyla exclaimed, ignoring his suggestion. "How exactly do you figure that's going to go? 'Hey dude, you're working for supernatural creatures. We know they pay you, but they're evil. We, on the other hand, are the capital-G Good Guys. Help us out?' Is that your plan?"

"Pretty much, yes," Azrael responded, ignoring her sarcasm, yawning, and closing his eyes. Gods, he looked warm and cozy, and she wished she could just snuggle up beside– whoa.

Flustered, Lyla stomped into the bathroom, where she poured some cold water over instant coffee, then returned to stand behind Sophie.

"Please tell me you've got a better plan..." she said, grimacing as she swallowed the badly blended concoction.

"I don't," Sophie replied, sincerely looking up into Lyla's face. "Azrael and I spoke on the way back. In his professional experience, the truth works best. The janitor probably already knows who he's working for. They're likely blackmailing him. And if he doesn't, one of us will show him their wings."

"And how exactly are you going to convince him to help us instead of the bosses who are either threatening him, bribing him, or even just signing his paychecks?" she retorted.

"Lyla," Azrael sighed, as he cracked one eye open, the blankets still pulled up all the way to his chin. "I make a living out of convincing lost souls to do the right thing. ..."

"Fair..." she retorted stubbornly. "Remind me, how did that work out for us in Denning?"

"No one likes a wise-ass." He yawned and turned his back to them.

"And no one likes being the third wheel to your guys' foreplay. Fuck it out already or give it a rest—" Sophie interjected.

"It's not foreplay!" they both interrupted.

"Whatever you say..." she smirked. Turning to Lyla, she added, "We'll observe the janitor over the next week and learn everything we can about him. Once we know who he is, who he loves, and what he lives for, we'll know exactly what will make him change his allegiance. Azrael is being a jerk, but he's right – persuading people to do the right thing is his area of expertise. If going back in time was what I was made for, this is what he was made for. He'll know what to say and do when the time comes."

"I guess..."

"Great," Sophie exclaimed, getting up out of her chair. "By my calculations, the human will be getting off his work shift in exactly four and a half hours, giving me just enough time to get up there and trail him back to wherever he goes. Goodnight, friends. Don't get too frisky while I'm gone!"

She was out of the hotel room in a whirlwind, leaving a deafening silence behind. All of a sudden, Lyla was extremely aware that she was alone with a pantless Azrael. In her bed. In a hotel room. And she had only one impulse: to silently climb under the sheets and see what happened.

"I'm going to take a walk," she hurriedly said, rattled by the situation.

Azrael replied with a light snore.

Lyla hurriedly collected her jacket and keys, and ran out of the room as fast as she could.

She walked into the brisk September night, relieved to escape the awkwardness, and began walking up and down various cobblestone streets. It didn't take her long to figure out the town: a river ran through the middle with a handful of streets on each side, and there was a cute town square with hills leading into the surrounding mountains. Ten minutes in either direction and one left the town and found themselves in fields, pastures, or woods. Walking helped clear her head. A year ago, the last time she'd been in this calendar month, she'd lost everything. She'd been in so much pain, nothing had mattered anymore. But now, she had things to lose again. And that petrified her. She had a father, whom she'd grown to love. She had a brother. She had whatever the hell Azrael was, and three little fledglings she'd do anything to see again. She had a cause, a purpose, something to live for.

Lyla found herself on a grassy hill overlooking the town. She sat there until sunrise, meditating, focusing. All they needed to do was get proof of the virus' existence to Hermes before his seven siblings came to visit the island. If they could do that, Hermes would be able to squeeze Demeter for information with the full force of the other Ten and their priests. They'd be able to stop the virus before it was even released into the world. She went over it in her head, again and again, until all she could see were the myriad of ways this could go wrong, all the blind spots in her plan she'd so deliberately ignored until now. For the first time since she'd been a child, Lyla found herself praying – to what, she didn't know – hoping against all hope and reason that something heard her and would protect them.

With the sun rising and the tiniest bit of hope in her heart, she finally returned to the hotel room with two energy drinks and some grocery-store pastries. Azrael was sitting under the window, cross legged, his eyes closed.

"Meditating?" she asked, as he opened his eyes.

"Trying to. Or at least trying to release my fears," he replied, taking the can she was offering. She sat down across from him at the foot of one of the beds and took a large gulp of her caffeine-saturated drink.

"What the hell are you afraid of?" she asked, incredulous. Azrael was big and stoic, she couldn't imagine him being plagued by anxieties the way she'd been all night.

"Gods, what am I not afraid of?" he replied, taking a sip he immediately spat out. "What is this?! Are you trying to kill me?"

"It's caffeine. The one coffee shop in town wasn't open yet."

"This is not caffeine. This tastes like poison for children. I'll add you to the list of things I'm afraid of."

Lyla chuckled. "Oh yeah, better sleep with one eye open. Big Bad Me is coming for you."

They sat in silence, chomping on their greasy pastries for a moment before Azrael sighed and continued.

"I'm afraid of making the wrong choices. All the time," he began. "I'm afraid this mission will do more harm than good. I'm afraid I won't be able to protect you if something happens. I'm afraid of seeming foolish and incompetent if we fail. I'm afraid of the guilt I will feel when Sophie dies. I'm afraid of her dying for nothing. I'm afraid of Jeremy and Julien not forgiving me for her sacrifice. I'm afraid of Hermes demoting me or out-right sacking me. I'm afraid of you not making it back for some reason or other. And sometimes I am actually afraid of you."

"What do you mean?"

"I'm afraid because I don't fully understand what it is that you are. It made sense to me when I thought you were an angel who needed help coming into her own. But that's not what you actually are. You're much, much more powerful than that. I know I can't really help you become what you're meant to be, because it's beyond my comprehension. And that makes me feel very small and scares me," he admitted.

"It scares me too," she said, looking at the quickly lightening sky through the window behind him. "My dad said that I'm basically a ticking time bomb."

"What does that mean?"

"It means I can unlock at any moment. So far, I've been slowly practicing one skill after another. But if I'm not careful, I could go from clumsy little Godling into full-blown superpower in an instant," she admitted.

"What would that look like?"

"My understanding is that I'd go boom and kill everything around me." She tried to say it as a joke, but it rang bitter even to her ears. She could feel his stare on her face as she looked away.

"That's why he watches you like a hawk even when you're safe from the Fallen..." Azrael mused. "And that's why he insisted I emphasize meditation in your training..."

"I guess. Gods, he'd lose his shit if he knew what we've done. Let me rephrase that: he will lose his shit when he finds out..."

"...because all of this is a potential trigger for your awakening." Lyla noticed his breathing picking up as he continued. "You really shouldn't have come here. This was a mistake."

"Trying to do the right thing isn't a mistake," she retorted. "We're not here to engage. We're just getting the evidence and getting out."

"True," he conceded, shaking his head, "But Lyla, I can't protect you from this."

"I know. No one can. Not even Hermes. All I can do is try to keep a clear head and hope for the best."

"Right," he sighed. "And the reason the Gods exist is because none of them self-destructed and killed everyone around them growing up, so it can't be that bad, right?"

She thought of arguing that they didn't know what percentage of Gods made it to adulthood, but why be a downer when he was trying so hard to hold on to some shred of hope?

"Right," she replied and leaned her head back against the

bed. She heard him shuffle and felt the heat of his large bulk as he sat down at her side. She turned her head and opened one eye to see him smiling and offering his hand to her. She took it, amazed yet again at how much larger it was than hers. It wasn't quite the hand of a craftsman, but it was equally calloused and battered. A hand that wielded weapons and had taken quite a few hits over the years.

"Not such a little fledgling anymore, are you?" he asked with a warm smile.

"I still feel like it most days, though," she replied and leaned her head against his shoulder, closing her eyes.

"I wish I could say that I won't let anything happen to you," he whispered after a moment. "But that would be a lie. This is far out of my ken. What I can promise you is that I'll stay by your side no matter what happens. That'll have to suffice for now."

"Even though I scare you sometimes?" she teased.

"Even though you scare me sometimes," he quietly responded, leaning his head onto hers.

"Thanks, Az."

They sat like that for a while, before Azrael's thumb started stroking the back of her hand. Funny how that same gesture had felt protective and sweet a few months ago. But today that one finger moving across her skin ignited every nerve ending in her hand. As her own breathing picked up, Lyla felt the pulse in Azrael's neck strengthen ever so slightly, drawing her in closer. Shifting her face right into his skin, she inhaled whatever pheromone made her lose her mind around him.

"Gods, you smell like something I want to eat," she whispered.

Azrael's thumb stopped for the loudest of seconds, before he reached over with his other hand and possessively grabbed her waist. Which was all the invitation Lyla needed to start kissing that delectable skin of his. Azrael's sharp inhale at the first contact of her tongue with his skin was accompanied by a hard squeeze of her waist. Gods, she wanted that hand to snake under her shirt... but instead, it held still while he turned to touch his forehead to hers, taking a deep breath.

"I think it's my turn to take a walk," he murmured, about an octave deeper than usual.

She wanted to grab him and force him to stay, convince him, charm him, seduce him... But what she needed to do was let him move at his own pace. Even when it was so very frustrating.

37

The next few days went by at a snail's pace. While Sophie busied herself documenting the janitor's day-to-day life, Lyla and Azrael spent their days sleeping and their nights talking without saying much. He kept a polite distance, which she begrudgingly respected. As for the mission, they were both full of self-doubt and anxiety. Bringing it up wouldn't help, so instead they tried small talk, which they were both absolutely terrible at. On Sophie's final nightly excursion, Lyla decided to show him the little hill she'd found, so they could watch a beautiful sunrise before all potential hell broke loose.

As the first rays of light started illuminating the horizon, she asked, "We've got this, right?"

"To tell you the truth, I'm not too worried about being able to infiltrate the facility and find our proof. As you said, this is stupefyingly simple because the Fallen have no reason to suspect us. I'm more concerned about Hermes' reaction and the fallout from changing things. Remember, we went back to a point in time where he trusted his siblings. And not only will he find out about Demeter's betrayal, but Artemis will be on the island too, who we now know was raving mad already... We could be saving one species by destroying another."

"Right," she sighed. "So, when you don't know what's going to happen and you keep imagining the worst possible outcome... Humans call that 'catastrophizing...'"

He turned around and playfully bumped her shoulder. "Oh, really?" he replied. "And angels call someone like you a 'little smart-ass.' Did you know that?"

They laughed, and finally the first sliver of a red disk appeared behind the easternmost mountain.

"I know we can't really do anything but our best right now. I'm just not used to sitting back and waiting. And I'm anxious to hear Sophie's findings," Azrael admitted, staring at the warm light illuminating the valley below them.

"Speaking of, what are your methods of persuasion for this guy?" Lyla asked.

"It all depends on whether or not he is aware of who he's working for," he explained. "If he is, option number one would be to appeal to his higher morals. Number two is to bribe him with something better than what the Fallen are offering. And number three is threats of violence."

"Is it really that simple? That's it? You're basically just an action movie hero with wings?"

He chuckled. "I have no idea what that is, though I like the sound of it. But to answer your question, no, it isn't that simple. And it's really all about option number one. To be entirely honest, I can't fully explain it. There's something about my magic as a priest of Hermes' that allows me to understand the beings I interact with on an emotional level and helps me to see what would appeal to their sense of ethics. Though, if we get lucky, he'll have no idea who he's working for. In which case, I think a simple apparition might just do the trick."

"What do you mean?" she asked, wanting so badly to ask follow-up questions about this sixth sense he was describing.

"We're in Italy. There's a good chance this man is Catholic. If he thinks he's working a regular job for regular humans, one of us showing him their wings might just be enough to convince him to do god's work, so to speak."

"Are you serious?" she exclaimed. "You'd manipulate his faith like that? And you think that would be enough for him to blindly help us break into his workplace?"

"I think it would, yes," he mused. "True faith is one of the most powerful guiding forces I have ever witnessed. If he is a man of faith, I'm sure he'd gladly serve a higher power that gave him direct orders. As for my conscience... No, I don't love the idea of using someone's beliefs like that. But who knows which one of us is right? If it's him and if there is such a thing as an all-encompassing, all-knowing god, I'd hope that this work I'm doing would actually align with god's will..."

She pondered that for a moment. As she looked at Azrael's stern profile, his closed eyes, his hair flowing around his shoulders with that wind that seemed to always pick up right after sunrise, his skin glowing almost orange, Lyla wondered whether he was thinking his way out of an ethical dilemma, or whether he wasn't ready to admit to himself that maybe he did in fact hope there was a higher guiding force to all of this.

38

As it turned out, turning the janitor would be exactly as easy as Azrael had predicted. Sophie's report was meticulous. By the time she filled them in a few hours later, she knew everything there was to know about Mario, the one-man cleaning crew. He had no family or friends to speak of, no one that could have been threatened by the Fallen, and no one who would ask questions if he disappeared. He was a loner who woke up, went to work, watched television, and went to sleep. Every single day like clockwork. Except on Sundays, because Sundays were for church. He was indeed deeply religious.

"He drives up an access road at the back of the mountain and hikes the last flat mile to work," Sophie reported. "His equipment is in a shed by the road. If we convince him to help, I could sneak into the shed, climb into a closed trash can, and he could smuggle me into the facility that way. If he cuts a hole through the plastic, I could take pictures and videos through a hole in the trash can. He sneaks me back out— no one would be the wiser, and we could bring that evidence straight to Hermes."

"All right," Azrael replied. "Which one of us should reveal

themselves to him?"

"Obviously, Sophie should," Lyla told him.

Both angels turned toward her, eyebrows raised.

"Well, you won't let me infiltrate the lab I'm sure..." she began to explain.

"You got that right," the other two answered in unison.

"And if it's between the two of you showing yourselves to a human, I think it should be a female angel sighting. Points for feminism," she finished.

Azrael laughed. "Fine. It's settled then. You got the job, Sophie. Don't fuck it up."

"As if," Poseidon's daughter replied. "Lyla, while I nap, I need you to find a camera phone. If I can turn Mario tomorrow morning then sneak in during his afternoon shift, we could be out of here by tomorrow night..."

After that, all they'd need to do is travel back to the island by human means. They'd discussed it during a long night of waiting: it would take a total of three trains into France and to the coast of Brittany, where a ship manned by one of Hermes' descendants ferried people back to the island. It would take about a week to make the full trip. After bringing evidence of the virus to Hermes, they'd have to hide out somewhere safe on the island until they returned to the moment in time at which they'd left. But they'd be safe. In nine days, she'd be waking up at home and the stress would be over.

"Sounds like a plan," Lyla replied, grabbed the hotel keycard and her wallet, and sauntered out of the room.

A shop full of touristy knick-knacks across the river directed her to a bus for the next town over, where she found an electronics store that sold her the cheapest, most primitive version of a smartphone. After explaining at length to the manager, whose broken English she had trouble understanding, that she did not need a phone provider, only the phone itself, thank you very much, Lyla was back on the bus and ready to get this adventure over with. The cheap device would do. It was all Sophie needed to get the proof that would change everything.

39

Waiting for their friend after the successful reveal of her angel wings was, predictably, hell. They knew it'd take her an entire day to meet up with Mario, infiltrate the lab, get her evidence, wait out his shift, and sneak back down the mountain. It should have been just one more day. Lyla and Azrael had both just spent the better part of a week sitting around and waiting in complete impotence. And yet, this final day seemed to last an entire week. They didn't speak. Just paced back and forth. They'd sit on a bed, get up, go to the window, check the sun's position in the sky, sit down on the floor... On and on they went – until Sophie finally walked back into the room.

Azrael rushed toward her immediately, but Lyla's nerves were too on edge to even move. She just sat in the corner, tensed up, and waited for Sophie's report.

The latter dropped her jacket onto one of the beds and sat down wearily.

"Did you get it?" Azrael inquired, eyes wide.

"I got the evidence. I have photos as well as a recording of Demeter's minions talking about the effect of the virus, as well as when and where it will be unleashed. And how they've been working out a variety of strains targeting each type of angel and lost in existence."

Azrael's entire body sagged in relief as he dropped down onto the bed next to Sophie. "I can't believe it was that easy," he sighed.

Sophie shifted next to him. Silently, she took the smartphone out of her inner jacket pocket and packed it into a Ziploc bag, transferring it into the backpack Lyla had brought back from New York. As she did, Lyla noticed the tension in her face. The way she pursed her lips. She was deliberating something.

"What is it?" Lyla asked, getting up.

Azrael slowly turned toward her. "What are you talking about?" he asked.

"Something is wrong," Lyla replied. "What happened up there, Sophie? What are you not telling us?"

Sophie slowly closed the backpack before looking up and responding. "We miscalculated." She took a deep breath before continuing. "They're experimenting on angels and humans in there. A handful of each."

Lyla saw Azrael's jaw muscles clench at the mention of human and angelic lab rats. But he just intently looked at Sophie, waiting for her to continue.

"They're going to release the sick test subjects in two days."

"What do you mean, 'release' them?" Lyla asked.

Sophie looked at them, pain etched into her face. "They're going to release them in a variety of places to study how quickly the virus spreads."

"But that doesn't make sense. I looked it up, the first case wasn't recorded until December."

"Maybe they'll infect less populated areas and the spread is going to be much slower than we thought? Or maybe these early cases aren't going to be flagged? Either way, we're too late. It'll begin before we're able to get reinforcements."

"No," Lyla shook her head. "No. We didn't come all this way to fail. There has to be something we can do. Az, you're the strategist. Come on, give me something!"

Azrael got up, silently walked to the window and looked out at the last rays of light in the sky. "Short of setting the entire facility on fire, which I will neither do nor let you do..."

"Of course we're not committing murder," Lyla exclaimed, stepping toward him. "But there's got to be another option."

Azrael turned around and looked her in the eyes. "No, Lyla, there isn't. I'm not considering setting anyone on fire. I'm just making a point. I've followed you this far. But this is the line. I need to get you home. We can't get involved any deeper or we risk exposure. And exposing you to the Fallen... I won't do it."

"You're afraid I'm going to run right in there and heal the test subjects, aren't you?" she uttered accusingly.

"Isn't that exactly what you have in mind?" he replied, looking her straight in the eyes.

"Well... not entirely. What about when they transport the test subjects to their destinations? Wouldn't they be most vulnerable then?"

"No," Azrael shook his head. "No, Lyla, you can't possibly be thinking about jumping them on their way down the mountain. We have no idea what their transport plans will be, or how much security they'll have."

"No, we don't," Sophie interjected, slowly thinking out loud. "But we do know that there's only one drivable road off the mountain. And I heard them say that all ten subjects will be escorted out of the facility at once and taken their separate ways from there. They're planning on burning the compound to the ground and destroying all evidence by Tuesday night."

That was forty-eight hours away.

"Not you as well!" Azrael snapped at Sophie, incredulously shaking his head.

"Like Lyla said," the older angel answered, "we came all this way. Let's at least exhaust our options."

"We don't have any options!" Azrael thundered. "We're done. This is over. It's time to cut our losses!"

"*Our* losses, huh?" the older angel thundered, jumping up. "But we don't really share losses you and I, do we? You can just go back to how things were. I, on the other hand, gambled my life for this. So, no, I am not okay with just giving up and turning around!"

"That's not fair," Azrael replied quietly. "You know that that's not fair. You took this risk. But I can't let Lyla take the same risk. Not with who she is. We were relatively safe so far, but this could go wrong in so many ways. I won't let her."

"You can't make me or stop me from doing anything," Lyla interjected. "I'm a loose cannon, remember? Besides, all I'm asking right now is to talk through the option of ambushing them. Just talk."

"The option? It's not a fucking option!" Azrael threw his arms up in frustration and turned to face Lyla. "There's three of us. And we counted fifteen of them. They could have extra security come join them for this. Possibly other angels the Fallen have turned. Maybe even demons. How, exactly, do you think two of us are going to hold them at bay while you heal ten sick patients? And how do we get away afterwards?"

"I don't know, okay? I don't know," she retorted, those hateful tears of vulnerability and powerlessness closing up her throat. "But what I do know is that I can't just walk away from this. Not when I know what's going to happen. Not when I know how they'll feel—"

"I'm afraid you'll have to. We are grossly outnumbered. We'd be playing right into the Fallen's hands if we got anywhere near that envoy."

Lyla racked her brain for some answer. Something. Some way to get out of this— when a knock sounded at the door. All three of them turned toward it in unison. It was past sunset. Who could this possibly be?

They all froze. The seconds ticked by as they exchanged questioning glances.

In silent agreement, Lyla, Azrael, and Sophie unanimously pulled out their wings as the knob slowly turned and the door creaked open.

"I'm afraid you already did," echoed the voice of the elk-antler-bearing creature standing in the door frame.

40

Demeter's doe eyes betrayed nothing of the chill in her voice, as she stepped aside and let six lethal-looking angels file into the room. Every single one of them had a larger frame than Azrael – priests of Ares', Lyla guessed. That answered the question of Ares' allegiance, then.

Azrael instinctively stepped in front of her, but they both knew this wasn't the moment for heroics. They weren't just out-numbered – they didn't know how many more were outside the door or how they'd been made.

"Tsss, Hermes' general got so emotional he didn't even hear us come up the stairs..." Demeter shook her head. "Escort them into the courtyard. This room is too small for a chat, and frank-ly, it smells like a tiger cage. Have you three been cooped up in here for ten days without opening the windows?"

As the Goddess spoke, two of her soldiers flanked Lyla, grabbed her by the elbows, and started walking her out of the room. She wanted to resist, but she felt their iron grips on her upper arms. Exchanging a look with Azrael, she followed their captors after a small nod from the latter. This room might be too small for a chat, but it was also too small for a good fight. They'd stand a better chance at escaping out in the open.

Or so she hoped, until they made it into the courtyard and she saw that every single side of the walled-in space was flanked with half a dozen of the larger angels. White wings spread and at the ready, hands crossed in front of them, they were just waiting for an order to attack. Lyla's head spun. Where had they gone wrong? And how on Earth were they going to get out of this?

Their escorts left the three of them standing in the middle of the courtyard and stepped back into a semicircle behind them. Meanwhile Demeter casually sat on a stone bench in front of them, draping the green vines that grew in and out of her skin over the rock. She reminded Lyla of a horrifying version of DC's Poison Ivy, lounging and gloating at her prey.

"I must say," the Goddess' voice echoed through the yard. "You got quite far. I respect all your hard work. Coming back from the future, finding our lab, observing our comings and goings, convincing Mario to help you, infiltrating the place... I would have loved to see what plans you devised for this ambush of yours, but I'm afraid I'm on a tight deadline, and I just cannot indulge in this any longer."

"How—" Sophie started.

"How do I know all this? Well... I really mean it, your plan would have worked out perfectly, if it weren't for the fact that I own this entire town. You were right about Mario's religious persuasions. But you see, we pulled that little trick on him and everyone else here the day we arrived. They've all been working for us ever since. And the moment three new English speakers arrived in town... in an off-season month I might add... they informed me, recorded your conversations from the next room...

thin walls, you see... and I've been one step ahead of you ever since. It has been quite entertaining, I must say – particularly listening to these two talk about their deepest fears and night-mares and get all emotional in the process..." she finished with a head nod toward Azrael and Lyla.

At that, she saw Azrael's entire body lean in toward Deme-ter, his upper lip pulling back as if to bare his teeth at her.

"Az," she tried to calm him down, but she felt the same deep violation at having had their greatest vulnerabilities made pub-lic.

"I know I am yet to officially meet you in a couple of weeks, Lailah. But you've grown into something else, haven't you? You must have traveled back quite a ways into the past. And yet, you're still as volatile as Lucifer warned us you'd be. Emotions are a hindrance, don't you know that yet, young fledgling?"

"Bite me," Lyla spat out.

"Oh, I just might," Demeter giggled with a white-toothed smile. "It's almost too easy to get a rise out of you. You see, when you arrived I considered spreading the virus more aggres-sively. Dropping ten infected patients in the ten most populated areas of the world... What a plan! But then, I realized that your return from the future meant that you were desperate. Ergo... my original plan worked out perfectly, didn't it? The virus killed millions, just as I'd planned?"

Lyla bit her tongue.

"But taunting you with a threat of releasing my test sub-jects... it was too sweet a temptation, to get to see you all riled up. And let me tell you, you all played your parts beautifully. Lailah with the savior complex, unable to leave a potential vic-tim behind. Azrael, ever so chivalrous, making it his life's mis-sion to protect the damsel in not-so-much distress. And Sophie, oh my dear, the resentment that's been building up inside of you over your self-sacrifice is just delicious. You're all ripe for the kind of canvas my favorite brother likes to paint on."

Oh Gods, she was planning on taking them to Lucifer. Lyla exchanged a look with Azrael who seemed as lost as she was. They were about to be dragged back to Hell. Without any reinforcements this time. Without anyone knowing that they were missing, that they even existed in this timeline. Panicking, Lyla started to look around and count. There were six angels behind them, twenty-four on the walls, and a Goddess right in front of them. Thirty and a big boss against the three of them.

She looked at Azrael again, as dark spots threatened to overtake her vision. Dizzy, she fell to one knee, and tried to catch her breath— when she saw it: Azrael going berserk, attacking all thirty angels by himself, flying through the air and throwing helter-skelter attacks in every direction, creating a distraction to allow her to fly away.

She couldn't let that happen.

As her vision cleared, she felt a warm hand on her shoulder, a wing around her back. Demeter was so sure of her victory, she'd ordered her soldiers to stand down for the time being.

"I got you," Azrael whispered into her ear. "I'm going to—"

"No," she snapped at him under her breath. "Don't you dare."

"What are you—"

"I saw what you're planning on doing. Gift of foresight, remember? Don't you fucking dare," she spat out, looking into his gold-green eyes.

"Lyla, I'm your only shot at getting out of here."

"No, tough guy. I'm your only shot at getting out of here," she whispered back. "Now get up, step back, and let me do the work."

His eyes widened, but he listened. He slowly got back up

and stepped away, making room for her to gather her magic about her. She was surprised that he'd let her take this shot, but she didn't have time to wonder about it. Instead, she took a few deep breaths and dropped into the meditation chamber in her mind, as Demeter's voice faded into the distance.

"Check on her... What's wrong with her?"

With her eyes closed, her body curled forward into a ball, and her wings draped around herself, Lyla could see the court-yard from a bird's-eye point of view. She saw all six priests who'd escorted them down rush toward her. She saw Azrael slowly an-gle the front of his body toward the closest corner to him, a dozen angels in his line of fire. She saw Sophie, who made up for what she was lacking in magic with martial arts training, and had fought alongside them in Hell, mirror him on her other side. And she saw the other dozen angels farther off step closer to Demeter.

In her mind, all of this happened in slow motion. Slow enough for her to gather all the rage, all the fear, inside of her, shape it into a ball of lava in her chest, and let it slowly roll up her throat and into her mouth. Right as the half-dozen angels approached her and got into grasping distance, she sprang up, slammed her wings back into them, and let that ball of hot fury roll off her tongue in a scream that hit Demeter right in the face.

She didn't turn around to see it, but she knew that the six soldiers were unconsciously slumped in a heap at the bottom of the wall, and that the ones who'd already been standing there had sprung aside in shock. Instead she turned toward Sophie. Azrael would be fine. By now, he'd have a protective shield around him, and would be fending off several adversaries. So-phie, on the other hand, had no magic to speak of and, without a weapon, she'd be defeated in a heartbeat.

Lyla sprinted toward her friend and took to the air, ready to take down the angels who were dog-piling on the time-traveler, when a barbed sting pulled her right wing back, extricating a scream of pain from her. Pinned back down to the ground, she tried to pull her wing out of this new vise, only making the agony more piercing. Something sharp was suffocating her very being, binding her wing, trying to cut through it. Now she understood why Hermes had lost all strength when Lucifer had plucked his feathers off his wings. This pain was debilitating. She could barely think straight enough to turn around and see the green vines snaking their way across the yard toward her – vines that seemed to grow out of Demeter, sent to bind Lyla. As she turned around on her knees, trying to fold her wings back into her body to free them from the shackles, another green plant crept its way up and around her torso, pinning her arms to her sides, and reaching her throat, cutting off just enough air that Lyla wouldn't be able to use any sonic attacks.

She turned toward Azrael to see that he had defeated most of his attackers, half of them unconscious dolls strewn around his corner of the yard. A couple of them were dead. She knew that, without knowing how she knew. Nothing about their demeanor betrayed the fact, and yet, she had absolute certainty that those priests had not survived Azrael's magic. Four of them, however, were left standing and those four incapacitated him in the split second he wasted looking for the origin of Lyla's agonized scream.

How had she thought that the three of them could defeat two to three dozen trained Ares priests and a Goddess? As her throat closed up, in part from being choked, in part from the disillusionment of failure, a tear made its way down Lyla's face. Azrael and Sophie were restrained, each in one corner of the yard, and she herself was finished.

The acrid taste of defeat made its way into her mouth like acid, as her vision threatened to go dark from the pain in her wings. They'd come all this way for nothing. They hadn't made anything better. They hadn't saved anyone. Sophie had sacrificed herself in vain, Azrael was about to die, and she'd become Lucifer's new plaything.

Demeter slowly walked toward her, the green plants that connected her body to Lyla's slithering around the ground in the process.

"That's enough, darling," she sweetly said, as she knelt in front of her and cupped Lyla's chin to look into her eyes. "Ares won't forgive me if I don't bring back at least some of his soldiers."

"Don't. Touch. Me," Lyla choked out between pained breaths. Demeter's hands were ice-cold, as if she'd been dead and immobile for centuries. Their chill poked through her skin like stalactites.

"Oh, but we're family, aren't we Lailah? Some line in that family tree goes all the way from me down to you... Or does it go up to you? I no longer remember such things," she mused.

Lyla understood what Hermes had been trying to warn her about. This was the madness. Beyond the vines and antlers, there was something deeply terrifying, something unpredictable about this female. It wasn't her power, it was her volatility that made Demeter the most dangerous creature Lyla had ever encountered. As she looked into those large, brown eyes, she felt her mouth dry up like sandpaper. With her tongue stuck to the roof of her mouth, she couldn't have said a word if she'd wanted to. Only a whimper came across her lips in spite of her attempts at breathing through the pain. Writhing on the ground, Lyla became nauseous from the torture searing its way through her very being.

"That's better," Demeter asserted, slowly standing back up and turning toward Azrael and his captors. "How's this one holding up? Did you break him?"

Lyla summoned all her strength to crack an eye open and look at Azrael. Two angels were restraining him, his arms folded back around his wings, effectively binding his magic, while the other two held out large blades, threatening to slice him open at the first sign of disobedience. His nose was bleeding, his hair was tousled and falling out of the bun he'd bound it back in, and a large gash at his temple was steadily dripping onto the ground. But he seemed fine overall. As she assessed his injuries, Lyla noticed his chest heaving with fury. He was barely containing himself as his eyes darted between the blades, Demeter, and Lyla herself. She locked eyes with him, then shut her eyes again. He'd known this was a fool's errand. He'd tried to stop her at every turn. He was only here because he'd been pulled in against his will. But now he would be the one paying the price. Lyla couldn't bear the thought that she'd led him right into a trap.

"He's fine," a gruff angel replied in a low voice. "But he'll stay still if he knows what's good for him."

"Good," the doe-eyed Goddess' echoey voice replied. "I have orders not to harm him or my niece. I wouldn't want to accidentally break my brother's toys..."

Lyla sighed in relief. At least Azrael wasn't dying right this moment.

"Her, on the other hand..." Demeter continued, as Lyla felt her glide right over her own body and stalk into the direction of the heap of angels she knew restrained Sophie.

Lyla opened one eye in spite of the pulsating anguish that simple motion caused her and looked toward her friend.

"Move," the Goddess ordered, shooing the soldiers out of the way, as she arrived in front of the powerless angel. Instantly,

Ares' children stood up and backed up into a semi-circle six feet behind Sophie, who was left kneeling on the ground, doubled over as if she'd been kicked in the stomach.

"You are a rare commodity, aren't you?" Demeter sweetly whispered, crouching in front of Lyla's friend. "How many of you are left?"

When Sophie didn't immediately reply, Demeter pulled her head up by her hair to be at eye level with her. "I asked you a question. How many of Poseidon's children are left?"

"I don't know," Sophie spat out, gasping for air. She must have gotten hurt in the few seconds Lyla's assault had lasted. "We don't exactly have a group chat."

"Well..." Demeter continued. "Either way, you lost your value when you used your power, didn't you? Now, you might as well be a feathered human." She said the word as if it were an insult. "When did you come from?"

Sophie's head fell forward, as if too tired to keep her neck up, and the larger Goddess twisted her fist in her hair to pull her back up. "When did you come from, feathered human?"

"Nine and a half months from now," Lyla interjected to help out her friend. Demeter's head snapped toward her in a motion so quick she could never have been mistaken for anything other than the apex predator she was.

"Nine and a half months..." she repeated, turning toward Lyla. "Interesting. You condemned this poor soul to sit around and wait for her own death for the better part of a year? You really are one of us, aren't you, Lailah?"

Lyla closed her eyes and let her talk, as she was trying to guess at the damage her brutalized friend might have endured. Was she bleeding internally or had they only knocked the wind out of her?

"Oh yes, I do know what and who you are. It's not really a big secret anymore," her mad ancestor continued without pause. "In fact, life's quite tedious in Hell these days. Lucy can't stop talking about you. 'Lailah here' and 'Lailah there.' It'll be a breath of fresh air to bring him another chew toy, so he can finally talk about something else. But what to do about this third traitor? Oh, what to do, what to do..." she paced back and forth, her voice echoing with each step, her shoulders slightly hunched like a cat stalking prey.

"You're the traitor," Lyla spat out through gritted teeth, in an attempt to distract her from pouncing on Sophie. She needed time. Time to think. Time to somehow keep her friend alive.

"Me?" Demeter exclaimed, as if legitimately insulted. "Oh no, sweet child, I am quite true to my nature and my people. It's the Ten who betrayed our way of life and our mission."

"You are one of the Ten," Lyla replied around the vine, choking her.

"I was one of the Ten. But I've been redeemed," Her Madness Incarnate replied as she spread her wings, each one extending ten feet from her sides.

Hermes' wings were always on display. Lyla had assumed that he couldn't fold them into his body the way angels did. Now she realized that that wasn't the reason he let them trail behind him on the ground. The Ten had been born on their planet with black wings like the rest of their species. But after they'd followed the Fallen onto Earth and rescued humanity from their attempt at destroying it in the crib, they'd been punished with white wings. Whether Hermes proudly wore his white ones as a sign of his integrity, or whether he wore them in shame as a reminder of his punishment, she didn't know. But, as Demeter unfolded her wings and Lyla discovered that they had reverted to their original pitch black while she'd betrayed the Ten, she realized that her father's choice was intentional, that he was reminding himself daily not to fall as low as his brothers and sisters had.

As the horned Goddess proudly displayed her wings, tendrils shot out of her right hand's fingertips, like blades of grass rapidly growing out of every appendage. The first couple of inches shot upwards, then tiny green leaves appeared, heavily wearing them down and curling them toward the ground. Those vines were growing in Sophie's direction at an alarming rate. She was about to kill her, likely by smothering her.

Lyla needed to think of something, and she needed to do it fast. Sophie would not die like this. She could not. It was bad enough that she'd sacrificed herself; the least Lyla could do to pay her back was to ensure she died on her own terms.

But it was more than that. She'd grown to love the angel, and to look up to her. Lyla admired her courage, her integrity. She admired her softness, the fact that Sophie wasn't apologetic about her vulnerabilities. When was the last time she'd had a female role model, if ever? She'd grown up in a world of men. Men's works were studied in school, men were the ones achieving things and furthering the world, while women were quietly erased. Even on the island, she'd been surrounded by males. Her father. Azrael. Jeremy. As much as she loved all three of them, she had desperately needed a female friend in her life, and Sophie had been a breath of fresh air. Lyla hadn't been raised by angels. She'd been raised by humans. She'd internalized this world in which she was supposedly less worthy, less capable, less likely to succeed, simply... less. And it made her so very sad to think about that world, and so, so very angry to think about the female in front of her who was trying to take away her friend.

She'd pushed these thoughts down her entire life, since the day she'd first gotten angry at the parts with which she'd been born, when she'd first realized that she'd been born on the "losing team," as she'd once thought of it. She was ashamed to have ever felt that way about herself. It made her so sad that she was afraid if she started crying about it, she might never stop. She could feel it like a stone lodged in her throat, growing larger and larger, righteous anger and sorrowful fury making their way out of her body.

As Lyla thought of everything Sophie represented for her, the millions upon millions of soon-to-be overlooked little human girls growing up right this moment, still oblivious to their disadvantage, blurred into one in her mind with this one female who needed saving right now, this one female she simply wouldn't allow to die. The vine around her neck was shredded to pieces as a scream of sorrow made its way out of her throat. She saw the green bits fly outward and hit the ground like the pitiful plants they were.

But she didn't stop there. She stood up, one strengthened step at a time, and spread her arms and wings, knowing Demeter's shackles could no longer hold her, freeing herself from the piercing pain the latter had inflicted upon her. The Goddess screamed with that same pain, as the ends of her green tentacles were pulverized. Taking a step back from the grey-winged female, she gestured to her soldiers.

"Don't move. Keep the other two in check. I want this one all to myself."

She sounded steady, but Lyla sensed the fear in her, the ever-so-slight doubt that she might be out of her ken.

"You sure about that, grandma?" she taunted her, as she stalked toward the Goddess.

"Lyla!" she heard Azrael shout from the corner of the yard. A warning? An admonition? She wasn't sure. But she ignored him and gathered her power about herself instead.

Healing was all in the imagination. She conjured up metaphors for injuries and diseases, and, as she healed them in the world of her mind, her magic healed them in reality. Maybe destruction was no different. Maybe she just needed to invoke weapons stronger than her opponent's.

"Back off, little girl," Demeter threatened, squaring off on her. "I promised my brother to bring you in alive, but that doesn't mean I can't kick you around a little first."

Lyla ignored the taunt. Her vision narrowed to the monster in front of her, the female who'd decided that power meant oppression and fear, who wanted to subjugate the world rather than uplift it. She'd had just about enough of those kinds of people.

Lyla spread her white wings to their fullest length and flapped them once in Demeter's direction. The blow went right through the Goddess, not raising a hair on her head, but the fountain behind her toppled over. And came crashing to the ground in a pile of rubble.

When had she become this strong?

"Lyla! Stop!" Azrael yelled. She understood: he was afraid she'd unlock. He was probably right. This was not the time or the place. But she ignored him.

Three of Demeter's vines shot in her direction but, picturing a machete in her right hand, Lyla swung it across them with a flourish of her right wing and the creeping plants dropped to the ground, precisely where she'd imagined cutting them.

Now she was certain that this was shock in her adversary's eyes. Shock and fury.

"How dare you?" the Goddess snarled. "I was the one who snuffed the life out of your mother, and I'd do the same to you right now if I were allowed."

She kept swinging new green branches in Lyla's direction. And Lyla cut them all off with a mere swish of her hand.

"Is that supposed to make me mad and lose my focus?" Lyla asked. "Nice try, movie villain."

"She was no match for me, and you're not either."

Lyla stopped, grounded her feet, and decided to halt Demeter's stalking approach. With one thought, she turned her wings into a steady fan, flapping her feathers ever so slightly, and created a wind tunnel the Goddess couldn't push against. As she quit approaching, she briefly lost control of her tendrils and they went flying behind her back, getting tangled in her dark wings.

"You were saying?" Lyla sweetly asked, imagining her arms stretching out all the way toward Demeter, grabbing the dozen vines flailing about and wrapping them around the crazy, old bitch.

Caught up in her own weapons, Demeter lost her balance and fell to one knee. Lyla heard a commotion behind her. But she no longer needed to look around to know what was happening: instead, she instinctively closed her eyes. No. She didn't just close her eyes. She closed an extra vertical lid over her eyes that she'd never known she had. Now, she saw everything that was happening. The priests had stepped toward their leader, afraid and unsure whether or how to step in. Sophie was back on her feet, which meant she had not been harmed beyond saving. As for Azrael, he'd used his attacker's momentary loss of focus to take to the skies and land right behind Lyla, which was the only place he thought he was safe from her assault. As if she'd ever hurt him...

"Lyla," she heard him yell over the rushing wind. "Lyla, please stop." It wasn't a command. It wasn't even a request. It was a plea. He sounded almost... sweet, impotent, completely aware of how outclassed he was in this moment.

And he was right. She knew that he was right. She needed

to stop. She didn't want to be dragged to Hell. She didn't want him to join her there. She didn't want Sophie to be snuffed out as easily as Demeter had threatened to kill her. And she didn't want the latter to get away with all of this and to live another day to add to the misery of angels, lost, and humans.

But the alternative was to unlock and raze this entire town to the ground. She could feel it inside her. The growing power, like a fire that had been ignited and wouldn't stop until everything was ash.

With those internal eyelids, she saw Sophie, standing behind her to her left. So frail. So scared. She'd kill her. If she unlocked, she'd have a chance at taking on Demeter, but she'd also kill Sophie. And Azrael. And every human in this town who'd been manipulated and used by these monsters.

She heard a gasp and realized she'd been choking Demeter this whole time. The Goddess was on her knees, her own weapons turned against her, vines trying to grow into her nose and eyes. One of the green snakes was sprouting over her lips, prying her mouth open. Lyla knew it would be the final straw if she sent the green plant inside her opponent. The Goddess fought her power, but the fire inside Lyla was growing. She could almost see a shimmer around her own body, pulsing as her magic tried to surge out into the world. Calling her a bomb had not been hyperbole. That was exactly what she was. And that was exactly how she'd explode into the world.

Ever so slowly, Lyla turned her head toward Azrael, careful to keep her body and the wind tunnel emanating from it directed toward her enemy. She saw the shock on his face when she looked at him, and she realized that her inner eyelids were still closed. She was scaring him. She must have had those same red and purple eyes on her extra lids as Apollo did, because she could tell that everything in Azrael's body wanted to run. She felt it as if it were her own sensation: the fear of a prey animal, the instinct to find cover from the monster in front of him. From her.

"I don't know how to stop," she finally admitted.

Behind her, she knew Demeter was near death's door. The soldiers were petrified. Too scared of her to intervene, and too scared of their leader to run. Ever so slowly, Azrael reached for her right hand. He just held it, as his other arm reached around the back of Lyla's neck, looking straight at her for consent. Hyperventilating, she allowed for the contact, and he pulled her in, touching his forehead to hers.

"I told you, I wouldn't run. I'm staying right here, little fledgling," he whispered. "No matter what happens, you're not alone."

She felt his breath on her face, his calloused hand on her skin. A tear escaped her shut eyelids. She wasn't alone. She hadn't been alone in a while, and she now knew she'd never have to be alone again. Azrael was breathing heavily, his chest heaving up and down, radiating heat in her direction. He was scared, and yet decided to trust her. She knew he wanted to say the right thing but couldn't find the words. Instead, he stroked the back of her head with his thumb. She could feel the roots of her individual hairs moving around with the massaging gesture. She heard it too, that soothing sound of another's touch stroking her hair. As her ears focused on that sound of someone caring, the shimmer radiating from her body slowly receded, until it was fully yanked back into her like an overextended rubber band and vanished. Her eyes snapped back open, and she fell to her knees, Azrael willingly sinking onto the cobblestones with her.

The last words she heard before drifting into the oblivion of absolute exhaustion were, "I can't kill you, but I will make you wish my brother would let me."

41

Lyla woke to the chatter of dozens upon dozens of birds as well as the soothing patter of waves gently breaking against rocks. Her eyes were shut, she realized, and her head hung to one side, too heavy to roll up. Her lids were red with the light of bright sunshine coming through, but those too were too heavy to lift. Gods, she was uncomfortable. She tried rolling to her other side, before realizing that she wasn't lying down. She was sitting up in some kind of upholstered chair. But she couldn't move her arms. They were crossed in front of her, and she couldn't for the life of her uncross them. Was this one of those nightmares where she lost control of her limbs? As she began struggling against the fabric holding her arms in place, Lyla felt her heart beat against her ribs like a caged animal.

"Oh, look, she's awake," a male voice echoed in her direction.

Lyla had heard that voice before. As her lungs struggled for air, her eyes shot open. Frantically, she looked around and took in her surroundings. She was sitting at a large banquet table on a sunny, pebbled beach. All around her were sand, rocks, and water slowly moving toward them and back, over and over again. The table was set with all the different glasses and forks and knives she'd never been fancy enough to learn about, but the food – heaps upon heaps of raw meat. She looked down and understood why she couldn't move: she was wearing a straitjacket, her arms crossed in front of her, the sleeves tied together behind her back. Across from her sat Azrael in the same predicament, awake and breathing heavily, but otherwise silent. On each side of the table sat three vaguely familiar Gods turned Fallen, their heads currently turned toward her, their various creepy eyes boring holes into her face. She only recognized Lucifer and Demeter. And above them... above them were hundreds of birds, flying, circling, singing. She'd never seen anything like it. She didn't know much about birds, but she recognized seagulls, sparrows, ravens, parrots, flycatchers, mountain chickadees, tucans... These weren't birds that were supposed to fly together.

Following her gaze up, Lucifer snapped his fingers and every last one of the animals stopped vocalizing mid sentence and came flying right down to the beach, standing still, obediently following an order.

"Birds come to me. They always have," the Fallen explained, as he called upon a parrot with a hand gesture. The green bird came to sit on his shoulder, cradling its beak in its owner's neck.

Lyla wished she could say it was less terrifying meeting him for the second time. But this was worse. Lucifer was just as fear-inducing now as he had been when she'd met him in Hell: his black wings draped over the back of a throne-like chair; his yellow goat eyes, with their rectangular pupils, staring at her from his cocked head. A head that looked bald at first glance, but was covered in a shiny carapace like a beetle, and sporting two backwards-curving horns. He may have shared some of the features of the human depictions of the devil, but he was so much more chilling. How creatures so free and light as birds could willfully obey him, she didn't understand.

Staring at Lucifer, Lyla opened her lips to ask where Sophie was, but her tongue stuck to the roof of her mouth, too dry from fear for regular speech.

"She's trying to say something," an overly sweet voice came from her right side.

Lyla snapped her head around just in time to see one of Demeter's vines creeping its way across the table toward her. The Goddess sat closer to Azrael than she did her, but Lyla could tell from the rage in those entirely brown eyes that it was her she wanted dead. And she could see why: there were deep marks around her neck, crawling up her chin and over her lower lip where Lyla had attacked her with her own plant-like appendages; she would have expected bruises and choke marks, but these injuries looked more like permanent scars etched into the Goddess' immortal skin. Lyla would have swallowed if she'd had any saliva left.

"Here, you need to drink, darling," Demeter continued, curling the vine around a goblet and, to Lyla's horror, lifting it up and magically pushing it across the table toward her face.

As the silver container got closer, Lyla tried to pull away. She could smell wine in there, but who knew what it was laced with. And she certainly didn't want that creepy plant anywhere near her own neck for Demeter to take revenge with.

"Come now, child. This is for your own good. Tsk. Those hatchlings... always so fussy at the dinner table, aren't they?" the recently Fallen Goddess said to Lucifer, as both playfully shook their heads. "We're just here to help you. This is for your own good. Now be a good girl and open your mouth. Or we can do it the hard way if you'd prefer."

As Lyla continued to fail at pulling away, the goblet came knocking against her lower teeth. Demeter tilted the wine down into her mouth, pushing a little too hard and letting the sharp edges of the chalice cut into Lyla's upper lip and skin, as the wine she still refused to swallow poured down her chin and all over the front of her white straitjacket.

"Look at the mess you made me make!" Demeter growled. In a flash, she was standing, her face inches from Lyla's, the chair she'd just gotten up from reverberating on the rocky beach.

"Now, now, sister," Lucifer chided. "We're not trying to scare her into joining us.... At least not yet..."

Demeter turned her head toward him at an inhuman angle and hissed. Before she could even look back at Lyla, Lucifer whistled, and two hummingbirds darted toward Demeter's face, pecking at her eyes with their elongated beaks. The Goddess pulled back, screaming, trying to catch the birds, but they were too small and too fast even for her, supercharged somehow by their demonic master. It was disturbing, watching the sweet, small avians feast on her eyeballs, droplets of blood dripping off their beaks and down onto her cheeks.

"Go home, sister. If you can't control yourself, you're not welcome at this table. Come back when you've learned better manners," Lucifer berated her, before recalling the birds with a flick of his wrist.

Lyla was equally as relieved to see Demeter walk away toward a small cottage fifty yards up the beach, as she was perturbed by the hummingbirds now casually sitting on Lucifer's horns, dripping blood down onto his face that he did not bother to wipe off. She had no idea how they'd get out of this one. Their hosts were unhinged. And yet, she wouldn't dare try to use her power on them again. Not when Azrael was so near.

"Bring out the other prisoner," Lucifer barked at one of the Fallen sitting across from him. The latter stood up, like an automaton, his hoofed legs clacking on the rocky path he took toward the cottage.

As they waited, Lyla's eyes caught Azrael's. He sat, entirely still, an ice-cold expression on his face, but she noted the trickle of sweat at his temple. He was just as petrified and impotent as she was. He couldn't use his wings or magic with the straitjacket on. She couldn't use her power, lest she annihilate Azrael, Sophie, and herself in the process. Would that be worth it if she took down Lucifer and Demeter too? Not when so many of the other Gods had turned, not when the Fallen had greater numbers than they did already. Lucifer might be their leader today, but someone would surely fill the power vacuum the moment he was gone. Even she knew enough of history and politics to know that taking out one tyrant was never enough when they were surrounded by dozens ready and willing to step up at any time.

The sound of hooves on stone pulled her attention back to the cottage. The Fallen was returning, Sophie in tow. Her face was red and slowly bruising, but those must have been the hits she took in the courtyard. It didn't look like she'd been abused since their abduction. She walked normally and looked as strong as ever. There was no straitjacket on her. Not even handcuffs. After all, she'd lost all her power the moment she'd taken them back in time, and, as Demeter had so cruelly pointed out, she had no more magic than a human now. Nonetheless, Sophie's grey wings were proudly unfolded behind her, a sign of her remaining dignity.

"Sit, sit, my dear," Lucifer manically addressed the angel, pointing toward the chair Demeter had vacated. Sophie cautiously sat down, throwing Lyla a glance in the process. She wished she could say something to her, anything to make this better, but the only words that came out were a whispered, "I'm so sorry."

"Now that everyone's here, let's have ourselves a nice little chat," Lucifer talked over her. "Go back to the house and prepare three rooms for our guests," he added, gesturing to the Fallen who'd brought in Sophie as well as to his three co-conspirators still sitting at the table. All four looked at him skeptically.

"Come on. Shoo," he added. All four black winged creatures departed, throwing glances over their shoulders as they walked toward the cottage.

"They're so nosy," Lucifer complained, leaning back in his chair and ordering the beach birds to fly up to the table. In one swift motion, they were all sitting on it, immobile but occasionally quietly tweeting, as if commenting under their breaths. Lyla looked at Azrael, whose gaze was following the little ones as if trying to predict what dangers could come from them.

"But this is a family matter," the Fallen added. Azrael's face snapped up to him, and Lyla noticed the wink Lucifer gave him as he snarled at the demonic creature. What in the actual twisted fuck was wrong with Lucifer that he'd somehow consider them family?

"Now. Lailah, let's not dance around the issue. You know what I want. And you know you're not leaving here until I get it."

He cocked his head in her direction, his yellow and black eyes boring into hers.

"Over my dead body," she replied, finally finding her voice again.

"No," he drawled, nodding toward Azrael and Sophie, "over theirs, actually."

"You and I have already played this game. You threatened me, and you threatened my loved ones, and I told you to go fuck yourself. And then I got away. I realize that hasn't happened for you yet. But maybe you should know, so you can reevaluate your negotiation tactics," she bluffed. It sounded so confident. So cocky. When had she learned to act that well? On the inside, she was shaking like a leaf, scared to death for herself and her friends.

"Then I can't wait to meet you again soon. Twice in a year? Lucky me... But I'm sure we can make this interesting. Because you see, the first time we met, this hadn't happened yet... Who knows how things will change? We could make history, you and I."

He was right. Maybe there'd be no second meeting this time around. Maybe she'd be his prisoner, not her father. Maybe it would be her feathers ripped out of her wings, one by one. Her back ached with the thought.

"The way I see it, you have two choices, darling niece. You can go through Hell and torture. There are two loved ones of yours here, and, from what you're telling me, I gather you already know my methods. So I'll let you fill in the blanks on that option. Or you can hear me out."

"Sure, let's hear it. This ought to be good," she snarked back.

"It is quite good, actually. The thing is... your father hasn't been telling you everything. In fact, I'm pretty sure he's been leaving out some very important details that...well...change everything," he told her, pursing his lips and shifting his head from one side to the other, as if deliberating an important question.

"He's been telling me everything I need to know."

"Really? Has he ever told you where we came from?"

The Gods and Fallen had come from another planet. The latter had been sent to destroy humanity, the former had come after them to save the human race. And they'd been duking it out on planet Earth ever since.

"Of course he has. As have all the history books I've read. You're going to have to do better than that," she spat back.

"Oh, but those books aren't telling the truth now, are they? No, you see, they're telling you what the Ten wanted their descendants to believe, so they'd follow them on their little crusade against evil old me."

He looked at her, his lips pouting under the thin fangs that protruded from them. Did he really think she'd believe him? Or get thrown off-kilter by his implications?

"I see. So it's a real case of their word against yours, then?" she chuckled.

"Now you get it," he exclaimed, rubbing his hands together in excitement.

"And who do you think I'm more likely to believe? The loving, caring God who treats others with kindness, or the Fallen I have seen torture, threaten, and maim people?"

"I do what I must," he growled back, aware he'd lost the argument. In one instant, all the birds went silent and preternaturally still, leaving only the eerie pitter-patter of the waves, irregularly rocking back and forth onto the shore.

"I guess you're not ready to hear me out then, are you?"

"Not now, and not ever."

"Suit yourself," Lucifer responded, standing up and casually throwing a pristine white napkin from his lap into a bloody dish. "I'm tired of this moment in time," he spat, turning and leaning over the table toward Lyla. "Luckily, as opposed to most of my siblings, I never lost my ability to travel in time. Backward... or forward."

Lyla didn't understand the threat, until Azrael jumped up and awkwardly stepped toward Sophie, his elbows bouncing left to right with the motion. But he was too late. Lucifer snapped his fingers and brought them nine and a half months forward, to a time when Sophie was no longer alive. Her lifeless body slumped head first onto the meaty plate in front of her, the blood dying her blonde hair pink. And she wasn't the only one who died. All of the birds dropped in one instant, their bodies rigid, their eyes wide open toward the sky.

Azrael stood behind Sophie's chair, helpless, unable to even touch her and place her in a more dignified position. As for Lyla, she just sat there, staring, eyes dry, but her breath coming in and out in sudden spurts as if she were wailing.

"I tried to play nice," Lucifer's cold voice echoed to her left, but she couldn't tear her eyes off the lifeless body of her friend. She'd known Sophie would die. But not like this. Not snuffed out in a moment, just to make her feel powerless and insignificant.

"Look at me," the Fallen growled, turning her chin toward him with his clawed hand. He stood by her chair, towering over her. He wasn't playing anymore, that much was clear. Gods, she wanted to scream at him. She could feel the power slowly heating up inside her chest again, that little ball of fire that could grow uncontrollably at any moment. She knew that the straitjacket wouldn't stop the power. It would burst right through it, shredding it like the Hulk's clothes, and burning everything in its path. But Azrael looked so vulnerable, his sweaty hair stuck to his temples as he helplessly crouched by their friend's side. She couldn't do this to him. For once, she'd have to keep her temper, so he at least could make it out alive.

"Sweet, sweet niece," Lucifer continued, never letting go of her face, his claws digging deeper and deeper into her skin. "You are going to stay here, be polite and fucking delightful, and you're going to listen to my version of history. I'll even let Azrael go. Or," he added with a nod of his head in the latter's direction, "he's next."

This was it. She'd tried to undo the past and make a better future, and all she'd achieved was getting her friend killed and getting herself captured. Lyla looked down, breathing heavily with tears that were yet to come, burning with the deep shame of having single-handedly ruined her father's meticulous plans for her. This whole time he'd been working to keep her safe from Lucifer and she'd run right into his arms herself.

"Do you concede?" the Fallen's cold voice rang in her ears.

She was beaten. They both knew it. But he'd make her say it.

As she opened her mouth to accept defeat, she heard Azrael's feet shuffle in the sand. Standing up straight, he said, "I'll stay. Let her go, and I'll stay."

Lucifer let go of Lyla's face at last and cocked his inhuman head toward the angel.

"What are you saying?" he whispered.

"You know what I'm saying," Azrael quietly replied. He spoke slowly, as if each word cost him, as if he could barely get them past his lips. "I'll do what I always refused to do. I'll stay. Indefinitely. I'll serve you. I won't fight you. I'll do anything you say."

"You'll finally work for me?' Lucifer replied, straightening up and turning toward Azrael.

"Yes."

"What–?" Lyla asked, searching Azrael's face. But the two males stood across the table from one another, gazes locked, as if they'd forgotten all about her.

"You'll do anything I say?"

"As long as you give me one hour with her, and then you let her go and don't come after her, yes."

"Come here. Let's test that." Lucifer beckoned him over to

his side of the banquet table. Without dragging his feet, Azrael walked toward him, each sandy footstep a punch to Lyla's gut.

"Kneel," the Fallen ordered.

Taking his last deep breath of freedom, Azrael obeyed.

"After three decades, you're finally bending. You love her that much?"

"Yes," Azrael answered the rhetorical question.

"Yes, who?" Lucifer asked.

"Yes, father," Azrael replied, closing his eyes.

42

A zrael?" Lyla asked through blurry eyes. She wasn't sure what she expected him to answer. Did she hope he'd somehow wink at her, tell her it was a lie and that everything would be ok? He did nothing of the sort. In fact, the angel did nothing at all, as Lucifer – his father – walked around him, kneeled – completely ignoring Lyla – and undid the buckles of his straitjacket.

Lyla's eyes widened at the gesture, expecting the angel to summon his wings and challenge the Fallen to a fight, to somehow get them out of there after all. But again, Azrael remained kneeling on the smooth pebbles, his eyes shut.

The only sign of emotion she detected was the bobbing of his throat as Lucifer barked, "Stay!" in his direction, a command fit for a dog, while he himself advanced toward Lyla.

"Az?" she asked again, her voice sounding so weak and pathetic to her own ears, like a child begging to be told that Santa Claus was real after all. She knew he heard her. She saw his face twitch and his eyes squeeze shut even tighter, before he bowed his head. That was as much of a response as she'd get from him.

She'd almost forgotten about Lucifer, until he produced a leather contraption out of thin air and held it up to her face. "Open your mouth," the Fallen commanded and she realized what it was: a muzzle – a precaution against her sonic magic. Gagged, and with her arms and wings bound, she'd be truly powerless. As if this was something she could still fight. She couldn't. Not without Azrael by her side. So what difference did it make? All fight gone out of her, she obediently opened her mouth as Lucifer inserted the bit, a protrusion from the mask that held her tongue in place and kept her from doing anything other than swallowing and whimpering. She closed her lips around the cold metal as the Fallen placed the leather mask on her face and tightened a variety of straps around the back of her head. She was surprised at the gentleness with which he touched her. This time, no claws dug into her skin. The brush of his fingers was almost tender. After all, he'd won.

"This isn't how I wanted this to go, Lailah," he sighed, attaching the last strap, crisscrossing it at the back of her neck and closing it around the front of her throat. The collar would choke her if she attempted to vocalize at all. "I can't say I'm disappointed to have my son back. But this was not my intention for you."

With those ominous and cryptic words, he grabbed her by the elbow, pulled her up, and guided her down the path toward the cottage.

"Come," he beckoned Azrael, who promptly stood and followed them, making no motion to revolt.

Lucifer guided her down stone steps into the basement of the house, opened what could only be described as a prison cell, and gave her a slight shove when she wouldn't step in. Not having any arms to balance herself with, Lyla tripped and her knees hit the hard stone ground, shooting pain up and down her legs. But that pain was nothing in comparison to the torment in her heart.

"One hour," the Fallen confirmed as he stepped aside so Azrael could let himself into his own prison.

His allegiance – for her life and one hour in the cell with her.

Lyla heard the gate lock into place and Lucifer's hooved legs climb back up the stone stairs, but she didn't look back. Not being able to make use of her hands, she struggled to get back to her feet, until Azrael crossed the distance between them and gently helped pull her up the rest of the way. Unable to speak or express herself in any way, Lyla looked at him, despair in her eyes, a muffled *Why?* coming through her muzzle.

"Why? Is that what you're asking?" he replied. "Will you sit down with me, please?"

But she didn't. Lyla remained standing in the middle of the cell, rooted to the ground, her panicked brain racing, trying to come up with a way they could both still get out of this.

"Lyla, it's too late. I made my deal, there's no going back on it. And I wouldn't go back on it, even if I could. Don't even think about asking me to take the contraptions off of you, I won't risk it. But will you please sit and listen to me? There are things I need to tell you, things I need to explain before we say goodbye."

She couldn't help the high pitched whimper that tore its way from her throat at the word "goodbye." She couldn't, she simply couldn't leave him here.

"Lyla, please. We don't have much time. Please, grant me that one last favor?" he asked, sitting down in the far corner of the cell, his knees drawn up to his chest, waiting for her. It was the pleading in his voice that broke her out of her paralysis. Slowly, one heavy step after another, she joined him in the corner, where he helped her awkwardly sit next to him.

"I know I hurt you by making this deal," he began. "I'm sorry. And I'm sorry that I took you by surprise. But I couldn't not make it. I hope you can understand that."

She shook her head. Yes, she did understand, because she'd have done the same thing; she'd have gladly sold herself for him. But she couldn't accept it. She couldn't even imagine the things Lucifer would make him do. She'd seen the fury in his eyes. The Fallen hated him – his son – for having defied him this long, and he was about to exact revenge for every single year Azrael had refused to work for him.

"You'd have done the same thing for me, and you know it," he gently chided her. "Lyla, I saw a way to get you out of here and I took it. I had to. You need to live. He wanted a weapon, and now he has one. He'll content himself with me. For a while at least. But I also had to... because I love you, Lyla. I love you more than I've ever loved before, and I can't bear the thought of you down here."

She knew all that. She knew it because she loved him too, and she couldn't bear the thought of leaving him here either.

After a long silence, Azrael continued. "I'm sorry I never told you. About my father. I was ashamed. And I was afraid Hermes would exile me if he knew who I had ties to."

He took another long break, nervously biting his lower lip and picking at his nails, then he finally broke his silence. "I guess since you can't answer me and I'll likely never see you again, I can tell you everything now..."

She wanted to scream. But all that came out was a muffled cry before the collar around her neck started closing off her airways.

"I told you I'd looked for my father when I came of age. I told you I hadn't found him. I lied. I did find him. But I had to keep it a secret. I would never have been able to work for Hermes if he'd known I was of Lucifer's line, that Lucifer had a direct connection to me, could track my inner workings at any time. He tried to win me over then. I renounced him. But today..." He shook his head. "I had to take his deal, Lyla. Please don't think less of me for agreeing to do his bidding. I had to get you out of here. I had to. Not just because of who you are. But because of who you are to me."

He paused and turned toward her, his face only inches from hers. Then he sighed and leaned back against the wall.

"Lyla, I don't know how obvious it is, but I've been in love with you since the day I met you."

He'd– what now?

"I never used to believe in love at first sight. But life made a fool of me the day I met you in New York and killed that demon with you. I don't know how, but when I saw you square off on the creature, I was done for. You burned so brightly, even in your rage. Even in your grief, you were fierce and beautiful. I couldn't get enough of the sight of you," he reminisced.

"And then Hermes put you in my care," he continued. "I hated him for it. I knew I could never be with you. That even fantasizing about it would be a mistake. I'm Lucifer's son, for the Ten's sake! And you are... well, you're you. Your father would never allow it. But he made me spend that time with you. And slowly, I started not just wanting you, but liking you. By the time we made it to the cabin, I craved your company like I craved air. And then... then you kissed me. Gods, I wanted to throw you on that couch and fuck you senseless. But I knew it would be a mistake. It wasn't lost on me that you had a crush on me. But having you and then letting you go? It would have destroyed me. So instead, I built up walls to keep you out. By the time we met again at the compound, I had even myself convinced that I didn't care much for you. But underneath... it never went away. The ache. The love. The way I can barely control myself when I'm around you. The way I constantly have to refrain from touching you, because everything inside me just wants to be close to you."

Lyla's mind was blank. Or maybe it was too full, she couldn't tell. She'd wanted Azrael so desperately and she'd had no idea that he reciprocated to this degree And now she was going to lose him forever, without even being able to say it back, without being able to touch him, the way she now knew he'd wanted to be touched not just recently, but for months.

"Lyla, if anyone's ever needed to survive and come into their own, it's you. We need you," Azrael interrupted her agonizing thoughts. "I couldn't leave you to the demons. I'd rather become one myself. Please forgive me."

How could she let him go in less than an hour? How could she possibly say goodbye? She wanted to scream, but even that had been taken away from her. She'd never see him again. At least not as he was. This male whom she'd loved in so many different ways, this male whom she'd wanted more than anyone ever in her life. She had maybe fifty minutes left with him before they'd tear her away against her will and turn him into a monster. With that thought, Lyla doubled over, struggling to get any air through her nose.

Azrael hesitated for a split second, before putting his hand on her back, and gently rubbing up and down her spine.

"I know, I know," he repeated. "I'll miss you too, sweet angel. But we're not quite saying goodbye yet, are we?"

She turned to look at him and shook her head. They were out of time. This torture didn't count as time.

"I mean it, Lyla," he countered, his voice shaking. "I can't think of what's going to happen tomorrow. I can't think of the things he's going to make me do. I can't think of the torture of being away from you, of not knowing how you are, of not being able to talk to you and laugh with you. I just can't."

With his plea, Lyla's airways cleared enough for her to sit up straight, silent tears streaming down her face, as she carefully controlled her breathing so the choker wouldn't tighten around her neck.

"Lyla. Lyla, please," he continued, gently wiping her tears away with the pads of his thumbs. "Will you do one thing for me? Will you give me these fifty minutes? Please."

Seeing the despair in his eyes, she swallowed her tears as best she could and leaned her head against his shoulder.

I love you, too, she tried to say.

"I know. I know, little fledgling," he answered. "May I?" he asked, hooking his left hand under her knees. She nodded and he swung her legs over his lap, wrapping his right arm tightly around her body and holding her close to his warm chest.

"I wish I could make it so that you never feel alone again," he whispered into the top of her head. "I wish I could make it so that you're never scared again."

She cradled herself against his neck, inhaling that fresh scent of his, trying to commit it to memory so she'd never forget his presence, whimpering with a mixture of despair and desire.

"I've dreamed of this so many nights, you know?" he stated, as if he was reading her thoughts. After a pause, he continued. "Sending you to bed the night before we went into Hell was a mistake. I've regretted it ever since. If only I could go back... I would hold you until the sun rose. I didn't sleep a wink that night. I was tossing and turning, thinking about bursting into that room and worshipping your body like it had never been worshipped before. But if I could go back, all I'd do is hold you and tell you that I love you, all night long."

Lyla turned to look into his eyes. She wanted a lot more than to be held and told that she was loved. She needed more. And she needed it now. It wasn't just that his words had reignited every single fantasy she'd shoved down, of him shoving her down and having his way with her. It was the desperation for one last memory, one last moment of intimacy to remember him by.

Azrael must have sensed the shift in her body. Scrutinizing her face and gently caressing her hair back, he asked, "I take it you don't hate the idea of me worshipping your body?" Her insides coiling themselves into a knot of fear, anguish, and of that same desire that was hiding between his words, Lyla swallowed and slowly nodded her admission.

"I'm sorry that it's too late for that now," he replied, unable to keep a little smugness out of his voice. "Gods, how I wish I'd taken the chance when I could."

Was it too late though? They had about forty-five minutes left... Lyla tilted her head trying her best to convey the suggestion with a slight lift of an eyebrow.

The male chuckled off the proposal. "I don't think a quick fuck with the devil's son in a prison cell befits a Goddess of your station..."

Please, she thought. *Please, I need this. Let me have this, just once.*

He disentangled his limbs from hers, trying to keep her at arms length, but Lyla grabbed the opportunity to throw a leg over his so as to straddle him. It would have been a lot sexier, if she hadn't needed him to catch her as she flailed and lost her balance.

"Lyla!" he shrieked as if appalled by her indecency. "You're muzzled and in a straitjacket."

But he caught Lyla's racy smile under the contraption, trying to convey the fact that it wasn't her first time tied up and gagged. Casually leaning back and intertwining his fingers at her lower back, he suggestively asked, "I take it you liked learning about those handcuffs in my bedside table last year then..."

Lyla's eyes widened as she vigorously nodded – yes, she'd thought about those handcuffs a lot... late at night... when she couldn't sleep... with a couple of fingers inside herself, wishing they were his. But this was so much more primal than that. She needed to be his and she needed him to know she was.

Azrael blew out a shaky breath, looking into her eyes. She could see the struggle in him. This wasn't how she'd pictured it either, but it was all they had. Lyla waited for a decision as he looked her up and down, scrutinizing her face, and making up his mind. Slowly, he closed his eyes and nodded. She waited for another agonizing minute before he exhaled the tension coiled up inside of him with a low moan, a mischievous little smile forming on his lips.

He lifted a hand to her face and slowly brushed it through her hair, grabbing a curl between his fingers and staring at it, taking another and carefully tucking it behind her ear, his fingers lingering around the shell of it a little longer than necessary. She'd felt this kind of touch from him twice before and she didn't think she could resist it a third time.

Lyla's eyes closed on their own, as a lone finger trailed down the side of her neck and her uncontrollable need had her lean her body as close into his as possible. "You little fiend," he whispered in her ear, playfully biting the lobe. Lyla's reply came in the shape of a muffled moan accompanied by an instinctive clenching of just about everything below her waist. She felt Azrael's cock twitch to life under her as he took her body's reaction for the invitation that it was.

"You might be incapacitated, but I'll stop the second I feel any discomfort in you, okay?" he whispered, looking into her eyes for a sign of acknowledgment. She blinked in response. Azrael sighed with satisfaction and dropped his face into her neck. "Thank you for trusting me, little fledgling," he murmured, as his tongue and lips began exploring her neck, biting into the leather strap of her muzzle, exerting the slightest amount of pressure on the choker, and digging his teeth ever so slightly into her soft skin.

Lyla heard his breathing hitch, then accelerate as he got hard under her. With that, she forgot everything. She forgot about Lucifer. She forgot that she wouldn't see Azrael tomorrow. She forgot about the war. She forgot that she was a God being that was likely to implode and take a chunk of the Earth with her. All that remained was her and the scent of this angel she so desperately wanted inside herself. As a hand snaked its way under her shirt and up her back, Lyla, mostly powerless to reciprocate, started circling his erection with her hips, dry humping him in a desperate attempt to create more friction.

She felt the continually more excited heaving of his chest, as he ever so slowly explored what skin he could access under the snug straitjacket. Her arms were bound so tightly around her torso that said access was grossly limited, but he made up for it with the featherlight touch of his calloused hands – that touch that was barely there, teasing like a cool breeze on a hot summer day and making her want more, more, more.

Instead of more though, she felt a shift in the large angel. Kissing every surface of her face he had access to, she sensed him trying to regain his composure and to slow down his breathing. Finally, he grabbed her hips and stopped her from undulating. "Wait, wait," he breathily whispered, lowering his head as he took a few deep breaths. Pulling back to look into her face, he asked, "Are you sure you want this?"

She nodded vehemently. Gods, yes, she wanted this.

"Like this? Here? With... everything as it is?" he continued, unsure.

She nodded again, pleading with her eyes for him not to drop her now, not when she was this vulnerable.

"Okay then." A smile spread across his lips and he readjusted both of them so he could pull out his beautiful grey wings and wrap them around her. "Your wish is my command, sweet fledgling."

Replacing the hands at her back with the touch of his soft feathers, the feathers she knew from experience to be so very sensitive, he began lifting the fabric of the straightjacket, looking into her eyes for any signs of disapproval. As he awkwardly pulled the shirt up under her tightly bound sleeves and over her breasts, which were pushed together, framed, and displayed by her crossed and locked arms, her nipples got even harder – not so much from the cool air hitting her as he stared down at her, as from the thought that she was dressed and yet exposed. Without quite pushing her chest into his face, Lyla tried to inch closer thrusting her breasts out, her shallow breaths betraying her need and expectation.

But she wasn't the one in charge.

Azrael pulled back with a grin. "So needy... You'd be begging me right now, if you could, wouldn't you?"

Yes, she would.

"What? Too proud to admit it?" he continued teasing her, when she didn't immediately respond. Lyla shook her head and ground herself into his erection in response.

"Is that a yes?"

She nodded.

"Yes, you need me really badly right now?"

Fuck, yes. Another nod.

"Yes, you want me to devour those beautiful tits already?"

Get on with it already. An impatient nod.

"All you had to do was ask..." he teased and ended his torment, diving head first for said tits. Sadly, her arms were bound so close to them that they didn't allow for much access, but that didn't stop him from grabbing her ribcage and pushing his thumbs under her arms to tease what little side boob he could access while nibbling on her nipples one at a time. She felt her breasts tightening, her nipples turning to rock under that able tongue of his before he began using his teeth, playfully at first, testing how far he could take things. When he bit down harder, she couldn't help the instinctual clenching of her sex, as the slight pain turned straight into lust.

Looking up at her from under hooded eyelids, Azrael whispered, "Fuck, it feels good to be this wanted by you..." He took a shuddering breath before adding, "Lean back into my wings, I've got you."

And get her he did.

Lyla leaned right back into his strong wings, the wings he'd once pointed out were larger than most males', as he feasted on her chest, sliding one hand down to impatiently knead her hipbone, while the other explored the back seam of her jeans, slowly making its way into her pants. His tentative touch grew stronger now, grabbing and massaging her flesh like he wanted to possess it. His head lowered, his torso contorting itself, as he tried to lick more exposed parts of her, while still cradling her back and head with his strong wings. He managed to reach her hip bone with his tongue, before Lyla started whimpering and wiggling on top of him in an attempt to signal that she needed more.

Noting the change, Azrael drew back and looked into her eyes. "Are you all right?"

She nodded vigorously, looking alternately at him and at her lap.

"You want me to take your pants off?" he guessed.

Lyla nodded.

Azrael looked around the cell. "I'm afraid the most comfortable place is still going to be my lap," he said apologetically.

She blinked. *I understand.*

"Stand up," he commanded.

With his help, she kept her balance as she stood, one leg at a time, realizing just how shaky she was on her feet. Azrael took the opportunity to kneel forward and, disappearing and reappearing his wings in the blink of an eye, ripped off his shirt, revealing that sweat-glistening chest she'd so often secretly imagined during training, but had rarely seen. Gods, he was sexy. Beautiful muscles aside, she noticed the lack of scars: he'd survived all the years of fighting by being better than his opponents, by almost never getting hurt, and by being under the protection and healing of Aphrodite's best priest when he did get wounded. Leaning in, Azrael looked up at her, as he slowly raised his hands to her waist line, undid the button of her jeans, and lowered the zipper one tooth at a time. He placed a kiss on the edge of her underwear, grabbing it in his teeth and pulling it down a tad, before growling, letting it snap back against her skin, and looking up at her.

"Gods, you're driving me crazy."

Yet, he took his time peeling the jeans off her legs and helping her step out of them, lifting and lowering one foot at a time, before doing the same with her underwear. She hadn't known that being undressed by someone could feel this erotic. It made her feel vulnerable, yet taken care of, to be placed in this position where she could do nothing but let him decide what was next. After dropping her underwear on top of the heap that were her pants, Azrael focused all his attention on her sex. She'd never seen him look at anything that intently. Standing there, her arms locked around her chest, breasts out, exposed and shaky from all the foreplay, Lyla held her breath, waiting for Azrael to make a move. After an eternity, he grabbed her hips, inched closer and licked once along her, all the way to her clit, as if both staking his claim and verifying this was in fact happening.

"I changed my mind," he snarled, flipping her around and shoving her against the wall behind him, leaving her head spinning. Yet, he still had the presence of mind to lift his wings and to place them between her back and the rough, cold, stone wall. Azrael pinned her there, one hand gently pushing against her lower belly, the other snaking around her thighs, kneading and caressing the place where her ass, thigh, and hip met in a silent promise to catch her if her legs gave out. As for his tongue... it seemed to know exactly where to go. Instinctively struggling against her restraints, tormented by the fact she herself could not touch, could not taste, Lyla threw back her head and closed her eyes, all of her attention focused on receiving pleasure. The hand that had been dancing across her belly snaked its way up to play with her nipples, while his other hand inched closer to her center, his thumb slowly making its way toward her wet core. Azrael chuckled against her as he realized just how wet she was. She wanted that thumb inside her so badly, but instead he played with just about every sensitive part of her vulva he could find, as his other hand dropped down to hold her lips open and give him better access to the clit he started rhythmically flicking his tongue against... which was all Lyla could take before exploding. With a muffled shriek, she came, the vocalization tightening the strap around her neck, pleasurably choking off her airways and putting her in that in-between place of the most intense orgasms. Her legs collapsed, as she managed to draw a deep breath through her nose and slowly remembered she was alive and had a body. Azrael, a feline smile on his face, caught her and lowered her into his lap, turning around to sit against the wall.

Cradling her in his wings, he murmured, "Don't get too cozy, I'm not done with you yet."

He wasn't? Lyla sluggishly opened her eyes. Still feeling the fluttering pulse in her clit, she wondered if she could take any more, but started stealing hopeful glances at the bulge in Azrael's crotch. "Not that," he commented, shaking his head. The disappointment must have shown on her face, as he explained, "Not here... Not like this..." Suggestively running his fingertips along the inside of her thigh, he added, "But that doesn't mean other parts of me can't be inside you..."

He threw a look at her from under lashes way too perfect for a big, strong warrior, and stopped, waiting for her consent, she presumed. In response, Lyla shifted her hips closer, trying to get those fingers exactly where she wanted them.

"Greedy, I see..." The fingers continued their slow trek up her legs until Azrael conceded. Burying his face in her neck, he pulled her against him with one hand, possessively grabbing her ass, as the other hand started exploring her entrance. He purred with satisfaction, teasing her with a finger tip. "Your neediness is intoxicating," he remarked, kissing the top of her clavicle, just where the straitjacket started. "I could just tease you all day like this..."

But even he knew that they were running out of time. Giving in to her needy whimpers, he plunged two fingers into her as he pulled her closer and straight down on top of his cock.

"That's it. Ride the palm of my hand," he instructed her, digging right into that spot inside her that most men couldn't find without a map and a flashlight. Having just had an explosive orgasm, everything inside her felt swollen and tender in just the most exquisitely sensitive way. His wings tightened around them, blocking out all light and cocooning them in their own little universe, as his other hand dug into her flesh with his barely restrained desire. She tightened around his fingers, relentlessly pushing herself into his palm for more friction.

"Oh Gods," he panted into her neck, "I wish it was my cock deep inside you, little fledgling. Fuuuuck." Feeling his entire body shake under and around her with the need for more, Lyla clenched around his fingers and came again.

In a sweet gesture, Azrael lay the weight of his head onto her shoulder for a few long seconds, his heavy, irregular breath warming the skin of her neck. Said breath hitched as she clenched around his fingers again. And again. And again. At long last, he slowly pulled them out and they sat for a moment, not daring to move, before he kissed her cheek and asked her to stand up.

On shaky legs, Lyla looked down at him, as he demonstratively sucked his own fingers. "Delectable," he smirked.

He helped her back into her clothes as mindfully and gently as he'd helped her out of them, zipping and buttoning her pants back up, as if wrapping a precious gift.

Finally, Azrael stood, gently pulled her top back over her chest and belly, and looked down at her. For the first time since she'd known him, they'd finally closed that distance between them. Azrael smiled and leaned down, running a hand through her hair. Before she could remember where they were, he leaned down, touched his lips to her ear, wrapped a wing all the way around her, and brushed its tip to her forehead.

"Thank you for letting me dream of you, little fledgling," he whispered, as she fell back into his wing, injected with magic that put her to sleep.

Epilogue

AZRAEL

Not sleeping with her in California had been a mistake. Not sleeping with her again in Italy had been equally as dumb. And finally getting to taste her, to pleasure her just enough that he could imagine perfectly what she'd feel like coming on his cock, what she'd sound like if she could vocalize her desire... that might have been the stupidest thing he'd ever done to himself. He'd hoped to leave her with something to remember him by. The territorial, primitive side of him had wanted to mark her as his, though he knew she'd never be. And some naive part of him had hoped that the memory would somehow keep him warm, keep him safe, keep his heart going as Lucifer inevitably chiseled away at it, piece by piece. She hadn't been gone an hour yet and he was already haunted by the memory. Right after he'd put her to sleep, one of Lucifer's lackeys had appeared and ordered him to take her upstairs to a portal. He hadn't been too surprised that he'd been allowed to bring Lyla back to the island himself. After all, he'd be more pliable if he had proof of her safety and well-being. What had surprised him was that Lucifer hadn't sent an escort along with him, that he'd let him leave his clutches to return Lyla to safety, certain that he'd come back, like the loyal dog he was to become.

He had come back. He hadn't even dreamt of disobeying the Fallen's first order. Even when he knew it for the dangerous test it was. Now that he hadn't used the opportunity to run and save himself, Lucifer knew that Azrael would do just about anything to keep Lyla safe. And that meant he could make Azrael do anything he wanted him to do.

He couldn't think about that. Not yet. He didn't want to think about what he'd have to do to continue ensuring her safety. Lucifer's imagination knew no bounds. He could already smell the gallons of blood his soul was about to be bathed in.

At least she'd be safe. At least she'd stand a chance. The world would stand a chance with her safe...

He tried to hold on to that. To remind himself that he'd had no choice, that his sacrifice was the only way to ensure that what they'd been fighting for for millenia would endure.

True as that may be, hooking up with Lyla had been selfish at best. Gods, he could still smell her on his hands. Laying on the cold ground of the cell he'd been returned to, Azrael held them up to his face, afraid he'd soak up her scent until there was none left on his skin, aware that either way the last reminder of her would be gone within hours. Azrael closed his eyes, letting the tears he hadn't shown her run down the sides of his face and into his hair. He could still hear her high-pitched whimpers as she'd lost all control and given herself over to him. As much as he'd dreamed, fantasized, and pleasured himself to the idea of making her moan, he'd never imagined she'd be so willing to entirely surrender to him. The way she'd made herself so completely vulnerable and had trusted that he'd catch her was intoxicating. To be able to take care of the little fledgling just this once, not just to pleasure her, but to prove to her that she was safe, that she could let go and he wouldn't let her get hurt, had made him feel... worthy.

Gods, how he wished he was. Maybe it would have been safer to keep her as a pipe dream rather than having evidence that their chemistry wasn't only real, but that she wanted him in exactly the way he wished to be wanted. Now he knew precisely what he'd never have again. He'd hoped to create a memory to warm his hands by in the harsh, cold days that lay ahead. Instead, he'd authored a dream so vivid and sharp that it would haunt him with what could have been but would never be. If only he'd successfully stopped her from going on her delusional crusade into the past. If only he'd had the courage to let her in sooner. If only he'd set aside his self-flagellation for just a moment. Maybe he couldn't have been with her long-term, but he could have stolen weeks, months... What he wouldn't give to get those months back now. She hadn't run screaming when she'd found out about his father. On the contrary, she'd handed herself over to him. The truth hadn't changed him one iota in her eyes. Yet he'd let that truth stand between him and happiness his entire life. Like a fucking idiot.

And now she'd pay the price with him. He wanted to believe that she'd be fine, that he'd given her a little distraction, something to remember he wasn't just a monster, a fun moment to get her through to whatever came next for her. But he wasn't fooled. The look in her eyes hadn't been that of a woman seeking a fun distraction. No, she was as head over heels in love with him as he was with her; there was no denying it. She'd looked at him in that way that no one had since Jeremy; like he was beautiful, trustworthy, honorable, deserving... loved.

As he'd laid her down in her bed on the island, still deep asleep from his magic, and tucked her in like the precious angel she was, he'd heard it: the little moan in the back of her throat, the acknowledgment of his presence, that her body knew it was him bringing her to safety and that it approved. There had been such promise in that sigh. That fleeting vocalization had contained an entire universe in it, an ephemeral dream of a shared life, of everything that could have been, of how they could have been, if only...

If only.

No. She'd wake up just as haunted as he was. Add that to his list of regrets.

Though he knew what came next, Azrael welcomed the interruption of his mental torture when he heard hooves descend the basement stairs. He scrambled to his feet, hurriedly wiping the tears off his face and tying his hair back into a bun. Lucifer could use him as a weapon, but he wouldn't give him the satisfaction of seeing his torment. By the time the metal door slid open, he was standing in the middle of the cell, arms crossed, wings spread out wide, his best "fuck you" face on. Predators couldn't help pouncing on weakness and vulnerability. He might have been dangling on top of a figurative meatgrinder, but he'd be godsdamned if he let them see his fear.

Lucifer's glowing yellow eyes appeared in the door. "You've been told what you are to do next?" he asked, leaning his body into the doorframe as if to make himself appear more palatable.

Oh yes, he'd been told. On his way to the island, he'd been informed of the atrocious task his father had in mind for him next. He'd thought perhaps he'd be eased into monsterdom, that it would be a gradual process. But he'd promptly been relieved of those false notions.

"Yes."

Lucifer cocked his head. "Any feelings about what you're about to do?"

"No." Azrael clenched his jaw so hard he might have chipped

a molar.

"She's safe, isn't she?' his father suggested.

"Yes," he conceded.

"What are you brooding about then?"

The Fallen was baiting him, trying to maneuver him into an argument to make a show of force. He wouldn't give him the satisfaction.

"You bought yourself my obedience. Not my feelings," he replied, his voice devoid of the emotions Lucifer was trying to coax out of him.

"Oh, son, I don't need you to give me your feelings. I have been privy to those since the day you were born. I know just how small and pathetic you're feeling right now. I know you're an endless pit of regret, rumination, and resentment. And I know your dispassionate expression is nothing but a façade for how afraid you are of the great things you and I are going to achieve together."

Azrael barely contained his scoff.

"Is there anything you'd like to say?" the Fallen asked, slowly approaching him, the clip-clopping of his hooves on the stone ground somehow more menacing than the smoldering threat in his eyes.

"If you have my obedience and you don't want my emotions, then what do you want from me?" he bit out, barely containing the urge to flare his wings at the enemy, as the latter kept creeping into his space until they were almost nose to nose. Menacing him would only set off the predator though.

Lucifer cocked his head, staring right into his eyes. It took everything Azrael had not to close them in an admission of fear, to not even blink as the monster assessed his every pore.

"They trained you well, I'll give them that..." the latter mused. "What I want is for you to grant me your most chipper and delightful company, is all," he added, suddenly switching into a completely frivolous registry with that unhinged flippancy that made the Fallen the most unpredictably dangerous creatures on the planet.

"Come on, son, follow me!" Lucifer joyously instructed him, turning back around to saunter out of the cell. "Great deeds await us!"

JEREMY

Jeremy sat by the side of Lyla's bed. This time, he didn't attempt to heal her. She'd need as much sleep as possible. And he needed time to prepare for the mental state his little sister would be in when she woke up. He could try to ease her pain, to take it away, but he wouldn't go there this time. She'd be in such agony that he'd be taking away her soul alongside her pain. He'd create a monster. Just like Lucifer was about to do to Azrael.

Azrael, who had carried her back from Hell himself, like a willing servant. Jeremy had felt such relief at the sight of the grey wings wrapped around his little sister. He'd gone out of his mind when he'd found her note explaining that she'd gone rogue. He'd surmised that Azrael must have followed her back. Seeing them both return in one piece had been the greatest relief of his life.

He hadn't understood why Azrael had silently carried Lyla to her cell. Why he'd carefully laid her down in her bed and tucked her in like a precious gift, not saying a single word. He'd kissed her forehead and whispered, "Goodbye, sweet fledgling," at which point alarm bells had gone off in Jeremy's head. Then,

Azrael had pulled out the little boot knife he'd carried around almost his entire life, never letting anyone – not even Jeremy – touch it, and he'd laid it on Lyla's pillow.

He'd proceeded to quietly leave the room and march to his own, Jeremy one step behind him. He'd sensed the agony coming off his friend, hoping that it was "only" his pain over Sophie's sacrifice. But he'd understood that it was more than that when Azrael had started packing up his room, stuffing a few spare clothes and a whole lot of blades into a small backpack.

"Please, talk to me," Jeremy had said into the silence.

Finally, Azrael had sat down on the edge of the bed he'd slept in his entire life. Jeremy had always hated the ascetic life his friend had chosen for himself, never owning more than he needed, never aiming for more than being a good general to Hermes. He may have covered it up with stoicism, but Jeremy knew Azrael's heart better than anyone. The male was so full of self-loathing that he had no idea of the amount of love he had to give. He'd watched him pine for Lyla for the better part of a year now, knowing how much good could have come from their union, and not being able to intervene. Azrael was even more thick-headed than Lyla. If he'd convinced himself to stay away from her, there was nothing Jeremy could have said or done to change his mind. Even when they'd been dating, Azrael had never been able to fully open up. Jeremy had loved him with all his might, but the insecure angel had always kept him at a distance. The thought went against everything Jeremy believed in, but maybe some wounds couldn't be healed. The amount of hatred Azrael had experienced in the first years of his life for the color of his wings might just have been one of those things.

At last, his friend had opened his mouth. The voice that had come out of it had chilled the blood in Jeremy's veins. It was cold, dead, devoid of any emotion.

"We went back in time to undo the pandemic," he'd started.

"I know."

"We failed."

"I know."

"Sophie sacrificed herself for nothing."

"I know," he'd replied, keeping the sorrow at bay until he could find out what else had Azrael so distraught.

"I have to go back," the latter had added, matter-of-factly.

"Back where?" he'd inquired, as it had slowly dawned on him, a truth that simply couldn't be.

"I made a deal," Azrael had finally admitted.

"With whom?" he'd asked, terrified of the next words that would come out of his friend's mouth, wanting to disappear, undo time itself, so he wouldn't have to hear it.

"With my father," Azrael had declared with a complete finality.

He hadn't understood at first.

"Lucifer."

And then he'd gotten it. Azrael had left in search for his father after their relationship had ended. He'd claimed never to have found him, but he'd returned changed. Everything about him had been more rigid, harsher. It explained his power. If he was the son of Lucifer and a priestess of Hermes', he was bound to be one of the most powerful priests to have ever been in the God's service. It also explained his reticence to get close to Lyla. Azrael had always known that he was on borrowed time, that sooner or later he'd be at his father's mercy. Jeremy's heart had stopped at the thought of the beautiful soldier caught in Lucifer's claws.

"Azrael," he'd asked, "what kind of deal did you make?"

"My allegiance for Lyla's freedom."

Oh, Gods. Of course he had.

"Azrael, listen to me. You don't have to go back. It's just words. You're both safe now," he'd tried to bargain.

"If I don't go back, they'll come down on this place with everything they have. Apollo was right. Ares, Hephaestus, Demeter, and Athena have joined forces with the Fallen. I saw them sitting by his side. Our numbers are depleted. Even with Hades and Apollo, we can't take them on. You know that."

No, they couldn't. In fact, they may have just lost the war. But that was a problem for another day.

"Why does he want you, then?" he'd probed.

Azrael had remained silent for a long while.

"Pride, I guess," he'd finally replied. "And because he wants to secure the lost tribes' allegiance."

The lost historically hated their ancestors, the Fallen. And they weren't particularly fond of angels either. Jeremy had scoffed. "No offense, but a mixed angel who gave decades of service to a God? They aren't going to listen to you."

"They will when I bring them the antidote."

"What are you talking about?"

"Demeter made an antidote to the virus. They've had it all along. Their plan was to deplete the lost's numbers until they'd be desperate enough to join. I'll start rounding them up and offering them the cure tomorrow."

He had seen the grief in every inch of the angel's face. Azrael had devoted his life to fighting for the Gods, to saving this world and all the beauty in it he believed was worth saving. And he was about to willingly join in its destruction instead. He would help enslave a people who had held on so tight to their freedom and neutrality, and in so doing he would hand victory to the Fallen.

"In a few weeks, the only victims of the pandemic will be angels and unwitting humans..." Jeremy had mused. He hadn't known what else to say. He hadn't known how to tell his friend that he loved him and that he'd do anything to rescue him, without causing him more undue pain.

Without a word, Azrael had gotten up and left.

"Goodbye, brother," Jeremy had whispered into the empty silence.

The next time he'd see Azrael, he'd be a broken male.

He hadn't known until just now that he was capable of pure unadulterated resentment. Now he understood why it was so all-consuming. He'd only seen it in others, and he'd never comprehended why they couldn't just let things go. Now he got it. It was a fire in his heart, threatening to consume the rest of him. Jeremy wanted to scream. He wished he possessed Lyla's gift for sonic attacks, so he could destroy everything around him with the might of his rage. Instead, he sat in silence, staring at his little sister, so completely absorbed he barely heard Hermes enter the room.

HERMES

Lailah would need as much sleep as she could get. He tip-toed into the room and signaled Jeremy to follow him out into the hallway.

"Azrael sold his freedom to Lucifer for her to be returned safely," the healer explained through choked tears.

Hermes nodded. He'd figured as much.

"He'll finally break him," he mused. It saddened him immensely, but he'd known it to be inevitable ever since the stubborn, grey-feathered fledgling had been left at the temple gates.

"You knew?" Jeremy asked.

"That Azrael is Lucifer's offspring? Of course I knew," he replied. "Subtract the animal features, and he looks exactly like his father."

"Why didn't you–"

"Kick him out, like he expected I would if I found out? Azrael is just as much mine as he is Lucifer's and I raised that angel a whole lot more than his father did," he growled, possessive territoriality edging into his voice.

"No. Why didn't you tell him it didn't matter?" Jeremy accusatorily interjected.

"Because that is a lesson for him to learn, not for me to teach."

"Well, he's learning it the hard way," came the harsh reply. The healer had never dared object to or even disagree with him before, but Hermes wasn't surprised to find out that Azrael was Jeremy's emotional line.

"I'm sorry it had to happen that way," he conceded. He was so very sorry. More than the angel could ever understand. This had all been about giving up control against his better judgment, about not intervening when every fiber of his being told him to, about letting things run their natural course for once. And it had been tearing him in two to watch the suffering, to share in it every step of the way. As he'd actively sat back, he'd been sensing his sanity slipping away, edging him closer and closer to the inevitable.

"That's my point. With all due respect, it didn't have to be that way," Jeremy bit back, on the verge of angry tears.

"Jeremy," he began, leashing his temper. "I don't interfere with your work. Don't interfere with mine. Azrael made his choices. Lailah made hers. Do you think I wanted this?" he asked genuinely. "Going back in time is the greatest mistake my kind ever made. And we get to regret our mistakes for all eternity. I love Azrael like a son. I always have. I didn't direct him or Lailah to do any of this."

"But you should have!" the healer fought back. The part of Hermes that was slowly coming off its hinges whispered in his mind to just throw the angel down the hallway. But the overwhelming part of his heart wanted to embrace him and to tell him that he looked so like his mother, that he couldn't look at him without his brain doing a double-take, thinking she was back. That, though he'd known the healer's father and invited him to work on his island, he'd always loved Jeremy as if he were his own son, and that he wished for nothing more than to create a whole world he could feel safe and happy in.

"You should have intervened!" the young angel continued railing against him. "You should have guided this! You should have done something!"

He'd never seen Jeremy lose his composure like this. He'd seen him affected in every way in which an angel could be affected by external circumstances. But he'd never seen him despair. A few hours ago, they'd discovered a note explaining Lailah and Sophie's mad time travel plan, and Jeremy had panicked. But now, with this reveal of Azrael's new allegiance, he was exuding the kind of dread priests of Aphrodite's weren't really supposed to be capable of.

"Jeremy... Jeremy..." he gently chided, as the latter collapsed against the wall, his fists balled up so tight his nails were drawing blood. "Get your plumage in order and your head back in the game... This is war. And war comes with casualties—"

"No," the angel interrupted him. He wasn't shouting this time. He was pleading. "No. No. No. Not Azrael. Don't call him that. Don't dismiss him like that. After everything he's done for you? Don't give up on him. Please, don't give up on him," he continued, devolving into a blubbering mess.

"I can't give up on my children. But he's beyond my reach now," Hermes explained, full well knowing that his explanation wouldn't satisfy the angel.

"And her?" Jeremy asked through a veil of tears. "This is going to wreck her. How much more do you expect her to endure?"

"Before what?" he replied, sitting down across from him. "Before I wrap her in bubble wrap? Don't you think I would if

I could? Don't you think my heart breaks every time she suffers? I hope she endures no matter what, because she must. She doesn't have any other options but to endure."

"She's not like you, you know?" Jeremy calmly replied. No angel ever addressed him this intimately. Anyone else would be wiping the tears off their face. But not Jeremy. He wore them proudly. "She wasn't raised by you. She wasn't raised to be a Goddess. She was raised human."

"I know," Hermes proudly replied. "It's her greatest strength."

"No," Jeremy shook his head. "You don't understand. It's going to be her downfall. She's not built to think about the big picture, to sacrifice for the greater good. She's built to care about today, and to burn brightly right now."

"Exactly," Hermes replied, pushing himself back up. As much as all of their pain decimated his insides, and empathically sharing this newly added ordeal with his daughter and the male he considered a son had edged him that much closer to his kind's psychosis, he knew she wouldn't just wake up to shine brightly today, but to shine brightly forever.

"Gods damn you, you're wrong about this..." the angel called after him.

"We'll see," he murmured, walking away.

LYLA

While the powers that be regrouped and strategized, while Jeremy despaired, while Azrael sold his soul to the devil and coerced every tribe of his own grey-feathered people to join a cause of death and destruction he'd dedicated his entire life to fight against, Lyla dreamed a lifetime's worth of dreams and nightmares.

The world was upside down, the air sucked out of everything, sound and scent gone. She flew up, up, up, away from the blast that followed her, away from the shaking earth, away from the fire and the melting ice. As she flapped her wings, floating into the unknown of a new world, Lyla turned her head, amazed to see the feathers at the top of her wings turn black, as if someone were dripping paint onto them, letting it run down the length of the appendages. Drifting beyond Earth's gravity, Lyla wrapped her formerly white wings around her body, letting them glide in front of her, as she gawked at the pitch black color taking over, eating away at the light in every single feather.

Bracing herself for the pain, she lifted an arm through what now felt like the softest water, reached for a remaining white feather at the bottom of her left wing, and plucked it, only to see it turn the color of the proverbial abyss.

Lyla stood in a field of the lushest green, looking up into a dark grey sky. She knew the sun was at its zenith, yet its rays were no longer reaching her. And from said sky rained the most portentous rain. She reached a hand out to receive the much-needed water, the water that would feed and cleanse her. A grey droplet fell into the center of her palm, only to fly away on a breeze. And another. And another. Not water. Ash. Ash rained from the sky. And then the feathers followed. Dozens... hundreds... thousands... tens of thousands of feathers, some white, most black, fell from the sky, covering the field until the ground below was as dark as the firmament above.

And then, came the funeral. There he lay, at peace at last. His wings wrapped around him like a soft blanket. Pristine. Intact. All blood and dirt and sin equally washed away. The last of his kind. The slightest smile on his face. He'd died with hope in his heart. Hope for a new ending.

She ignited the funeral pyre with a song long forgotten:

I am you now and you are me...
If I should fail, you take my sword
All that is mine will be yours
Do not fear those we leave behind
The blood that runs in your veins, it is mine...
I am a stone falling through black water
My fall, it never ends...
Come paint my face, come take my hand
I do not wish you to understand
Someday you too will go to war

And by that time, may you not fear death anymore... [*]

She didn't fear death anymore.

She watched the blaze, as his wings combusted: kindling for the rest of his body. She watched his skin frizzle and broil. She watched as all his strength and magic turned to another pile of ashes. Shaking worlds one moment, ash the next. Ashes in a world of ash.

But then a blade of grass grew. A seed found enough water. A seed, carried by a bird of unknown origin. A seed of hope. It grew one root. Out of one came many. And then a stem broke through the earth. It grew into a miraculous sapling. The sapling grew into a tree. The tree bore fruit. And in the fruits, hundreds of seeds, hundreds of reasons to hope. From destruction had come new birth. New life. A new world. New feathers. Grey feathers. Black feathers. Down. Claws. Fangs. Antlers. It was all beginning, just as it had always been meant to.

And then he grew old. Him. She'd never thought she'd see the day. At first it was a line or two on his face. Then black hair turned to silver and silver turned to white. He shrunk somehow, every flap of a wing, every gesture slowing down, as he and time finally became good friends. One day he was gone, the others soon to follow.

Only she would stay, forever standing in a field of faded ash. Until someday their blood would wash the ash off her body. And at long last, the rain would wash away the blood.

After a lifetime's worth of dreams and nightmares, Lyla blinked her eyes open. On the pillow, near her head, lay Azrael's childhood knife, glinting in the morning sunlight.

---

[*] The Devil Makes Three. "Paint My Face". *Chains Are Broken*, New West, 2018.

Ophelia Wolf firmly believes that all stories float in the ether waiting to be told in whatever medium captures them best. She's a novelist who also writes for the screen and has worked as a director for theater, opera, and film. Originally from France, Austria, and Germany, she kept on moving west: she received a philosophy degree in London, went to The Juilliard School, became a New Yorker for almost a decade, and finally landed in Los Angeles where she is happily setting down roots and currently working on the final installment of the *Gods & Angels* series.

For more information and updates on upcoming merch as well as the release of the final installment of the *Gods & Angels* trilogy, visit:

https://opheliawolfdirector.com/

Or follow **@gods_and_angels_book** on Instagram